Y0-BQI-929

ASHWORTH & PALMER

BOOKS BY THOMAS HAUSER

Ashworth & Palmer

The Trial of Patrolman Thomas Shea

The Execution of Charles Horman

ASHWORTH & PALMER

THOMAS HAUSER

WILLIAM MORROW AND COMPANY, INC.
New York 1981

Library of Congress Cataloging in Publication Data

Hauser, Thomas.
Ashworth & Palmer.

I. Title.
PZ4.H383As [PS3558.A759] 813'.54 80-13086
ISBN 0-688-03700-3

Printed in the United States of America

First Edition

1 2 3 4 5 6 7 8 9 10

BOOK DESIGN BY MICHAEL MAUCERI

For Christine DiFrancesco and Catherine Hazard

Despite the incidental use of actual names and places, the characters and incidents portrayed in this book are wholly fictional.

PART ONE

I

When I was a small boy growing up in Nebraska, my father used to take me down to the railroad tracks to watch the trains roll by. Starting with the time I was about three, every day after work he would walk me down to a spot where the tracks split the prairie in two. We'd sit perched on the edge of a bluff and wait for a train to come into view.

I learned to watch the sky. The trains usually came at sunset, and it was hard to measure the fields at that hour. The shadows played tricks on my eyes.

The sky was more faithful. Let others stare at the endless wheat. I sat on the bluff and waited for the first glimpse of smoke rising from the engine toward the heavens. When it came, I would leap to my feet and point excitedly toward the horizon. My father's pipe would be lit by then, and the thin wisp of smoke from his tobacco lifting upward remains as much a part of me as the smoke of the advancing train rising in the distance.

Those are the earliest memories I have. When I got older, I made the trip on my own at least once a day. I never thought of the trains as leaving. Whether they went east or west made no difference. They were always coming home.

We lived on a farm outside of Lothridge. There's no use your looking it up on the map because it was out in the sticks and only had a hundred people. Later on, I went to school in Winthrop Township.

I had what most people would call an exemplary upbringing. My high school grades were in the low nineties, and senior year I made honorable mention halfback on the All-County football team. I won a full scholarship to college, graduated magna cum laude, and enrolled at the University of Nebraska School of Law. I pushed hard for grades in law school and was one of ten first-year students chosen for the Law Review. All through my life, whatever I've done, I've tried to do well. My father taught me that when I was young, and like so much of what he preached, I've done well by its preservation.

My father was a good man. He never sought to harm anyone. He was totally devoid of malice. Ill will and vengeance were foreign to his character.

He was an honest man of extraordinary integrity.

He was admirably open to new ideas and curious about them. He was tolerant and gentle. For a Nebraska farmer who never got beyond high school, his range of interests was remarkable.

He always tried to be fair. As far back as I can recall, I followed him out of respect, never fear or obeisance. When he ordered something done, it was with a word of explanation and a reason as to why things had to be so.

He was the only person in my life who loved me without reservation, and I loved him in return.

The summer after I finished law school, I came home to watch my father die.

He told me the day I got back to Lothridge. After work, when the sun began to fall, he asked me to walk with him to the spot where we used to watch the trains. As we walked along the road, he draped an arm on my shoulder and began to reminisce—about his parents and how he met and courted his bride; her death two years earlier, and the day I was born. We reached the bluff and, when the first wisp of smoke appeared on the horizon, he said the doctors had told him he would be dead by autumn.

I won't trouble you with too much of what followed. As the disease spread, his mind deteriorated rapidly and fell prey to periods of aimless wandering. The doctors criss-crossed his stomach with scars and tubes cutting into his bladder and intestines. In a matter of weeks, he was unable to move on his own from bed to the window. His speech became seriously impaired, and soon only a few of us were able to understand him. Oftentimes, a day or two passed without his being aware of his surroundings. Oozing bed sores swelled across his body, and for a time I found it difficult to look at him. I was more comfortable when I saw him in pajamas. They cosmetized his degeneration and covered the tubes cutting into him.

The infections grew worse. Liquid waste mixed with excrement. His urine bag, normally yellowish orange, turned brown with increasing frequency. His fever would rise, sometimes as high as 104 or 105 degrees, and when it subsided he would lie there, a little weaker and closer to death, not remembering what had transpired the day before, knowing only that he was leaving one void and entering another. Often, when the fever subsided, he would ask someone to hold the morning newspaper up in front of him while he turned his head from side to side. He never asked for his glasses. He could not read without them. The balance of good and bad in living had tipped against him. For his sake, I began to hope he would die.

I spent almost all my time with him those last few months. It was a far from selfless vigil. I was soaking up every bit and piece of him I could find, desperately trying to pull some final meaning from his life.

We spoke for the last time on a Sunday in September. He was lucid, but weaker than before. He could hardly speak, and it strained him even to turn his eyes from side to side.

"I want to die," he said. "Will you help me?"

I turned away involuntarily, then back to face him.

"I want to die, but I can't do it alone. Will you help?"

"Are you in any pain?"

"No."

"There are people who love you. You know that, don't you?"

"I do."

I put my hand on his forehead.

"I won't get any better, and I don't see the point in lying here. I want to die. There's nothing more left to live for."

I told him two things—that I loved him and still got pleasure out of being with him, and that I would never let him suffer. He fell asleep with my hand on his forehead.

That night I went back into his room. He was lying in bed awake, with his eyes open, staring at the ceiling. The urine bag was filling rapidly with dark brown fluid.

"I want you to know," I said, "I meant what I told you this afternoon. Even now, I get a great deal of pleasure out of being with you. I feel a tremendous amount of warmth and love."

"So do I," he answered.

"You've been a perfect father."

Those were our last words together. That night, the fever came again. The following morning, my father died.

II

I've always wanted to excel. I also like to win. I won't put a value judgment on either quality, but midway through my final year of law school they led to a remarkable turn of events.

Like all third-year law students, I had begun to interview for a permanent job. My grades were good (I had risen to number two in the class), and the Dean of Students had described my credentials as "unusually desirable." As a local boy made good, I was in position to choose among the best firms in Nebraska. Thus it was that, one cold December night, I found myself in Omaha being wined and dined by William Hutchins of the esteemed firm of Hutchins, Culpepper & Woods.

"Tom," Mr. Hutchins said at the close of dinner, "we'd love to have you with us next June. And mark my words, you couldn't choose a finer firm than Hutchins, Culpepper & Woods. Every one of our twenty lawyers is a respected member of the bar. Our work is challenging, and no one in the state of Nebraska does it better."

I nodded, and then Hutchins sought to administer the coup de grace. Invoking the name of the most fabled of the giant Wall Street firms, he closed with the words "Hutchins, Culpepper & Woods is the Ashworth & Palmer of Nebraska."

The Ashworth & Palmer of Nebraska! Over the years, certain names have achieved a grandeur of their own. Harvard, Tiffany, maybe a dozen other institutions are synonymous with class. Within the legal profession, Ashworth & Palmer was *the* name. Maybe not everyone agreed. Just as some educators are loath to accept the notion that Harvard is "the best" university in America, some lawyers are of the opinion that no one firm can be ranked above the others. But any random sampling of attorneys would find that Ashworth & Palmer is the consensus choice for "number one."

The firm is legendary. On the night William Hutchins and I sat sipping after-dinner cordials at the "best" restaurant in Omaha, Ashworth & Palmer employed two hundred thirty attorneys, virtually all of them former law review editors from Harvard, Columbia, or Yale. The firm's forty partners made between two and four hundred thousand dollars a year. Beginning associates one month out of law school were paid thirty thousand dollars annually with "appropriate" bonuses and raises thereafter. The roster of firm clients included the most powerful corporations in America, and the firm had a reputation for *never* losing a major case. I could go on, but the most compelling proof of the matter lay in the fact that William Hutchins was seeking to impress by calling his firm "the Ashworth & Palmer of Nebraska." There was no doubt in my mind that lawyers the nation over often engaged in similar hyperbole.

In retrospect, what followed was inevitable. Thanking Hutchins for his offer, I promised an answer within the month. Later that night, I drafted a letter to Messrs. Ashworth & Palmer, Ten Wall Street, New York, N.Y. In essence, I told them that I didn't care what schools they hired from; that whoever their associates were, I was as good as the best and better than the rest (although I didn't phrase it quite that way). I enclosed a copy of my résumé and ended with the offer to fly to New York at my own expense for a personal interview if one was necessary. It was a good letter. Two weeks later, the Dean and several faculty members received lengthy telephone inquiries from Ashworth & Palmer regarding my credentials. Four days after Christmas, the following letter arrived at my door:

> Dear Mr. Henderson,
>
> It is with great pleasure that I offer you a position as a first-year associate with the firm of Ashworth & Palmer. Your duties, should you accept, will involve the preparation of major cases for trial. I would appreciate your notifying us as soon as possible with regard to your decision.
>
> Sincerely,
> James G. Moffitt
> Chief of Litigation

It was that easy. All it took was twenty-four years of hard work and a little guts. I telephoned my acceptance to Moffitt immediately, then settled down for my final semester of school. After graduating in June, and not knowing of my father's illness, I went home with the intention of paying a short visit. His passing left me very much alone.

In early October, I sold the farm. Except for some books and a few personal mementos like the family photo album and my father's watch, I gave away everything to neighbors, distant relatives, and friends. Then I packed my belongings, said good-bye to trees my parents had planted before I was born, and journeyed to New York to begin the rest of my life. On the first Monday in November, having settled in a comfortable one-bedroom apartment on Riverside Drive in Manhattan, I made my appearance at the offices of Ashworth & Palmer.

Ten Wall Street was the first in a wave of modern office buildings constructed in downtown New York. Sixty-seven stories high, encompassing an entire city block, its tenants included the most prosperous law firms, investment bankers, and brokerage houses in America. Legal arrangements for the financing and construction of Ten Wall had been supervised by Ashworth & Palmer. When the building opened in June 1961, the firm promptly occupied floors sixty-four through sixty-six of the towering steel and glass structure. Only the Officers' Club (an elegant dining room reserved for members of the business elite and their guests) held higher ground.

Entering the downstairs lobby at Ten Wall for the first time, I stopped just inside the revolving doors. It was warm for November, and I hadn't worn a coat. After much deliberation the night before, I was dressed in a gray suit, light blue shirt, and conservatively striped tie. Naturally, I had brought an attaché case, which was empty except for two lined yellow legal pads. Whatever else might be said, I was confident I looked like a lawyer.

The first bank of elevators across the lobby to my right bore the sign, "Floors 60–67." One of the elevators was open, a flashing white light just above indicating "up." I stepped inside, pushed a button for the sixty-fifth floor, and stood facing forward as the door closed after me. Seconds later, the car stopped, and I exited out onto a finely tooled parquet floor. Straight ahead, above an imposing pair of heavy glass doors, a series of raised bronze letters spelled out the legend, "Ashworth & Palmer."

Slightly intimidated, I pushed ahead and approached the long, leather-topped reception desk just inside the doors. As I did, a well-dressed woman in her late forties seated behind the desk looked up inquiringly.

"My name is Thomas Henderson," I said. "I'm supposed to start work here today."

Immediately it struck me that I had been unduly formal. Everyone I knew called me Tom, and I had no desire to be called Thomas by anyone.

"Yes, Mr. Henderson," she said. "We've been expecting you. Mr. Moffitt's secretary reported that you would be with us today."

At least they hadn't forgotten I was coming. In mid-summer, I had called Moffitt to tell him I would be delayed by my father's illness. Moffitt had seemed somewhat uncertain as to just who I was and instructed me to make arrangements for a starting date with his secretary.

The receptionist's nails were color coordinated with her dress. Large oil portraits of two men (who I assumed were the firm's founding fathers) dominated the far wall.

"Mr. Moffitt's secretary will be with you shortly," the receptionist advised. "In the meantime, perhaps you could make yourself comfortable in the waiting room to your right."

It was less a suggestion than a command. Two young lawyers went by without breaking stride. I nodded in their direction but was unable to establish eye contact with either one.

The waiting room was an alcove located off the reception area in such a way that a visitor could not see directly into it from the desk or glass doors. Crossing to it, I shifted my attaché case from one hand to the other and stepped inside. Straight ahead was a large picture window stretching virtually from wall to wall, ceiling to floor. All of downtown New York was laid out before me—jagged caverns formed by huge buildings, thousands of people scurrying on the streets below, the sparkling waters of New York Harbor glistening in the morning sun. And smack in the middle of it all, as though placed in the harbor by Messrs. Ashworth & Palmer themselves, stood the Statue of Liberty, her upraised arm pointing toward me on the sixty-fifth floor.

"Hey, Henderson," I said softly, "I think you've made it." And I wondered if maybe Clement Ashworth and Noah Palmer hadn't once felt the same way as young men come to New York to seek their fortunes. Then I remembered my firm history.

Clement Ashworth had been a native of Boston with Brahmin blood and infinite social connections. Noah Palmer, a New Yorker, had been of slightly lesser birth. In 1854, the two men, then both in their early thirties, entered into an agreement to practice law as partners. Their understanding (which was committed to writing since neither man fully trusted the other) called for them to work jointly on all cases and divide the spoils of victory based on which partner had brought in which client and how many hours each had worked.

Ashworth and Palmer were both exceptionally fine lawyers. They were also inordinately greedy men, and the firm soon had more business than it could handle despite the fact that both men worked eighty hours a week as a matter of course. Thus, in 1858, they hired two lawyers five years out of Harvard to work for them. The new attorneys were paid on a salary basis and had no share in the firm's profits. One worked for Ashworth, the other for Palmer, and for purposes of profit sharing, the hours each toiled were attributed to their respective masters. Thus, Ashworth worked his protégé to the bone to maximize his own share of the firm's income, and Palmer did likewise. In time, the firm of Ashworth & Palmer grew to accommodate the unprecedented number of twelve attorneys, and Ashworth declined an appointment to the United States Supreme Court, explaining to then-President Grover Cleveland, "I make more money than all the Justices of the Supreme Court put together."

Having fashioned a firm in their own image, the two partners were satisfied to a degree. However, as the years passed, they grew troubled by the knowledge that someday (as happens to all men) they would die. Thus, in 1893, having achieved septuagenarian status and not wanting their creation to follow them to the grave, they sought to ensure its perpetuation by offering a partnership to one Thaddeus T. Hughes—a hardworking lawyer who had spent twenty-seven years in their employ. Hughes received word of his impending promotion to the partnership with great pride and inquired whether the firm's name would be changed to Ashworth, Palmer & Hughes, whereupon he was instantly fired. On June 1, 1894, the fortieth anniversary of the firm's founding, Ashworth & Palmer at long last inducted a third partner—one Wallace T. Dunn—but not before Mr. Ashworth and Mr. Palmer amended the firm's partnership agreement to guarantee in perpetuity the following:

(1) The formula for division of profits among the partners could be changed only by unanimous vote of those present at the firm's annual June 1 partnership meeting.

(2) The selection of partners could be made only by a unanimous vote of those present at the firm's annual June 1 partnership meeting.

(3) The name of the firm would remain Ashworth & Palmer forever.

Ashworth died in 1901 at age eighty. Palmer followed him to the grave five years later. Yet the firm continued to prosper. By 1925, it had five partners who had come up through the ranks and twenty salaried lawyers. Foremost among the partners was Russell Ford—brilliant, aggressive, and well connected. Owing largely to Ford's genius, in the depression era when many firms foundered Ashworth & Palmer enjoyed continued growth. For every client that went bankrupt and disappeared from the legal scene, Ford added a solvent bank or major industrial corporation. By 1950, Ashworth & Palmer employed fifty-five associates (young lawyers on salary), twenty-seven of whom worked for Ford. Thus, seventeen partners divided fifty percent of the profits, while Ford (pursuant to the partnership agreement) took home the remaining half.

A lesser man might have been satisfied with his lot in life, but Russell Ford was not. On June 1, 1954, the hundredth anniversary of the firm's founding, Ford proposed to his partners that the firm name be changed to Ashworth, Palmer & Ford. At age seventy-four, he too had come to realize his mortality and wanted a monument on passing. The motion sparked bitter debate. Ford was not a popular man among his colleagues, most of whom had come to fear his wrath and despise his hold over their personal fortunes. Moreover, the proposal ran directly counter to the firm charter, which decreed that Ashworth & Palmer should remain just that in perpetuity. After ten hours of heated debate on Ford's motion, the partners adjourned for dinner and began to caucus informally among themselves. As they spoke with one another, a consensus evolved. At 9 P.M., the partnership meeting was reconvened, and Ford's proposal was turned down by a vote of sixteen to one with one abstention. As expected, Ford stormed out of the room in a rage and went home to bed. Arriving at work the next morning, he was met by a delegation of partners who informed him that "by unanimous vote of those present at the firm's annual June 1 partnership meeting" he was no longer a partner at Ashworth & Palmer. Ford later also learned that, "to prevent the rise of another Russell Ford," his former partners had voted unanimously to share all profits equally thereafter. Thus, literally overnight, Wall Street's finest law firm became its first "egalitarian" one as well.

The waiting room resembled a niche in the furniture wing of the Metropolitan Museum of Art. A long Chippendale sofa, patterned in blue and white silk damask with a highly polished mahogany frame, graced one wall. Opposite the sofa, a small mahogany desk with a brown leather top and gold tooling stood alone. There was no chair by the desk—a clear indication that it was for viewing only. Two uncomfortable-looking ribbon-backed chairs with blue and gray damask seats complemented the sofa.

Like the reception area, the room was paneled in walnut. A small plaque to the left of the sofa read, "This room contains furniture from the office of Noah Palmer, 1854." There was no mention of Ashworth's furniture, which I suspected was on display at the Victoria and Albert Museum in London. A page of venerable handwritten parchment hung in a glass-covered frame above the desk. Having withstood the ravages of time, its title was clear: "Agreement of Partnership Between Clement Ashworth and Noah Palmer, June 1, 1854."

Seating myself on the sofa, I glanced at a delicately carved wood end table to my left. A heavy brass ashtray rested on top next to a cut-glass bowl filled with thin chocolate-covered mints. The atmosphere suggested that, however inviting the mints might be, it would be inappropriate under any circumstances to take more than one.

"Mr. Henderson?"

I looked up and saw a well-dressed, middle-aged woman, wearing a tailored beige dress and single strand of pearls, standing in the doorway. Her brown hair was medium length and carefully set.

"My name is Katherine Whittle," she said.

I stood up and smiled.

"I'm Mr. Moffitt's secretary. Mr. Moffitt is tied up in a conference this morning and won't be able to see you. He asked me to show you around." Without waiting for a response, she turned and walked toward the reception area.

"The firm has three floors," Mrs. Whittle explained as I accompanied her down a long corridor with blue carpeting and grasscloth-covered walls. "Sixty-four, sixty-five, and sixty-six. We're divided into four departments. Corporate and litigation are the largest with ninety lawyers each. Our tax and real estate divisions are considerably smaller. As you know, we have two hundred thirty lawyers—forty partners and one hundred ninety associates. There's also a nonlegal staff of secretaries, messengers, file clerks, library assistants, telephone operators, and the like, numbering just over three hundred. We have five foreign language translators for international work."

I nodded and she went on.

"You'll be assisting our litigation partners in the preparation of cases for trial. Most of your work will involve federal securities and antitrust law. There are fifteen litigation partners, and each one has a number of associates assigned to work for him. As a general rule, associates work exclusively with one partner for a period of two years and are then rotated to another. It's an apprentice system, which will enable you to become familiar with one or more cases and develop an expertise in a particular area of the law. It also allows for fuller evaluation of an associate's abilities when decisions on partnership are made.

"This is Mr. Moffitt's office on the right," she said, pointing toward a closed door beyond a secretarial alcove. "As you know, he's the head of our litigation department. All of our litigation partners have offices on either the sixty-fifth or sixty-sixth floor. The litigation associates are similarly located."

"Will I be working for Mr. Moffitt?"

"I don't think so. My understanding is that you've been assigned to Mr. Hunker." Nothing more was volunteered on the subject, and I decided that I would learn about Mr. Hunker when I was supposed to.

The firm offices were awesome. Ashworth & Palmer took up three floors of the third largest office building in downtown New York, and Mrs. Whittle (I assumed it was Mrs. because of her ring) was an efficient guide. One by one, she pointed out the firm library (one hundred forty thousand volumes—the largest private law library in the world), supply room (a veritable treasure trove of scotch tape, stationery, and yellow pads), file room (two thousand cabinets, five file drawers each, manned by twenty clerks), and so on. Ashworth & Palmer, I learned, employed one man whose sole function was to cash checks for lawyers. "Common sense," Mrs. Whittle explained. "An associate's time is billed to clients on an hourly basis. If you went to the bank to cash your own checks, the lost time would cost the firm forty dollars. Multiply that by forty partners and one hundred ninety associates cashing one check each week, and you'll see that having a cashier is cost efficient."

The firm duplicating room had five mammoth copying machines with seven battered-looking old men to run them. A dozen smaller copying machines were scattered around the three floors. In addition, each floor had a Xerox Telecopier to reproduce documents by telephone from anyplace in the United States.

Occasionally, Mrs. Whittle and I would pass one or more well-dressed men scurrying in the opposite direction, and she would stop politely to introduce me as "Mr. Henderson, our new associate." Invariably, the other party was presented as "Mr. X—a fellow associate," or "Mr. Y—he's a partner." I was not introduced to any nonlegal staff, although we did cross paths with a number of secretaries and messengers.

"This is the steno pool," Mrs. Whittle announced as we came to a huge windowless room off an inner corridor on the sixty-fifth floor. Looking inside, I saw about forty women of varying ages sitting at closely set desks. Most of them were typing. A few sat reading magazines or newspapers. "After you've been here a few months," she continued, "you'll be assigned your own secretary who will sit in the alcove outside your office. In the meantime, you'll be expected to use the steno pool."

"Do I have to make arrangements in advance for day-to-day use?"

"Goodness, no!" she exclaimed. "The pool operates in three shifts—nine A.M. to five; five to one A.M.; and one A.M. to nine. There will be someone available for you at any time, day or night, three hundred sixty-five days a year including Christmas. The same holds true for copy-machine personnel, messengers, and telephone operators. The office never closes."

We continued past several large conference rooms, each one elaborately furnished with long tables and leather-backed chairs, expensive-looking oil portraits on the walls. At the far end of a corridor on the sixty-fourth floor, she pointed toward two swinging doors straight ahead. "The firm lunchroom is in here. Associates and nonlegal staff find it convenient. It's much less expensive than the neighborhood restaurants and takes considerably less time."

"Where do the partners eat?"

"At the Officers' Club upstairs."

The remainder of our conversation, like that which had preceded it, dealt with firm-related matters. I learned that I was one of thirty-seven associates starting work at Ashworth & Palmer that fall. Thirty-four of "us" were graduates of Harvard, Columbia, or Yale. The outsiders were myself, a former editor-in-chief of the Stanford Law Review, and a woman who had been number one in her class at the University of Chicago.

"Each case," Mrs. Whittle explained as we went on, "is given a number for billing purposes. So is every associate. Your number will be 6590.

"This is the men's room," she noted as we came to a door marked, logically enough, "men." "There's one in the same location on each floor. Obviously, you may use it any time you wish." She paused for effect. "Down the hall, there is a door marked 'private.' That is the partners' men's room and is reserved for use by partners. Once, a young associate who didn't know better went in by mistake . . ." Her voice trailed off as though the young man had never been heard from again.

At half-past eleven, the tour came to an end. "I've arranged for two associates—Jordan Caine and Jim Britt—to take you to lunch," Mrs. Whittle said. "They'll pick you up around noon. Mr. Hunker will call you later in the day. Meanwhile, let me show you your office."

Walking at the same brisk pace employed all morning, she led me to the southern end of the sixty-fifth floor. There, just beyond a secretarial alcove, I saw a closed door and, to the right, a nameplate—a thin strip of brass five inches long and one inch wide that could be inserted or removed from its metal holder with ease. In raised black letters set against the gold, it read "Thomas C. Henderson."

I thanked Mrs. Whittle for the tour and stepped inside. The room was about twelve feet long and eight feet wide. A large walnut desk stood straight ahead with a formica-topped credenza to one side. Two empty six-foot shelves stretched along the wall to my right, one shelf at eye level, the other slightly below. A steel-gray file cabinet was lodged in the corner to my left. A comfortable brown-leather swivel chair rested behind the desk. On the floor, in the center of the room, were two cartons of law texts and notebooks I had shipped to New York from Nebraska. Behind the desk was a picture window. And, beyond that, was the same view I had seen from the Ashworth & Palmer waiting room ninety minutes earlier. Granite and glass towers . . . the blue harbor . . . the Statue of Liberty with its torch pointed directly toward me. All in clear view from my office, *my office,* on the sixty-fifth floor at Ten Wall.

"Hey, Henderson," I told myself, "you've found a very impressive home."

III

Jim Britt came to my office shortly after noon. He was about my height (six feet even), on the stocky side, with dirty blond hair and a smooth complexion. Waiting for Jordan Caine, we covered the obligatory personal minutiae. Where had I gone to school? Was I married? I learned that Britt had attended Columbia as an undergraduate, earned a legal degree at Yale, and had been at Ashworth & Palmer for eight years. He was married with two children. Ten minutes into the conversation, the third member of our party arrived.

"Sorry I'm late," Jordan said. "Moffitt's meeting was slated to end at eleven, but we got hung up on a subsidiary corporation our illustrious client has set up in the Virgin Islands. Moffitt thinks it's a conduit for illegal payments to United States government officials. Naturally, the client denies it."

"And?" Britt queried.

"And I think it's a can of worms we're better off not opening," Jordan answered. "But that's not the way Moffitt does business. He wants to know all the facts all the time. Maybe he's right. At least that way, if any bodies are buried, he'll find them before the Department of Justice."

"And if he does?"

"You know Moffitt. If it can be done legally, he'll rebury them halfway to China."

Jordan Caine was a shade over six feet tall with black hair and strong features. His voice was deep. He seemed anxious to impress. Waiting for the elevator, I learned that he had been a Law Review editor at Harvard, clerked for United States Supreme Court Justice Potter Stewart, and spent the last five years with Ashworth & Palmer. At age thirty, married with no children, he was five years my senior.

"The best food nearby is a seafood place called Lindemann's," Jordan said as we reached the street. There was no dissent, and we walked several blocks to a fashionable-looking restaurant on the corner of Nassau and Wall. Inside, the clientele was almost exclusively male. Everyone was well dressed. There were linen napkins on the tablecloths.

"Don't worry," Britt told me as we were seated. "The firm will pay for lunch. It's part of your orientation."

The maître d' placed menus in front of us. Jordan ordered Nova Scotia salmon and filet of sole. I did likewise. Britt opted for bouillabaisse preceded by a double Jack Daniel's on the rocks. Then Jordan picked up the conversation.

"The purpose of this lunch is to tell you a little more about Ashworth & Palmer. The firm feels that new associates will fit into the system more easily if they know what to expect. Obviously, most of what you learn will be assimilated on a day-to-day basis, but a quick introduction from an associate's point of view does help.

"Ashworth & Palmer," he continued, "is made up of superachievers—people who have been on top in college, law school, and everywhere else their entire lives. These people are driven to excel, and you're one of them. At age twenty-five, you've earned the right to tell people that you work for Ashworth & Palmer, but that privilege, unless renewed, will expire in eight years."

Britt's drink and the Nova Scotia salmon arrived. I pushed the capers and chopped onions covering my portion to one side and began to eat. Jordan went on.

"The firm operates on the principle known as 'up or out.' It does not have permanent associates. At the end of eight years, an associate's work is evaluated by partners in his department. If his performance measures up to the standards of the firm and if the economic need exists, he'll be offered a partnership. If not, he's asked to seek other employment. Being a partner at Ashworth & Palmer is, in every sense, 'making it.' There's no other place in the world quite like it. It's a lifelong guarantee of power, prestige, and financial security. The firm income is divided equally among the partners. This past year, each partner took home three hundred and ten thousand dollars.

"The decision regarding who will become a partner rests on three factors. To a large degree, you'll be judged on your ability as a lawyer and the quality of your work. Next, there are a number of less tangible items—social graces, whether or not you're perceived as a team player, and so forth. The third key is hard work. The people who run this firm are driven men. They average sixty or more hours a week in the office and aren't about to share their profits with someone who does less. Each week, the firm posts a computer printout listing the number of hours every associate has worked over the previous seven days. To have any chance at all of making partner, your name has to appear near the top of that list on a regular basis."

"What are the chances . . ." I started to pose the question, then stopped.

"What are the chances of making partner?" Jordan prompted.

I nodded.

"About one in fifteen."

"Do you want to make partner?" I asked.

"Yes. And so do you or you wouldn't be here."

I turned toward Britt. "What about you?"

"I'm the wrong person to ask," he said. "In the world of up or out, I'm out. I was passed over at the partners' meeting last June."

I felt quite clumsy.

"It's not as if you're looking at a dead body," Britt half joked. "I'm told that life after Ashworth & Palmer does exist. I'll move on to a pretty good job somewhere else. The firm has connections all over the country."

"Do you regret coming here now that it's over?"

"Not really." He took a long sip from his already half-empty glass. "You see, for most of my life I've been number two. I have a brother who's three years older than I am. When I applied to college, I was rejected by Princeton so I went to Columbia. Then I made dean's list but not Phi Beta Kappa. I was accepted at Yale Law School but turned down by Harvard. I graduated cum laude but missed out on Law Review. For eight years at Ashworth & Palmer, I've been with number one. No one can ever take those years away from me."

"That's a pretty negative view," I protested. "Columbia, Yale, dean's list, and cum laude are more than most people accomplish."

Britt shook his head and took a slurp of Scotch. "It's nothing. Everything through the end of law school is a game. The word 'accomplishment' doesn't fit."

He was starting to slur his words a little, and I hoped he wouldn't order another drink.

"Look, Tom," he continued. "None of this is meant to detract from what you've *accomplished*." He accented the word. "I'm sure you were one of the better law students at the

University of Nebraska, and your letter to the firm, which Moffitt showed around, was a creative piece of writing and gave us all a chuckle. But as a lawyer you're like any other first-year associate. You know zilch. You have no clients. You wouldn't be able to draw up a set of interrogatories if your life depended on it, let alone figure out where to file them. You're one hundred percent dependent on the partners to train you, pay you, and give you a job reference in the likely event that you're chewed up and spat out eight years from now. They own you. They'll run your life down to the nth degree. And believe me, if you don't know your place now, in the next few months you'll learn it. You'll see. Compared to a messenger or a secretary, you're pretty hot stuff. Compared to a partner, you're shit."

The waiter placed our entrées in front of us. Jordan looked exceedingly embarrassed.

"The fish is good," I said after a few bites.

Britt, who appeared to have drifted into another world, began running a spoon through his bouillabaisse, periodically lifting chunks of scallop and shrimp to his mouth.

I couldn't think of anything to say.

"Are you married?" Jordan asked.

We had already covered the subject once, standing by the elevators.

"No. Yourself?"

"Yes. . . . My wife's name is Barbara."

There was another silence.

"How does the firm bill clients?" I finally asked.

"On an hourly basis," Jordan said. "At the end of each day, all partners and associates fill out computerized diary cards listing the cases they've worked on, along with a breakdown of the total hours worked. Each case and each client has an office number. For example, the client I'm spending most of my time on now is American Steel. Its number is 3124, and the case is the seventy-ninth we've handled for them. Ergo, the case number is 3124-79. Once diary cards are filed, the computer goes to work. Partners' time is billed to the client at one hundred twenty-five to two hundred dollars an hour. Associates are billed between sixty and ninety. The billing rate depends on seniority."

"That's a lot of money," I noted.

"It makes for some interesting mathematics. As a first-year associate, you'll be billed at sixty dollars an hour. If you work fifty hours a week, which is average, you'll generate a hundred and fifty thousand dollars a year. Your salary is one-fifth that. Maybe another fifth goes to overhead. The rest is profit."

"Why do clients pay a hundred and fifty thousand dollars a year for someone like me?"

"They don't," Jordan answered. "They pay upwards of a million dollars a year for *teams* run by an Ashworth & Palmer partner. The firm only handles large litigation—cases worth millions of dollars to a client. Generally, we litigate for three or four years, then settle on terms favorable to our side. Occasionally, a case has to be tried, but that doesn't happen too often. Large litigation culminating in trial is a five-to-ten year battle, and a full-blown trial can cost ten to twenty million dollars. Very few of our opponents have the resources to fight that sort of war. Over the past two decades, Ashworth & Palmer has handled several thousand cases. Twenty-three have been considered *major*—by that I mean nationally known cases with legal fees totaling five million dollars or more on a single matter. All of Wall Street keeps an eye on those cases. Of the twenty-three, Ashworth & Palmer has won four, settled fourteen on exceedingly favorable terms, and lost one. Four are still pending."

"Who lost the one?"

"Lonnie Hunker."

A waiter cleared away the dishes, and Jordan, in not so subtle fashion, ordered coffee for *all* of us. When mine came, I pushed it to one side. Britt drank his.

"The partner you work for structures your life," Jordan advised. "He can make it good or he can make it bad. For the next two years, what you learn about the law and what you learn about being a lawyer will depend on your relationship with Lonnie Hunker. Clearly, it will be in your best interests to make that relationship a good one."

"You talk about my job and my life as though they're one and the same."

"If you expect to make partner, they will be."

I nodded my understanding.

"There's one more thing I should mention," Jordan added. "The firm frowns on socializing between the sexes within the office. It would be highly inappropriate for you to date one of our half dozen women attorneys, not that any of them are worth dating."

"What about nonlegal staff?"

He looked at me as if I were joking. "That would be like the master of a manor dating the domestic help."

"Thomas Jefferson had a son by a slave," I offered.

"If you want to get a little on the side like Thomas Jefferson, there's nothing I can do to stop you," Jordan answered. "But you'd better be very circumspect about it. I should add that, in the five years I've been here, I've never seen a secretary and an associate having lunch together in the firm cafeteria. That goes for motherly secretaries who look like Eleanor Roosevelt as well as the good-looking ones. The firm likes its associates to put some distance between themselves and the nonlegal staff. I'm not saying that's the way things should be, I'm saying that's the way they are."

The waiter laid our check on the table, and Jordan reached for his wallet. "I'll take it," he said. "Firm protocol calls for the junior man to pick up any reimbursable item, but today you're the guest."

The bill came to thirty-nine dollars plus tip. Jordan paid in cash and pocketed the receipt for his expense account records. "Good luck," he said as we walked back to the office. "And remember, it's a challenge."

The two boxes of books I had shipped from Nebraska were on the floor in the center of my office where I had left them. Bending over, I tested the cartons and realized I'd need a scissors or letter opener to cut through the tape.

Given to logic, I straightened up and set about exploring the desk. The right-hand drawer was cluttered with paper clips, pencils, and small white memo pads. No scissors. The center drawer held more of the same, along with an assortment of gum-backed labels and rubber bands. Obviously, my predecessor had been weak on organization. Miraculously, I found a pair of scissors in a drawer to the left. With great ceremony, I cut through the tape on the cartons and was in the process of returning the scissors to their home when a thin strip of brass on the bottom of the drawer caught my eye. Looking more closely, I saw a gold nameplate with the name "Peter Forrest" inscribed in black.

I don't know. Maybe it was Britt getting drunk at lunch. Maybe I had suppressed my anxieties about big-time competition more than I cared to admit. But suddenly I was scared. Here was a guy, apparently named Peter Forrest, who had sat in the same desk in the same office that I was about to occupy, and, after God knows how many years, all that was left of him was his name in black letters inscribed on a piece of brass.

The tremor passed, and I unpacked my books, placing them one by one on the polished hardwood shelves. They took up less than a third of the space. The walls were painted white and looked bare. I made a mental note to bring some pictures in for color.

The door opened and a frail-looking, white-haired man

wearing baggy slacks and a gray messenger's coat entered. "These are for you, Mr. Henderson," he said, placing a packet of pale blue computer cards and a loose-leaf notebook containing mimeographed pages on my desk.

"What's your name?" I asked, extending my right hand.

"Bill," he answered, clearly surprised by the inquiry. Somewhat deferentially, he shook hands and backed out of the office.

Each computer card was the size of a postcard, with my name printed on top next to the number "6590" and the designations "date, client number, case number, hours spent." The bottom half of each card was empty, save for the inscription "describe services rendered."

I put the cards to one side and looked down at the loose-leaf notebook. Its cover bore the words "Firm Manual." Affixed to it by means of a paper clip was a pink two-by-four-inch routing slip with the following typewritten message:

> TO: TCH [That's me!]
> FROM: JGM [James G. Moffitt, I assumed.]
> I advise you to become familiar with the contents of this manual as soon as possible.

Obediently, I picked up the volume and turned to page one: "The Ashworth & Palmer tradition of excellence," the first paragraph read, "will be furthered by strict adherence to the policies and procedures outlined in this manual. Under no circumstances should they be cast aside in favor of the personal preference of an individual associate without the prior knowledge and consent of the partner to whom the associate is assigned."

There followed several more introductory warnings, after which the manual got down to basics: "The only legal matters to be undertaken or performed by an associate are those matters assigned to him by a partner. The sole exception to this rule is that, with the consent of a partner, an associate may without fee represent himself or a member of his immediate family."

Next came the matter of time charts, also known as diaries: "An associate must account for all time from the moment he enters the office until leaving for the night. Legal work carried on at home, in court, or elsewhere must also be reported. All time entries must be made on the firm's computerized cards in one of three categories—(1) work billable to a client; (2) office matters such as orientation sessions for new associates; or (3) personal matters (e.g. lunch and occasional diversions such as leisure reading of the daily newspaper during office hours). A 'personal' diary card should also be filed in the event an associate is ill or on vacation. Should an associate fall more than one week behind in the submission of diary cards, his paycheck will be withheld until the delinquency is rectified. At a bare minimum, each associate is expected to generate forty hours of billable time each week."

There was more. Specific instructions on how to sign letters to clients ("sincerely" or "sincerely yours"); the admonition that, within the office, casual dress would not be tolerated. Clearly, Ashworth & Palmer associates were expected to lead regulated professional lives. For about an hour, I studied the guidelines. Then, at 4 P.M., the telephone on my desk rang for the first time, and I was summoned upstairs to meet with Lionel J. Hunker.

IV

"Should I knock?" I asked his secretary.

"There's no need. Mr. Hunker's expecting you."

I opened the door and stepped into an office three times the size of mine. Royal blue drapes and gold carpeting leapt out at me. A tall, heavy man with thick blond hair and tortoise-shell glasses sat behind an oak desk at the far end of the room. "I'm Lonnie Hunker," he announced, rising from his chair. He was about my height, with sloped shoulders and a huge stomach that hung over his belt. Wearing a gray pinstripe suit, white shirt, and crimson silk tie, he looked like someone who would be very much at home in front of a jury.

"I'm Tom Henderson."

We shook hands, and Hunker motioned me toward a chair by the desk. He was in his mid-forties, and judging by the twenty-five or so bound volumes of the Harvard Law Review displayed on the bookshelf built into the wall behind him, he had gone to Harvard. A framed certificate hanging to my right indicated that Hunker was a member of the American College of Trial Lawyers; another that he had been admitted to practice before the United States Supreme Court. Autographed photos showing Hunker shaking hands with Gerald Ford and Hunker standing beside Chief Justice Warren Burger were also in evidence. A color portrait of Hunker with his wife and two children graced the desk. The blue drapes were pulled shut the length of the room.

"Edwin Hardesty will be with us in a minute," Hunker said. "He's the other associate who started work at Ashworth & Palmer today. The two of you have been assigned to work with me on the Union Construction Company case." The telephone buzzed, and he picked up the receiver. "Okay, I'll take it. . . . Hello, Frank . . . On that merger, there are several steps we should consider to avoid the appearance of a Clayton Act violation. First . . ."

As the conversation progressed, I focused on my new boss. His voice was remarkably resonant. Even on the telephone, he spoke in perfectly structured sentences, not once letting a participle dangle. He never broke off in mid-sentence to start a thought anew.

Several minutes into the conversation, the door opened, and another associate, about my age, entered. Hunker, still talking on the phone, gestured for him to sit, and the fellow did, nodding in my direction. He was my height (all lawyers at Ashworth & Palmer seemed to be six feet tall), with broad shoulders and a slender waist. His hair was brown, eyes blue.

Hunker said good-bye to whomever it was he had called "Frank" and studied the new arrival. "You must be Ed Hardesty."

"Yes, sir."

"Have you and Tom met?"

"Not yet," Hardesty answered.

The two of us shook hands.

"All of us here at Ashworth & Palmer under the age of

sixty are on a first-name basis," Hunker said. "I hope you'll both call me Lonnie."

The buzzer sounded again, and he picked up the telephone. "Okay, put him on. . . . Hello, Lloyd, I think we've got a deal. I won't know for sure until noon tomorrow, but it looks good. . . . I'm pleased, too. You'll do a splendid job. . . . My best to Ethel. . . . Good-bye.

"All right," he said, turning back toward us. "Let me tell you about the case. One of Ashworth & Palmer's clients is the Union Construction Company, also known as UCC. It's the largest consulting engineering firm in the country. UCC designs and then builds electric power plants, transportation terminals, and dozens of equally complex facilities. In most instances, the company has vigorous head-on competition, but in one area it's pretty much alone. UCC is the only major designer and builder of sewage treatment plants in the United States."

A quizzical smile crossed Hardesty's face, and Hunker picked up on it immediately.

"Lest you take this case lightly, let me explain to you what that means in terms of dollars and cents. Nationwide, Americans use three billion gallons of water a day—an average of one hundred fifty gallons per person. Virtually all of that becomes sewage. Residential waste water includes everything from yesterday's bath and the contents of your toilet to leftover soup. Industrial waste is greater in quantity and far more toxic. There are very few services more fundamental to our society than the proper treatment of sewage. Without water treatment plants, our lakes, rivers, and streams would become typhoid-infested repositories for deadly wastes. Sanitation as we know it would cease to exist.

"Any reasonably competent engineer can design a series of sewers to bring waste water from throughout a community to a given place. But once the sewage is channeled to a particular location, it has to be sanitized, and that treatment is an expensive proposition. Depending on size and a number of technological variables, a large waste water treatment plant costs between thirty and one hundred million dollars. Over the past decade, the Union Construction Company has sold over two hundred of them. Two years ago, the Department of Justice filed suit against UCC, claiming that it has unlawfully monopolized the sewage treatment market. If we lose this case, our client could be forced to make payoffs to local municipalities amounting to one billion dollars."

Satisfied that we had been properly impressed, Hunker went on. "All right; lesson continued. Contrary to popular belief, law school did not teach you to *think* like a lawyer. It taught you how to *intellectualize* like a lawyer, how to read cases like a lawyer, and how to use fancy words like 'interpleader' and 'remittitur.' Thinking like a lawyer is something different. It requires angling for every advantage, looking for every loophole, always trying to be one up on your adversary so you can screw him if you have to while making sure that he can't screw you. It also means presenting your case in terms that a judge and jury will sympathize with.

"Now, the Justice Department is going to come into court and argue that UCC forces cities, states, and small municipalities to buy sewage treatment plants at inflated prices. It will argue that, by virtue of its monopoly power, UCC has overcharged every taxpayer in the country, and in these times of inflation that's a troublesome argument. The only way we can combat the government's appeal to emotion is with hard facts. There are ten Ashworth & Palmer lawyers besides the two of you working on this case. All of them have become experts on sewage treatment, myself included. We're preparing to show the court that the Union Construction Company is one of the best-run corporations in the United States, offering first-rate service to more than two hundred million Americans at the lowest price possible. You can add to our factual presentation by learning about the industry and then helping to get the facts in shape for trial. Tomorrow morning, I'll send you each a set of materials on the case. I want you to read them thoroughly. Then you'll be sent to Union Construction Company headquarters in Cleveland for a two-week marketing and technological seminar run by the company solely for your benefit. You'll be the only two students in attendance. Once you get back to New York, we'll put your knowledge to work in the legal process. You'll meet the other Ashworth & Palmer lawyers on the case and help get this thing ready for trial. Any questions?"

"This might seem like an extraneous issue," Hardesty said, "but are we the good guys or the bad guys in this case?"

"Pardon?"

"What I mean is, has the Union Construction Company violated the Sherman Act?"

"Ed," Hunker answered, "that's for the court to decide, not us. Besides, you're missing the point. In fifty percent of the cases a lawyer handles, his client is in the wrong. Whenever there's a dispute, one side has to be wrong and the other right. Or if the issues are split, it will be sixty-forty in your favor one time and sixty-forty against you the next. Lawyers are technicians, not moral arbiters. You'll find that most people here enjoy their work because it's a challenge, not because of any cause or belief. We're interested in winning battles, not fighting them. Any other questions?"

There were none.

"All right, then," Hunker said, rubbing his hands together. "Let me just add one note regarding your personal advancement within the firm. Ashworth & Palmer is the best law firm in the country. I'm convinced of that. I used to think a seat on the United States Supreme Court would be better than a partnership at Ashworth & Palmer, but now I doubt even that. The point I'm making is this. You're in the big time. You're about to jump into the deep end of the pool, and you have two choices. You can become totally involved in your work and succeed, or you can treat it like an average job, in which case the rewards you reap will be limited. The Ashworth & Palmer system works best when dealing with highly motivated associates. The associates who advance the furthest are the ones who work the hardest. Welcome to the big time, and good luck to both of you."

Hardesty's office was two doors down the corridor from mine, and he invited me in to chat. His room was a virtual copy of my own; the same view, an identical desk, credenza, chairs, filing cabinet, and bookshelves. The only noticeable difference was that his carpet was brown and mine was a sort of dim orange.

"What do you think?" he asked, sitting on the edge of the credenza.

"About what?"

"The firm . . . Hunker . . . everything."

"It's quite a place," I said. "Maybe they lose a couple of cases each year for tax purposes, but overall they seem pretty efficient."

Looking back over the previous eight hours, we compared notes. The firm, Ed told me, had never elevated a woman or a black to partnership. It had six women and two "minority" associates. I recounted having lunch with Jordan Caine and Jim Britt, to which Ed allowed that the associates who took him to lunch had described Jordan as "a real comer." "They told me that making it at Ashworth & Palmer depends on brains, drive, and a willingness to eat it. From what I understand, Jordan Caine has all three. In addition to being very bright, he really wants it."

"Is that bad?"

"Not necessarily," Ed answered. "I'm just not sure it's for me."

The door opened, and an elderly man with silver hair stood before us. His eyes were deep blue. Nothing about him was fragile. If not for the wrinkles on his face, he could have passed for middle-aged instead of old. A gold chain extended from a loop on his navy blue pants to a nearby vest pocket. As a younger man, he must have been extremely handsome.

"My name is George Witherell," he announced. "May I come in?"

On the left-hand side of the Ashworth & Palmer stationery, the firm's forty partners were listed in order of seniority. The name George W. Witherell headed that list. A quick glance toward Hardesty indicated that he too was aware of our guest's stature.

"Yes, sir," we said in unison.

"Good. I always like to meet the new associates. Judging by the nameplate outside, one of you must be Edwin Hardesty. The other is no doubt Thomas Henderson, although I have no idea which is which."

We introduced ourselves, and Witherell made himself comfortable in the chair offered. "You're from Nebraska, aren't you?" he said, looking in my direction.

"Yes, sir."

"Farm country?"

I nodded.

"That's good. From what I hear, farm life makes an achiever out of you. The work is constant. Animals have to be fed seven days a week whether you feel like it or not. You harvest crops when they're ready or not at all. If that doesn't prepare you for the rigors of Ashworth & Palmer, nothing will."

Halting for a moment, he bent over and rubbed the inside of his left knee. "I have a few aches and pains these days. I'm not eighty-four years old for nothing. . . . Anyway, what I came by to say is I hope you young men take advantage of everything this firm has to offer. I learned long ago that, to be a good lawyer, good intentions aren't enough. To be effective, a lawyer needs two additional assets—competence and a love of the law. The first is relatively easy to attain. The second is quite a bit harder. I hope you two young men learn to love the law. Meanwhile, I suppose you both think you're pretty hot stuff, don't you?"

We sat silent.

"Well, you are. You're bright, talented young men, or else you wouldn't be here. That's a given. It's possible there will be times during the next few years when the going gets rough and you get down on yourselves a little. Don't let it happen too often. That's all I have to say, other than I hate blow-away cards that fall out of magazines. If you young men can construct a legal argument that will eliminate blow-away cards, you'll be very successful lawyers. Good day to both of you."

"He's quite something," I said when Witherell had gone.

"I'm not sure I belong here," Ed answered.

"Come on."

"No, really. I've been here for eight hours, and except for the last few minutes all I've heard is how great it is to work sixty hours a week for eight years to become a partner. No one seems human. George Witherell is the first person to come by unassigned to say hello. And that line Hunker gave us about the fabric of society depending on our ability to save the nation's number-one manufacturer of sewage treatment plants leaves me cold. Society as we know it couldn't exist without garbage collectors either, but I wouldn't want to devote my professional life to learning how to be one. I'm twenty-five years old, and something inside me says I should spend the next two years tramping around Africa or Asia, not studying sewage treatment plants in Cleveland, Ohio, or sitting here looking out at the Statue of Liberty."

The door opened again, and an aging messenger—they all seemed to be at least seventy—entered with an envelope in his left hand. "This is for you, Mr. Hardesty. Mr. Henderson's is on his desk."

Ed took the envelope, opened it, and after a quick reading handed me the contents.

> Dear Ed,
>
> Let me officially welcome you to Ashworth & Palmer and offer my regrets on being unable to meet with you today. Hopefully, the enclosed will emphasize our pleasure at your arrival.
>
> Sincerely,
> James G. Moffitt
> Chief of Litigation

Stapled to the letter was a check for one thousand dollars.

"I guess it's like Lonnie Hunker said," Ed murmured. "This is the big time."

"Hey," I told him. "Ashworth & Palmer isn't all bad. In less than a day, you've already made one friend. I'm just a farm boy from Nebraska, but I'm loyal and my dinner conversation is pretty good."

"Go pick up your check," he said. "Then let's get some dinner. If nothing else, we can afford a good one."

On the way back to my desk, I passed the most incredibly good-looking woman I'd ever seen. I stared awkwardly; she smiled and walked on.

V

Tuesday morning I arrived at work to find my desk underneath twenty inches of paper topped by a pink Ashworth & Palmer routing slip:

> TO: TCH [Me again!]
> FROM: LJH [Lionel J. Hunker]
> Read these materials thoroughly.

Leafing through the pages, I saw a dozen or so court documents followed by a larger number of intra-office memoranda bearing such esoteric titles as "Sewage Treatment Technology" and "Relevant Market Definition." One of the more intriguing memos was a fairly lengthy tome entitled "Problem Areas: Where They Are and How to Combat Them."

Twenty minutes later, Hardesty stuck his head into the room. "I got the same crap," he announced, looking at the mess on my desk. "What do we do with it?"

"According to the routing slip, we read it thoroughly."

"I was afraid you'd say that."

Actually, it wasn't so bad. The papers had been arranged to give us an overview of the case, and most of them were mercifully intelligible. The government's argument, as set forth in the summons and complaint, was that UCC had bought out some competitors, selectively cut prices to destroy others, and then used its monopoly position to raise prices beyond the normal competitive market level. In addition, the Justice Department claimed that lack of competition had led to a situation where UCC had all but stopped trying to improve its product technologically. Needless to say, Ashworth & Palmer vigorously disputed the charges, arguing that UCC had gained economic strength simply by turning out a better product than anyone else. Each side had then demanded that the other produce mountains of case-related documents. Thereafter, three Ashworth & Palmer lawyers had been assigned the task of reviewing documents, while the remaining members of the "team" were put to work in other areas. Two associates developed an expertise in sewage treatment technology. Four more studied the UCC marketing system. A tenth had begun work in conjunction with a Harvard Business School professor who was being paid to prepare economic testimony to the effect that UCC's prices were "fully consistent with competitive market levels."

"For ten points and an all-expenses-paid trip to Cleveland," I announced to Hardesty over lunch Tuesday afternoon in the firm cafeteria, "name the first major city to use underground sewers in modern times!"

"London," he answered.

"Right you are! Followed by?"

"Paris, Boston, and New York."

"Mr. Hardesty!" I exclaimed. "You're a genius. Now for a twenty-point bonus! What is the life expectancy of a sewage treatment plant?"

"Thirty years."

"Brilliant! Mr. Hardesty, you're incredible! But do you know how many tons of sludge are generated each year by sewage treatment plants in New York City?"

"Two hundred and fifty thousand."

"Mr. Hardesty, I'm going to buy you an ice cream sandwich. This has been a truly impressive performance!"

And so it went. For the rest of the week, we spent ten hours a day reading about sewage treatment, breaking one hour daily for lunch. It could have been worse. Any subject becomes interesting if you develop an expertise, and, for what it was worth, we were certainly developing an expertise in sewage treatment. (Actually, it was worth quite a bit. At week's end, we calculated that Ashworth & Palmer would bill the client six thousand dollars for our combined efforts.)

Also, I was getting to know Ed Hardesty pretty well, and he was nice, honest, and unassuming, with the ability to laugh at himself. "I was an All-Ivy middle-linebacker at Harvard," he confided to me one afternoon, "but I wasn't really that good. Ivy League football is pretty weak. I only weighed two hundred pounds, and that was at my peak. In a tougher league, I would have been pushed around something awful. Still," he noted, "it's ironic that Ashworth & Palmer put me on the sixty-fifth floor. That was my number in college."

"Do you think they matched it on purpose?"

"I hope not. I've gotten tired of being stereotyped as a dumb jock."

"No problem," I said. "We'll tell everyone you're a bright jock instead."

"Thanks."

Sunday night, we flew to Ohio. Contrary to Hunker's report, UCC's headquarters were not in Cleveland, but in an ugly industrial suburb called Unger, twenty miles north. There we spent the better part of two weeks under the watchful eye of Bud Daley, UCC's product sales manager, who shepherded us from one orientation seminar to the next.

"The government doesn't understand the risks we've taken," Daley complained our first morning together. "Sure, prices are high, but that's because we've made an enormous capital investment in our business. And with present-day inflation, the time lag between the date an order comes in and the date we deliver kills us."

Daley was a stubby, balding man, whose primary job was to sell product accessories to municipalities after they had ordered the basic sewage treatment plant. He wore a bicentennial tie and talked admiringly of an item he had once seen on display in the Century Plaza Hotel gift shop in Los Angeles—a clear plastic toilet seat embedded with quarters and half-dollars. "Hey," he said one night after we'd had a couple of drinks together in the hotel bar. "You want to know the truth? Whatever we charge, the public still has to buy from us. People can't stop shitting and taking baths, can they? But," he added quickly, "our prices are fair."

At the end of two weeks in Unger, I had aeration basins, control gates, pumping stations, and sludge drying beds coming out of my ears. Back in New York, I found someone in the steno pool to type up my notes, brought in some photographs to liven up my office, and spent Thanksgiving and Christmas with Ed Hardesty at his parents' home on Long Island. The first week in January, I declined an invitation to register for a pottery course Ed was taking to "meet chicks." As things developed, the second week of class he met "a gorgeous woman," but she spurned all offers to go out with him, and after four or five attempts he gave up trying.

"Why did you stop asking her out?" I chided one night over dinner.

"That's like asking the United States government why it stopped sending troops to Vietnam," he answered. "It was a losing battle."

In truth, even if she had been willing, Ed wouldn't have had much time to spend with her. Almost without trying, we were in the office *a lot.* In response to a myriad of court rulings, UCC had been forced to accelerate the pace at which it turned over documents to the government, and the three Ashworth & Palmer associates assigned to review documents prior to production were badly in need of help. Armed with our newly acquired knowledge of the sewage treatment industry, Ed and I were assigned to join them.

For five weeks, we sat cloistered in a windowless chamber on the sixty-fifth floor with Richard Watkins, Carole Shiner, and Arlen Cohen, the three associates previously assigned to document review. None of us had an individual desk. Instead, we shared a long wooden table which wobbled distractingly because, at thirty to fifty thousand dollars a year, we weren't smart enough to stick a folded piece of paper under the one table leg that was shorter than the others. The room was lined with loose-leaf notebooks on flimsy metal shelves. Every document in the case—and there were several hundred thousand of them—had been arranged in those books by date, subject matter, author, and recipient. As the final stage of our review began, we were instructed by Hunker to prepare indices of the documents and affix adhesive-backed red dots to those pages deemed "most troublesome" to UCC.

Inevitably, a gallows humor developed among us. Watkins—a fourth-year associate whom Hardesty described as "the only person I know who could get constipated in Mexico"—didn't share in the mirth. He was extremely stiff and resented being given the same work as beginners. Arlen Cohen and Carole Shiner, though, were good company. Arlen was a third-year associate, who planned on leaving the firm and moving to Massachusetts as soon as his wife finished her Ph.D. program at Columbia. He and Hardesty got along famously, Ed suggesting that Arlen's nickname should be "Ice Cream." ("Ice Cream Cohen, get it?"—We all groaned.) Arlen, for his part, would frequently request that Ed "take the football mouthpiece out of your mouth so we can understand what you're saying." Carole tried to converse on a more sophisticated plane but was eventually dragged down to our level. In essence, except for Watkins, we were making fun of ourselves—the brightest young lawyers in America, spending ten hours a day sticking red dots on documents.

Mercifully, in mid-February the review ended. Spurred on by a court-ordered deadline and Hunker's exhortations to "get the job done," the five of us agreed to set aside seven consecutive days during which we would "do or die." Arriving at the office on a Sunday morning at nine, we reviewed documents till 10 P.M., went home, slept, got up, came back the next morning at nine, and repeated the process daily until the following Saturday night. Meals were eaten communally at the review table—sandwiches brought in by the messengers for lunch; dinner ordered from a neighborhood restaurant at night. As permitted by the Firm Manual, every morsel was billed to the client. Each night, just before leaving, we'd route our handwritten indices, scrawled on lined yellow paper, to the steno pool via messenger. By 9 A.M. the following morning, they'd be neatly typed, waiting on our review table with five photocopies as requested. Toward the end of the week, I was so sick of proofreading indices aloud that I found myself reading "comma" as "coma." Still, we persevered and, Saturday night at eleven, the task was complete. Several days later, the firm's weekly computer listing of hours showed that the five of us had logged ninety-one hours each over the seven-day period. Jordan Caine dropped by my office to congratulate me on "making the Top Ten," and Hunker commented approvingly that I "sure must have burned the midnight oil." Still, I noted that, during the same seven-day period, half a dozen associates recorded even longer hours.

I had begun to watch the computer listing with regularity. My own average work week was hardly light. Monday through Friday, I arrived at nine in the morning and stayed until eight at night, with an hour off for lunch. Saturdays, I put in half a day. The total came to a little over fifty hours each week, which placed me around sixtieth out of one hundred ninety associates. Jordan Caine, by contrast, averaged sixty to seventy hours a week with flurries of seventy to eighty.

"You know something?" Ed told me one day at lunch in the firm cafeteria. "You're becoming like them."

"What makes you say that?"

"Because all you talk about are billable hours."

I shrugged.

"No, really!" he pressed. "It's true. You've changed."

"How?"

"In a lot of ways. Look, this place has taught us a lot, I'll grant you that. In a little over three months, we've learned what it's like to tackle the problems of a major industry, even if it is sewage treatment. We've seen how an office mobilizes incredible intellectual resources and turns out everything from strategy memoranda to fifty-page indices without a typographical error. We're surrounded by highly motivated, intellectually aggressive people who have taught us a level of professionalism I never knew existed. But sometimes I wonder about the direction in which we're being channeled. This place uproots people psychologically, and I'm not quite sure what's happening to us."

"You've lost me," I said.

"Look at the firm's partners," Ed answered. "Before coming to Ashworth & Palmer, their record of achievement was incredible. Ellis Slattery is the firm's public utilities specialist. Thirty years ago, at age twenty-four, he published a novel. James Moffitt is fifty-three. In 1952, one year out of law school, he managed Dwight D. Eisenhower's campaign for the Presidency in Illinois. Seven Ashworth & Palmer partners clerked for United States Supreme Court Justices. These men could be leading America. Instead, they're worrying about the effect of backwash holding tanks on prices in the sewage treatment industry."

"Maybe that's the kind of case they like."

"Or maybe that's the kind of case that pays. Look at the firm's litigation. James Moffitt and twenty associates are defending the largest manufacturer of steel in the United States. The case is ten years old. American Steel is paying Ashworth & Palmer six million dollars a year to stall, because it's safer for them to pay us than go to trial and risk losing a judgment. Half a dozen more lawyers here are representing corporate executives accused of stock fraud or bribery. Two of our clients are manufacturers of clay pipe who want to merge with one another. There's nothing wrong with that, but it's hardly crucial to the future of America. Jim Britt has spent the last year seeking to resolve the burning issue of whether or not proceeds from the sale of four hundred boxcars were properly calculated as an income item two years ago on the consolidated balance sheet of the Great Western Railroad Company. Is that what you want to do with your life? And one thing more," he added almost as an afterthought. "I've been here for almost four months, and I still haven't met James Moffitt."

In truth, neither had I. So, being me, that afternoon I called Katherine Whittle and asked for an appointment with the firm's Chief of Litigation.

"He's very busy," she said.

"I know," I told her, "but it's important."

"All right. There's an opening on his calendar at eight-thirty tomorrow morning."

That night, it occurred to me I wasn't quite sure why I wanted to see James Moffitt or what I would say to him—only that something was wrong. Before going to bed, I took a lined yellow legal pad from my attaché case and jotted down several thoughts. There was some coherence to them, although not a lot, and I decided to sleep on it. Obviously, at two hundred dollars an hour I shouldn't plan on taking up too much of Moffitt's time. I'd have to be brief and to the point.

At eight twenty-nine the following morning, I presented myself to Katherine Whittle. "He'll see you now," she said, after announcing my arrival over the intercom. I thanked her and stepped into the office, where James G. Moffitt rose to greet me.

"It's a pleasure," he said, shaking hands and offering me a seat. "What can I do for you?"

The room contrasted markedly with the others I had been in at Ashworth & Palmer. Everything was glass, crushed velvet, and chrome. Moffitt's desk was a large, glass-topped table with chrome supports. The chairs were orange and brown velvet with chrome legs and arms. The carpet was a plush burnt umber. Moffitt himself was shorter than I had expected but with inspirational good looks that made him appear part father figure, part politician, and part friend.

"I'm not happy at Ashworth & Palmer," I said.

Grave concern crossed his face. "Why not?"

His office window faced uptown. All Manhattan north of Wall Street stretched out before me . . . the Empire State Building . . . City Hall.

"I have doubts about a number of things," I said. "For

one, I don't feel any identification with the work I'm doing. It doesn't seem to matter to anyone here which side of a case we're on as long as we're paid and we win. Then there's the mood of the office. Everyone emphasizes the number of hours they work more than anything else, and most of the people I've met are terribly aloof. I've worked for Lonnie Hunker for over three months. I see him in the corridors maybe once a week. Other than that, all I get from him are pink routing slips with orders attached. I just don't feel comfortable here. Maybe I wasn't cut out to work at Ashworth & Palmer."

Having said my piece, I sat back and braced for the counterassault that never came.

"You know," Moffitt said gently, "twenty-five years ago I was very much like you. In fact, I left Ashworth & Palmer shortly after I got here. You didn't know that, did you?"

I shook my head.

"Well, I did," he said. "I'd been here about two months. I was a midwestern boy from Des Plaines, Illinois, via law school at Harvard, and as soon as I arrived at Ashworth & Palmer I was assigned to work for Russell Ford. He was the nastiest man I'd ever met. After eight weeks, I'd had it. I packed my bags and took a long bus ride home with the intention of setting up a shingle somewhere outside of Chicago. Then George Witherell flew out to see me. Among other things, he told me he didn't think Russell Ford would be long with the firm, which proved to be right. But more important, George passed along a few thoughts about the law and Ashworth & Palmer. Maybe I can do the same for you.

"Being a lawyer here has its rewards. Perhaps the most obvious are power, prestige, and money, all of which come with being an Ashworth & Palmer partner. But I've always felt there are more meaningful considerations. You see, I have a deep-seated commitment to the legal process. I firmly believe that, for all its defects, our system of justice is a good one. Sometimes the end result of a legal battle is unfair but, surprisingly often, equity and reason prevail. I derive a tremendous satisfaction from contributing toward that end.

"I suppose it's true that, working at Ashworth & Palmer, one tends to develop what you might call an affinity for big business. And maybe if I had started out with the Justice Department I'd be a famous trust-buster by now, rather than working on the other side. But our legal system is built on lawyers defending divergent points of view. The average Legal Aid attorney knows that ninety-five percent of his clients are guilty. His job, if he can do it, is to take a rapist or heroin pusher and get him off scot-free, yet very few people question his morality, quite possibly because he only makes one-third of what you as a first-year associate are getting paid at Ashworth & Palmer. Our morality is the same as that of a Legal Aid lawyer. We're participating in the system, and just because we represent corporations doesn't mean we're bad. And no profession outside the law is any better. Advertising men promote useless products. Newspapers oversensationalize to sell copies. I won't bother to dwell on politicians."

He had a very direct, easy way of speaking that grew more compelling as he went on.

"Next, and I'll be quite frank with you, Tom, you know what I like about the law? It takes a lot of skill and intelligence to do it well. It's a fabulous intellectual game, and not everyone is qualified to play it. Sure, we work long hours. That's part of the game. In fact, I'll be the first to admit that there were times as an associate when I worked past midnight when I didn't have to, just to curry favor. But long hours aren't the determining factor in deciding who makes partner. Jim Britt—and Jordan told me about his display at lunch your first day at work—Jim Britt averaged sixty-five hours a week for eight years. But his work quality was mediocre, so he didn't make partner. It's how good you are and what you produce that counts, not how many hours you spend at your desk."

Framed on the wall to my right, a pompous-looking British judge with a white wig and flowing red robe looked down at me. Above his visage were inscribed the words:

The law is the true embodiment
Of everything that's excellent.
It has no kind of fault or flaw
And I, my Lords, embody the law.

"There's something else that's also very important to me about Ashworth & Palmer," Moffitt continued. "Watching the growth of young lawyers and the sense of satisfaction that comes when someone such as yourself moves ahead. I liked your letter to the firm. I liked the initiative and drive it represented. And I like your coming in to see me this morning. It tells me that you're self-motivating, a self-starter. We need people like you at Ashworth & Palmer. You're the future of this firm. Don't let your self-doubts throw you. You've been here for less than four months. Give yourself and us a fair chance."

What can I say? There was a sincerity and a vitality to James Moffitt that sold me completely. In that moment, I wanted to be like him.

"Tom," he said, sensing that our conversation was near an end. "At last count there were several hundred thousand lawyers in the United States. I dare say that many of them are happy and successful in their work, despite not being partners at Ashworth & Palmer. But please, leave yourself the option of making this firm your permanent home. Don't coast. Do the job right. For as long as you're here, whether it's for one year or forty, do the best job you possibly can.

That way, there won't be any regrets on that far-off day four or five decades from now when your legal career is over."

A little after noon, Hardesty came by to see if I wanted to have lunch.

"I can't," I told him. "I have plans with Jordan."

VI

In the weeks that followed, my relationship with Hardesty changed. We continued to work on the UCC case and every few days had lunch together, but the ties between us were strained. Ed resented my growing acclimation to Ashworth & Palmer and the fact that I was diversifying my friendships. Meanwhile, with more conscious effort than I cared to admit, I was putting some distance between us. More and more, I found myself spending time with Jordan Caine. Word among the associates had it that Jordan was a "sure bet" for partnership, and being with him served several purposes: (1) he was a fount of knowledge regarding the Ashworth & Palmer system; (2) it didn't hurt to be seen in his presence by a partner; and (3) when all was said and done, Jordan was quite bright and interesting to be with. Also (and this is as good a time as any to bring the subject up), his secretary was one of the most exquisite-looking women in the world.

Beth Anders was five feet seven inches tall with high cheekbones, piercing blue eyes, long honey-colored hair, narrow hips, and breasts that may be politely described as "ample." Generally, she dressed in slacks, but on those days when she wore a dress to work it was clear that her legs were incredibly good. She was twenty-two years old and carried herself with the self-assurance of a woman mature beyond her years. On several occasions during the late fall and winter, I had seen her in the firm cafeteria—usually in the company of a black woman who I later learned was Carole Shiner's secretary. Beth Anders was the woman I had passed in the corridor at the close of work my first day at Ashworth & Palmer. One day in February, when I dropped by Jordan's office for lunch, I saw her sitting outside his office and learned both her identity and whom she worked for. The extent of our conversation was as follows:

ME: Hi! Is Jordan in?
HER: Yes.
ME: Thanks.

Jordan told me her name over a pastrami sandwich. In response to my further supercasual inquiries, he added that her typing and shorthand were excellent and repeated his earlier warning against dating within the office. Something in his manner suggested a proprietary interest.

On average, the women at Ashworth & Palmer—lawyers, secretaries, and paralegals—were remarkably unattractive. Beth Anders made up for all of them. On more than one occasion, I found myself standing in the corridor talking with a lawyer whose head would suddenly turn, and I would correctly postulate that Beth Anders was approaching from behind. Many a time, my own head reacted in similar fashion. Yet her looks were seldom discussed. At Ashworth & Palmer, one sought to avoid the reputation of cultivating interests that might conflict with a professional attitude.

My conversations with Beth Anders were limited to "hello" and other pleasantries. She seemed capable of so much more. Whenever I saw her talking with someone—usually a messenger or another secretary—her face was radiant and animated. Everything she said, even comments on the weather, sounded right. Yet I never saw her talking with a lawyer other than Jordan, who was her boss.

The firm published an office directory, listing the home address and telephone number of each Ashworth & Palmer employee. One night, I looked under the heading "nonlegal staff" to find her:

Ms. Beth Anders
(Secretary to Mr. Caine)
311 Bleecker Street
New York, N.Y. 10013
(212) 351-2114

I thought about her a lot. I still do.

Meanwhile, the Union Construction Company case dragged on. One by one, company executives flew to New York for debriefing on what they had done over the past ten years and why. Fifty thousand more documents were reviewed and, where warranted, red dots were affixed. One afternoon, Arlen Cohen and I spent four hours moving boxes around the file room for which UCC was billed one hundred thirty dollars an hour. In truth, the whole question of billing was a joke. Rarely did any associate on any case file a diary card reading "personal—*New York Times*—one quarter hour." Invariably, all firm clients were billed for work done on their behalf *and* the breaks taken in between. One afternoon, Carole Shiner and I sat around bitching about how boring it was to review documents. Then the conversation turned to office gossip, movies we had seen, and the fact that most partners looked as though their shoes were too tight. Carole volunteered the information that when James Moffitt went on vacation the previous year, he had "asked" an associate if the young man would "mind stopping by the apartment" to water Moffitt's plants two or three times a week. The associate, of course, had performed as requested.

After Carole left, I filled out my diary cards for the day. One entry read, "UCC, conference with Ms. Shiner, one hour." Carole recorded a similar entry—"conference w/ Mr. Henderson re document review." Our chat had cost the client one hundred thirty dollars. Later that month, Arlen Cohen and I entertained a UCC marketing representative who was in New York helping to prepare the case. Safe in the knowledge that we were on expense account, we took him to a good restaurant for dinner and to the theater afterwards. The following morning, Hunker instructed us to bill the client not only for out-of-pocket expenses but also for the hours spent at dinner and the show.

Outside the office, things could have been better. I had the normal complement of dates, but no one special entered my life. On occasion, I fantasized about the prospect of socializing with Beth Anders, but except for Jordan none of the lawyers seemed to have any contact with her. And the only information my guarded inquiries could gather was already obvious—that she had a ready smile and was absolutely gorgeous.

"I'm married," Arlen Cohen reminded me one afternoon when I brought the subject up. "*You* talk with her if you want to."

"She has lunch occasionally with my secretary," Carole Shiner advised. "That's all I know. I really don't get into my secretary's personal life."

One day, I asked Jordan if he and Beth Anders ever ate lunch together.

"Does any other lawyer here eat with his secretary?" Jordan demanded.

"Not that I know of."

"Then why should I have lunch with mine?"

Reluctantly, I concluded that, given office mores, Beth Anders was off limits. Meanwhile, Hardesty finally landed an appointment with "the gorgeous bitch" from his pottery class, but reported back glumly that at dinner she had ordered a shrimp cocktail, steak, asparagus, and a fourteen-dollar bottle of wine, all of which he had to pay for. And when he brought her home, she quickly picked up her cat and held it in her arms so he couldn't kiss her goodnight. Relations between us continued to deteriorate. More and more, I had the feeling that I was fitting nicely into the Ashworth & Palmer mold. My work quality was good, and people seemed to like me. By contrast, Ed was growing increasingly disenchanted and seemed perpetually at odds with Lonnie Hunker.

In truth, Hunker was not the easiest person in the world to get along with. As an associate, he had played the game well, regularly logging seventy hours a week before making partner. But he was the sort of person who seemed to derive pleasure from the personal misfortune of others and rarely showed consideration for anyone but himself. As Arlen Cohen once said, Lonnie Hunker enjoyed tapping ashes from his cigar on other people's lives.

Basically, Hunker's failings fell into three categories. First, he treated the associates who worked for him in extremely patronizing fashion. His view of the world was that good subordinates were invisible except when called upon, and that the ideal subordinate was one who would count out loud from one to ten thousand without question if so instructed. He was totally unwilling to discuss the merit (or lack thereof) of the assignments he gave and seldom returned my telephone calls or those of anyone else less important than himself. The only way an associate could gain access to him was via a written memorandum, and if Hunker didn't like what a memo said, he simply failed to acknowledge its receipt. Moreover, on those rare occasions when an associate was granted a personal audience, Lonnie did his best to establish psychological superiority. One of his favorite tactics, well-known throughout the office, was to stare at an associate and say solicitously, "You have a slight twitch in your eye. Are you all right?" I should add that, on one occasion when an associate suffered a severely broken leg and was in the hospital for six weeks, Hunker never inquired about his welfare. He did, however, send a messenger to the hospital with three thousand pages of depositions for the associate to digest.

Problem number two with Hunker was that, despite being an Ashworth & Palmer partner, he didn't seem to be a very astute lawyer. Several times at "team meetings," I listened as he cited a case, misinterpreted it, and then gave us half a dozen reasons why *he* was right. No one was ever able to convince him that he might be wrong. On more than one occasion, it occurred to us that making Hunker a partner might have been a serious Ashworth & Palmer error.

And last, quite frankly, Lonnie Hunker was a revolting excuse for a human being. His personal habits were disgusting. He was absolutely devoid of manners. "Please" and "thank you" were foreign to his vocabulary. Once I had the misfortune of sitting opposite him at a "team luncheon." Bite number two was in his mouth before bite number one was down the gullet. He never chewed his food if it could be swallowed whole or mashed between his side molars like trash in a New York City sanitation truck garbage compactor. At one particularly disgusting moment, I watched in amazement as a piece of pot roast dripping with grease escaped Hunker's mouth. In one fell swoop, his tongue reached down to steady the meat and he vacuum-sucked it in. Then he belched.

Despite his failings, it seemed in my best interests to accommodate Hunker. He was my boss, and my future depended on getting along with him. Eventually, I would be transferred to another partner, and as long as I didn't make waves I would survive. In fact, as strange as it might sound, Hunker appeared to like me.

Hardesty was less fortunate. Like most bullies, Hunker needed a whipping boy, and Ed was it.

"How many hours' sleep did you have the night before you wrote this?" Hunker demanded. We were at a mass meeting of all eleven Ashworth & Palmer lawyers assigned to the UCC case. The client was paying one thousand dollars an hour so Hunker could stand in a conference room on the sixty-fifth floor and wave a memorandum Ed had written the previous day on membrane-lined aeration basins. In truth, the memo was quite good, but it ran counter to Hunker's belief that membrane-lined aeration basins were an example of improved technology; thus it was unwelcome.

"I had seven hours' sleep," Ed answered.

"Seven? This reads like you had two. Maybe we should hang an 'Out of Order' sign on your head."

There were a few nervous giggles. The rest of us sat silent, even though we knew Ed's analysis was right.

"Thanks for standing up for me," Ed announced when the meeting ended and Hunker had gone. "With folks like you around, at least I don't have to worry about getting into heaven. There will be lots of empty places."

Then, as we left the room, he drew by my side. "Thanks to you in particular."

That afternoon, I went to see George Witherell. Why? Because I wanted to talk, and he was the only person at

Ashworth & Palmer I thought I could trust. Jordan was too calculating. Moffitt, I was beginning to suspect, turned his concern for young lawyers on and off like a faucet. George Witherell seemed to care. Other than brief conversations in the corridor, we hadn't talked since my first day at work, but he knew my name (he always said "Hello, Tom," which was more than most partners), and the door to his office seemed open.

"Could I make an appointment with Mr. Witherell?" I asked his secretary—a plump fiftyish woman who guarded the door.

"There's no need," she said. "You can go right in. He's not busy at the moment."

Witherell was sitting at his desk with the *New York Times* spread out in front of him. His office was a monument to elegance. Deep greens and blues dominated the room. On the wall behind him, a large gilt-framed painting showed Russian nobility dressed in stately evening attire disembarking from a horse-drawn carriage in the snow.

"It's about time," he announced, looking up from the newspaper. "You young lawyers are so busy and self-important that you never come to see me. What can I do for you?"

Suddenly I realized the need to choose my words carefully. Witherell had been with Ashworth & Palmer for fifty-five years, Lonnie Hunker for twenty. Strong bonds of mutual interest must have been forged between them.

"I've been thinking about your advice of last November," I began. "Primarily the difference between loving the law and simply being competent. I've been working on the UCC case for almost half a year now, and I haven't found much to love. Mostly, I've been studying sewage treatment technology and putting red dots on documents. I don't feel as though I'm growing as a lawyer, and I question whether any of us working on the case has the respect of the man we work for. I want to succeed at Ashworth & Palmer. I want to be a partner. But sometimes I think I'm missing the point of what this firm is all about."

Witherell waited until he was sure I had finished, then leaned back and rubbed his eyes. "I get tired sometimes," he said. "At my age, it happens with increasing frequency." He rubbed his eyes again. "Don't worry. I haven't forgotten your question."

Twenty seconds passed.

"As far as putting red dots on documents," he began thoughtfully, "there's nothing I can do to help. It's part of the job. Clients retain us because we're one of the few firms in America with the discipline and ability to learn an industry inside out. Step one of that learning process is reading documents, and step two is organizing what you've learned. If you were representing a tenant who lived in substandard housing, you'd want to know about every leaking pipe and piece of chipped paint in the apartment. You'd study the lease and every canceled check, housing summons, and complaint letter you could find. We do the same thing here, only on a larger scale.

"As for respect—and that's your word—as for respect, I've always assumed that all of our partners respect the associates who work for them. You'll have to be a little more precise in stating your problem."

I was now very much on the spot with no safe path to follow.

"I don't know," I fumbled. "I guess Lonnie Hunker has a pretty patronizing attitude toward us. At least, I get the impression that—"

"Respect is a two-way street," Witherell interrupted. "How do you feel about Lonnie Hunker?"

The spot I was standing on was growing ever smaller and more perilous.

"I find him difficult to relate to."

"That," Witherell said, "is a lawyer's answer. However, since you are purportedly a lawyer, I'll accept it. Off the record, let me tell you a little about Lonnie Hunker.

"Lonnie came to Ashworth & Palmer in the late 1950s. He wasn't the brightest associate we had back then. He was far from the most polished. But one thing about him stood out. He wanted to be a partner here more than any other associate I've ever known. He worked seventy hours a week for eight years. Except for Christmas, Thanksgiving, New Year's Day, and the Fourth of July, he rarely took a full day off. November 25, 1963, was a day of national mourning. An assassinated President of the United States was laid to rest. Lonnie was in the office at eight o'clock that morning. He worked until midnight. Ashworth & Palmer associates are allowed three weeks' vacation each year. Lonnie Hunker never took more than one. He relished the month of August because most associates were away then. That way, if an emergency came up, he was more likely to be called upon to handle it, which gave him extra experience and added exposure to partners. At one point, the pressures of work became too great for him to handle and, at his wife's urging, he sought psychiatric help. The firm had a medical plan which would have covered the cost completely. Lonnie never filed for payment because he was afraid, if we found out about his treatment, it would be held against him in the competition for partnership. His job is his life. His partners mean more to him than his wife and, I dare say, the associates who work for him mean more to him than his children.

"There are those who think we did Lonnie Hunker a disservice by making him a partner. The law can be painfully complex, and it just might be that at times he's in over his head. Not everyone can be a hotshot lawyer from Nebraska like you. But he's our partner, and we'll stand by him. The partnership is the most important thing any of us have, and it's far more important to uphold that partnership than to punish or reward individual partners."

He paused to make certain that the import of his remarks had sunk in, then continued. "I've heard it said, and maybe it's true, that the Ashworth & Palmer system institutionalizes partners not caring about the feelings of associates. But Lonnie Hunker doesn't get paid for being a nice person. And, conversely, Thomas Henderson is being paid quite a large amount of money to do a professional job. I suggest that, for the sake of your own future within the firm, you endure your two years with Lonnie Hunker as professionally as possible. Learn as much as you can from him, do your best, encourage him to think of you as a loyal ally. And because partners in this firm tend to stick together, I would think it inadvisable for you to share your feelings with any present or prospective partner other than myself. I, for my part, will keep your remarks in confidence."

Our conversation at an end, I rose to leave. "Young man," Witherell said, staring me back down into my chair, "there is one other matter which I would like to discuss. Last November, I suggested that you devise a legal argument which would lead to the elimination of blow-away cards from magazines. It is now late March, and I am still waiting for your solution."

March turned to April, and life at Ashworth & Palmer went on. The week after Easter, I got my own real live secretary, who was twenty-four years old and average in every respect save her name (Julie Swerzbinski) and her hyphenation (which was truly creative—e.g., Ashw-orth & Pa-lmer). Still, she made my job easier than before and was far superior to Eva Mueller (Hardesty's secretary), whom Ed described as "the only German who won't follow orders." Indeed, rumor had it that Hunker was on the verge of asking Ed to write memos out in longhand because he couldn't read Eva's typing.

Jim Britt left the firm in early May to take a job with a twelve-man office in midtown. As a parting gesture, Moffitt sent him a check for five thousand dollars and the promise of small case referrals in the future. That was the way things worked at Ashworth & Palmer. The firm had shed another piece of shriveled skin, and Britt would remain dependent on Moffitt's good graces for his livelihood.

Coincidental with Britt's leaving, Harris Boyd, one of Ashworth & Palmer's two black associates, was assigned to the UCC case. One night at dinner after a long document-indexing session, Harris drank too much and told us all that he regarded Martin Luther King as an embarrassment.

On the first day of June, attention focused on the firm's annual partnership rites. The deliberations were, of course, held behind closed doors, and thereafter all eighth-year associates were summoned one by one to Moffitt's office. (In addition to being Ashworth & Palmer's Chief of Litigation, Moffitt was also the firm's designated "Grim Reaper.")

John Bonnist was an associate who had spent eight years assigned to utility rate-increase cases. The work was deadly dull, but he had been a good soldier and never once complained. Moffitt told Bonnist that he had been passed over "because you lack breadth of experience." Maxwell Coy, a corporate associate, was bypassed because "you don't have that cutting edge" (whatever that meant). The most unusual exchange of the day occurred between Moffitt and Burt Bailey, an extremely bright, albeit somewhat loud, litigator who had worked like hell for six years and then eased up the last two to save his marriage. "You didn't have the guts to keep it up," Moffitt said. "You did it for six years, and then the job got too tough for you."

"It's not that the job got too tough," Bailey is reported to have answered. "It's that the job eats shit."

And so it went. Eight years earlier, thirty associates had started as a class at Ashworth & Palmer. Nine had dropped out before their day of reckoning. Of the remaining twenty-one, two were anointed.

"You've just been handed a fifteen million dollar prize," Moffitt told Richard Norwood, a Yale alumnus and senior associate on the American Steel case. "Congratulations on making the grade." A corporate department associate named Todd Casterline was similarly rewarded.

The remarkable thing was how fully the firm's decisions on partnership were accepted. Except for Burt Bailey's momentary outburst, the defeated candidates chose simply to grin and bear it. "I guess it goes back to when we were kids," John Bonnist said philosophically. "We were all conditioned to accept authority. Take playing Giant Steps, for example. We never questioned the right of the leader to tell us how many pinwheel steps or scissor steps we could take. Those with authority have an absolute right to preordain the winner. That's life."

Two days after the partners met, Moffitt told Jordan that his name had been "often mentioned" in discussion about the firm's future. "And for a sixth-year associate," the Chief of Litigation said, "your future looks exceedingly bright."

That same afternoon, George Witherell cornered me in the corridor and announced, "Your name came up in conjunction with the long-range plans of the firm. You will be pleased to know that Lonnie Hunker spoke quite favorably of you."

Lonnie Hunker might have been saying good things about me, but Ed Hardesty's humiliation continued. "The number on Ed's football jersey in college was sixty-five," Hunker announced at a team meeting held the last week in June. "But Ed couldn't count that high. For four years, he saw that big six and that big five next to one another, and he thought his number was eleven."

There was the usual response of nervous laughter from

some and silence from the rest of us. Hunker, having told his joke, turned to the subject of an upcoming conference with Samuel McAleer, the Judge assigned to the UCC case. McAleer was in charge of the case for all purposes and had grown increasingly irked by the snail's pace at which the litigation was proceeding. In an effort to speed things up, he had telephoned both sides and ordered, "I want you people active over the summer. That means no delay or sloughing off. Be in my courtroom this Friday at two P.M. prepared to negotiate a schedule that will bring this case to trial within the next two years."

Following the Judge's telephone call, Hunker had ordered that an Advisory Memorandum be prepared. Its purpose was to set forth UCC's side of the case and explain how Ashworth & Palmer was proceeding "as expeditiously as possible in the face of unreasonable and burdensome demands by the government."

"I've arranged for the memo to be hand-delivered to Judge McAleer's chambers Thursday afternoon," Hunker told us at the close of our defense team conference. "That way, he'll have a full day to study it before we meet with him on Friday. Hopefully, our arguments will have sunk in by then and McAleer will be leaning in our favor."

"I have a question," Ed said.

Hunker's face was a portrait of exasperation. "What is it?"

"Don't we have to serve a copy of the memorandum on the government?"

"That would cost us the advantage of surprise," Hunker said. "Can I go on now?"

"I don't understand," Ed persisted. "A party to litigation can't sneak documents into court without showing them to the other side. Everything we file with the court has to be served on the government first."

Ed was right, of course, and all of us knew it. "All right," Hunker muttered, retreating slightly. "Why don't you serve a copy on the government by mail? Send it out Thursday afternoon."

"That doesn't make sense," Ed said. "The court session is Friday, and you know how bad the mails are. The government won't get our papers until after the weekend."

"I know," Hunker smirked. "That's the point. We can say we served the memorandum, and the government will still be in the dark."

"That's unorthodox, to say the least," Ed pressed.

"Look," Hunker snapped. "I'd love to continue this conversation because it's very psychedelic and all that, but we have work to do. Serve the memo by mail on Thursday afternoon. Someday, in the unlikely event you're made a partner, you can do things your way. In the meantime, we'll do them mine."

Friday afternoon, we assembled in court—all eleven of us—to watch Lonnie Hunker perform before the Judge. McAleer was a slight, gray-haired man in his late fifties, physically unprepossessing, with a decidedly quiet manner, but the long black robe he wore indicated that he was in charge. Hunker bowed and scraped as though appearing before Oliver Wendell Holmes.

The government was represented by Alexander Beibel, a senior attorney in the Antitrust Division of the Justice Department, who appeared with two followers. "Your Honor," Beibel announced as the proceedings began. "I have a complaint to make. This afternoon, moments before coming to court, I received a document entitled Advisory Memorandum of Law from Ashworth & Palmer *in the mail.* I have not had time to read it. Indeed, were it not for the swiftness with which our fine postal service operates, I would not have received the memorandum at all prior to this conference."

The Judge was looking directly at Hunker, and the Judge looked pissed.

"Now, Mr. Hunker knows the rules of the game," Beibel continued. "He's well aware of the fact that litigation is not a contest of cheap surprises, and his office is ten short blocks from mine. Furthermore, as I understand it, Ashworth & Palmer employs a fleet of twenty-five ablebodied messengers. I would appreciate it if Your Honor instructed Mr. Hunker to serve all future papers in this litigation by hand. An incident of this nature should not occur again."

"Goddamn it!" Hunker bellowed, turning toward Hardesty. "I told you to serve those papers by hand."

For a moment, there was silence.

"That's not true," I blurted out. "You told him to mail them."

Hunker's face turned crimson.

"Mr. Hunker," the Judge said. "I hardly think it's worth the court's time to get bogged down in this matter. Thus, I will simply instruct you to make certain that this type of thing does not happen again. Get your ship in order. Do you understand?"

"Yes, Your Honor."

"Very well, then, let's proceed—without reference to your so-called Advisory Memorandum."

We returned to Ten Wall Street as a group.

"I'd like to see you for a moment," Hunker said to me as we stepped off the elevator on the sixty-fifth floor. Obediently, I followed him upstairs and entered his office, where he closed the door behind us. We stood by the drapes.

"What happened today must never happen again," he said. "You're a bright young man with a promising future, but you have a lot to learn. Lesson number one for the day —a good marksman always paints the target around the hole he has shot. Lesson number two—deceit is built into competition. That's all I have to say to you right now. This incident will not be mentioned between us again."

Hardesty was waiting for me when I returned to my desk.

"Thanks," he said. "You just earned one gold star from me and about a thousand black marks from Hunker."

"I'll take that trade anytime," I told him.

We shook hands, and his face broke into a broad grin. "By the way, congratulations."

"What for?"

"After eight months as a litigator, you've finally spoken your first words in open court."

Riding home on the subway at the close of work, I felt pretty good. It was too early to tell what repercussions, if any, would follow as a consequence of my speaking the truth, but at least my self-respect was intact. In the lobby of my apartment, I checked for mail (there was none), then went upstairs to change into a sport shirt and pair of jeans. It was seven o'clock and still light outside—another warm, breezy Friday night alone in New York. On impulse and with no particular destination in mind, I rode the elevator back down to street level and began to walk. Riverside Drive was my favorite street in the city, and I soon found myself flanked by tall stately apartment buildings on one side, Riverside Park on the other. "Maybe Hunker will hold a grudge forever," I told myself, "but at least I did what was right, goddamn it! At least I did what was right."

Then I realized that God rewards those who are just. Directly opposite me, on the corner of Riverside Drive and 79th Street, waiting for the light to change stood Beth Anders.

VII

An associate doesn't waylay a partner in public and begin a conversation. Rather, the choice lies with the partner. If he stops to talk, then the associate does likewise. If the partner walks on, then the exchange is limited to pleasantries. It's the same with associates and secretaries, except here the associate holds the power. A place for everyone and everyone in their place. As Jordan Caine once said, it's not the way things should be, but that's the way they are. If I didn't make the first overture, office protocol would require Beth Anders to pass me by.

I waved from across the street, and she acknowledged my presence with a smile. The light turned green, and she began to cross. I waited on the curb for her arrival.

"Hello, Tom Henderson," she said.

She knew my name.

"Hello, Beth Anders," I answered, proving that I knew hers. "What are you doing in this neighborhood?"

She was wearing brown corduroy slacks and a white sweater. Her honey-colored hair, parted down the middle, fell in swirls beneath her shoulders.

"I had drinks with a friend," she said. "Afterwards, I felt like walking." Her teeth were white and perfectly straight, her complexion flawless. "What about you? I thought all lawyers worked until midnight."

"I live nearby," I explained. "And we get time off on Friday for good behavior."

"I'm glad you've been good."

Then there was silence. . . . We had run out of conversation. . . . Time to say good-bye.

"Would you like to take a walk?" I half pled.

"Sorry," I knew she'd say. "I'd love to, but I have plans for dinner and I'm late."

"Sure," she answered.

There's a winding path that leads through Riverside Park to the water's edge. We followed it and sat by the Hudson River.

"How many years have you been at Ashworth & Palmer?"

"Five," she told me.

"What did you do before that?"

"I was in high school."

"Do you like the firm?"

"It's okay."

We were relating (or not relating) on two levels. Physically, I couldn't take my eyes off her. Intellectually, I couldn't think of anything to say.

"How long have you worked for Jordan?" I finally asked.

"Almost the full five years. I was in the steno pool for six weeks, and then he took me on assignment."

"What's he like?"

"A charming meat grinder."

A single gold chain hung loosely around her neck.

"You know something?" I said. "Last week the American Bar Association conducted a poll of Wall Street lawyers, and you were voted the most beautiful legal secretary in New York."

("What a dumb thing to say," I told myself.)

She laughed. "Did you vote?"

"Twice. Both times for you."

For whatever reason, that broke the ice. "My father's a bartender," she told me as we exchanged basic data. "I grew up in Queens. My parents still live there with my younger brother. He's sixteen. I have an older sister who's a nurse."

"Why did you become a secretary?"

"When I graduated from high school, I was seventeen. My grades were good, but neither of my parents had gone to college, and school didn't seem important. I guess all I really wanted was to get married and have children. I figured that, being a secretary, I could make a good salary and work in a nice office with bright people until the right man came along. Four years later, when he hadn't arrived, I realized it might be a long wait, so I got my own apartment and kept the job. That was eighteen months ago."

I told her about growing up in Nebraska, that I was an only child, that my mother had died three years earlier and my father the previous autumn. Suddenly she was easy to talk with, and I found myself reminiscing about the night almost twenty years earlier when my father had woken me up at midnight because our dog was having puppies. I watched three of them being born.

"I like it that you're from Nebraska," she said.

"How come?"

"It makes you less threatening than the other lawyers."

We sat by the river for over an hour and then, because it was getting late and the parks in New York aren't safe after dark, we walked back toward Riverside Drive.

"Have you eaten?" I asked.

She shook her head.

"I have some cold cuts in the refrigerator at home. We could pick up a head of lettuce and make a chef's salad."

"That would be nice," she said.

One block east of the park, we stopped at a small delicatessen where I bought some lettuce and a box of mushrooms. Then we walked to the sixteen-story red-brick building I called home.

"Good evening, Mr. Henderson," the doorman said, nodding his approval of my companion.

"That was Patrick," I explained on the elevator going up. "Of all the doormen, he's my favorite." The car stopped on the eleventh floor. My apartment was two doors down the hall. "Let me put the lettuce and mushrooms in the kitchen," I said as we stepped inside. "Then I'll give you a guided tour."

Actually, there wasn't much to show. The apartment was functional but hardly a candidate for treatment in *Better Homes and Gardens*. The foyer served as a dining area. Beyond that, a narrow walk-in kitchen housed the usual appliances. A twelve-foot-square bedroom was off to the right with a spruce-green carpet, teak dresser, and walnut desk. Two bookshelves lined with records and books stood just inside the bedroom door. My stereo was on the dresser. The largest piece of furniture in the bedroom was a walnut platform bed lodged against the left wall. Half a dozen plants in clay pots added color to the windowsill. A dozen photos brightened the walls.

The living room was larger with a deep blue carpet. Two mahogany end tables flanked a pine-green sofa with a circular swivel chair off to the right. Two more chairs rested against the far wall. Four posters I had picked up at a midtown art sale gave the room some color. There was a bathroom off the foyer by the bedroom door.

"It's a little bare," I admitted as the grand tour ended.

"I should have brought more odds and ends from Nebraska, but eventually I'll build a new collection."

We had gravitated to the living room, and Beth seated herself on the swivel chair by the sofa. "Would you like a drink?" I asked.

"Some wine if you have it."

"Red or white?"

"It doesn't matter. Whatever you think goes with chef's salad."

I left her to examine the sparsely populated wine rack in the foyer. "How about Almaden red?" I called out. "A delightful claret at two dollars and sixty-nine cents a bottle."

"Fine."

I pulled the cork, filled two glasses, and returned to the living room, handing one glass to Beth and seating myself on the sofa.

"Cheers," she said, leaning forward to touch glasses.

"Something incredible happened today," I told her, taking my first sip.

"What?"

"We were in court—all eleven of us on the UCC case—and Lonnie Hunker lied to the Judge."

"About what?"

"Whether he had told Ed Hardesty to serve some papers by mail or by hand. It was a minor thing, but he blew it way out of proportion by lying about it and trying to place the blame on Ed."

She was looking at me without talking. Both of us were sipping at a fair rate.

"Hunker's a slob," I said. "He lurches around the office shoving his chest out with his stomach sucked in, but it doesn't work. He still looks as if he ate too much Chinese food for dinner. If God made a list of people he was ashamed of creating, Lonnie Hunker would head the list."

"So why do you stay?"

"Because it's my job. And it's Ashworth & Palmer. And I want to be a partner."

Our glasses were near empty, and I reached for the bottle.

"Just a little more for me," she cautioned.

"What's Jordan like?" I asked for the second time in as many hours.

"Very controlled. He dominates his environment as completely as possible. Like all Ashworth & Palmer lawyers, he races people through doors and occasionally knocks someone over to get off the elevator first." She looked up from her wine. "That's the bad side. On the good side, he can be utterly charming, and all things considered, he's not a bad boss. He treats me as though I have some intelligence, which is more than most lawyers do. Sometimes he gives me paralegal assignments. Once he assigned me the same work as a first-year associate. I had to prepare an index of trial testimony. For about a week, I felt just like a lawyer."

"How come I never see you talking with the other lawyers?"

"They never talk with me. Every now and then, one of them makes some sophomoric comment about my sweater being too tight, but that's the extent of it. A lot of lawyers at Ashworth & Palmer are socially retarded."

"What's your definition of retardation?"

"Someone who knows the names of forty partners and a hundred Supreme Court cases but can't remember the name of a single messenger."

I was starting to feel the wine.

"Why do *you* stay?" I asked.

"I told you. Jordan's not a bad boss—and the pay is good. Being a secretary is all right and, believe it or not, being a legal secretary is a step up the ladder. If I tell people outside the office that I work in a law firm, they're impressed. Besides, what else am I going to do? My only other work experience is three years as a part-time cashier at Zuckerman's

Stationery Store when I was in high school. In case you're wondering, being a secretary is better."

"Don't you get tired of the work?"

"Why should I?"

"There's no advancement. You've been doing the same thing for five years. A secretary is a secretary is a secretary."

Her blue eyes narrowed. "Do me a favor," she said. "Try thinking of me as a person and not a secretary. We'll get along much better. I'm trying to like you, but sometimes I think you can't view me outside the context of Ashworth & Palmer."

"I didn't mean it that way."

Artfully, she changed the subject. "Why is Patrick your favorite doorman?"

"Huh?"

"In the elevator coming up, you said that Patrick was your favorite. How come?"

"I don't know. I guess it's because he's brighter than the others and he always says hello."

"I'm like Patrick," she said. "I'm bright and I always say hello. And I'm hungry. Can we make the salad?"

With Beth looking on, I rinsed the mushrooms and lettuce in cold water and deposited them on the formica-topped kitchen counter next to a large wooden bowl. Then I took a package of neatly wrapped ham, turkey, and Swiss cheese from the refrigerator and began to slice.

"Not bad," she said. "Can I help?"

"You can open another bottle of wine."

"All right, but you'll have to drink more than half."

"Agreed."

I reached into the refrigerator for the salad dressing, and Beth disappeared into the foyer to examine the wine. "You only have one bottle of red left," she called out. "Is it all right to use it?"

"No problem."

"Where's the corkscrew?"

"On the kitchen counter."

Bottle in hand, she returned.

"Let me set the table," I said. "Then I'll light the candles and dinner will be ready."

"What candles?"

"The candles I'm about to put on the table."

Moments later—salad mixed, wine poured, lights off, candles on—we sat opposite one another.

"You know," she said, "when I first came to Ashworth & Palmer, I was in total awe of the lawyers. I hadn't been that scared since I was in first grade looking up at the kids on the sixth grade playground."

"And?"

She shrugged. "When I look at sixth graders now, they don't seem particularly intimidating. The same holds true for lawyers. They can hire and fire, but they're no different from the rest of us. For some reason, most lawyers think their secretaries look up to them, but that's bullshit. I happen to think Jordan is all right, but you should hear the way some secretaries talk about their bosses. You know what we talk about in the ladies' room? How did this guy ever get out of law school when he can't even write? Look at the way so-and-so fawns over Moffitt. And why it is that every man in the office stares at my chest, but none of them ever come over to have lunch with me in the cafeteria. Last month, Ellis Slattery's secretary was blabbing about a blouse he gave her for Christmas, wrapped in a box from Saks Fifth Avenue. When she went to return it, they told her it came from Gimbel's."

We finished eating.

"Would you like to listen to some records?" I asked.

"The stereo, as I recall, is in the bedroom?"

"I'm afraid so."

"All right."

"Can I bring the candle in with us, or would that be too obvious?"

"No more obvious than anything else," she laughed.

I put on four records—one Elton John, two Simon and Garfunkels, and an album of love songs by The Beatles. Beth sat on the carpet, arms folded, with her back against the bed. "Who are the people in the pictures?" she asked, pointing to a photograph on the wall.

"My parents."

"They look like nice people."

"They were the best."

"Do you miss them?"

I nodded.

Even in the dark, her eyes looked blue. The candle picked up the highlights in her hair. "It's funny," I said. "One of the things I remember best about my father is his telling me that I had a face the color of strawberry ice cream the day I was born."

The music seemed to be growing louder. Paul McCartney was singing.

"Have you ever slept with anyone at Ashworth & Palmer?" I asked.

There was a long silence. "It's none of your business," she said at last, "but the answer is no."

"I'm sorry," I fumbled. "I didn't mean to embarrass you. I tend to make a jerk of myself when I drink too much."

"That's all right. It was an honest question."

The light from the candles reflected off her face. The shadows on her cheeks were unexplored valleys begging to be touched. Every line and ridge was etched to perfection.

"You're beautiful," I said. "You know that, don't you?"

"Yes."

"What does it do to your life?"

"I don't complain about it. Sometimes it's hard to deal

with people who can't see beyond looks, but overall it's an advantage. I try not to overuse it."

"If I kissed you, would you kiss me back?"

"Sure."

Our lips came together, and my hand dropped to her breast.

"Just one thing," she said. "I want to make sure you understand, the wine has nothing to do with this."

Very easily, with no sense of urgency or doubt, we began taking off our clothes.

"Don't forget your socks," she warned. "Socks are definitely uncool in bed."

"How about watches?"

"They're permitted."

Her bra and panties, both white, fell to the floor. A miniature red rose was embroidered on each. Both of us were naked. One of life's lessons is that dreams and fantasies aren't bound by the same rules as reality, but on rare occasions they do coincide. This was one of those moments. In every way, Beth Anders was perfect—warmer and gentler than I had imagined, even more beautiful without clothes than with them. Her legs were long and hard. Reaching out, I ran my hands across her stomach and back. Every inch was smooth and firm with muscles stretched taut in a way that suggested strength.

"You're quite something," I said.

"I know."

"But you have big feet."

"Size ten."

Honey-colored hair fell gently beneath her shoulders, framing a face that was flawless. Her breasts were firm and perfectly shaped.

"Are you good in bed?" she asked. "I've never been seduced by a lawyer."

"I have good nights and bad ones like everyone else. But the two of us can get it right if we practice enough."

We got it right on the first try. And the second. Just before I drifted off to sleep, I realized that for the entire evening reality had seemed suspended. And then I wondered what effect the whole thing would have on my future at Ashworth & Palmer.

PART TWO

VIII

Hardesty sat behind his desk, mouth agape, listening to details of my conquest. "What happens next?" he inquired.

"I don't know. She left Saturday around noon. I meant to call her Sunday night, but by the time I got home from dinner it was too late. I like her, I really do. But I feel funny about dating someone from the office, particularly a secretary. If word gets out, the powers that be could be very unhappy."

"I didn't notice a section on dating in the Firm Manual."

"Unwritten rules are the worst."

"You're right," he admitted. "God forbid you should get caught using the partners' men's room."

"Be serious," I prodded. "What happens if Beth and I start dating, and she blabs about it all over the place?"

"That's what you seem to be doing."

"I am not. The only person I've told is you."

"The only person you've seen is me. It's nine thirty-seven on Monday morning. You didn't arrive at work until nine-ten. Your suit jacket was hung on a hanger by nine-eleven, and you were in my office at nine-twelve. Outside of the receptionist, I'm the first person you've had the opportunity to tell." His eyes narrowed. "You didn't tell the receptionist, did you?"

"No, I didn't tell the receptionist."

"That's good. You have more self-restraint than I thought."

"Go to hell."

"Look," Hardesty counseled. "Be reasonable. For starters, it's conceivable that Beth Anders is as uptight as you are, which means she won't say a word. Second, and this might come as a shock, you shouldn't rule out the possibility that she doesn't regard sleeping with a lawyer as worth talking about. And last—maybe, just maybe—*she* doesn't want to see *you* again."

The first two possibilities were okay. Number three was sufficiently disconcerting that I decided to wander down the hall and pay a courtesy call on Beth Anders. As usual, she was behind her desk in the alcove by Jordan's office.

"Hi," I said.

"Oh, hi!" she answered, looking up from the magazine in front of her. "How was the rest of your weekend?"

"Not bad. What about yours?"

The intercom buzzed. "Just a sec," she told me, picking up the receiver. . . . "Sure. I'll be right in. . . . Sorry," she said when the receiver was back in place. "Jordan wants to dictate some letters. See you later."

Somewhat irked, I returned to my office where Hardesty sat waiting. "Hunker wants to see the two of us as soon as possible," he announced.

"What about?"

"I don't know, but he sounded agitated on the telephone."

"Fabulous. When do we go?"

"I assume that 'as soon as possible' means now."

Hunker's office looked the same as it had my first day at Ashworth & Palmer. I sat in a chair by the windows (which were still obscured by drapes), and Hardesty took a seat to my right. Hunker faced us from behind his desk. It was the first time the three of us had been alone since our introductory session eight months earlier.

"Tom . . . Ed . . ." he began. "I need your help but, more than that, I'm about to hand you a unique opportunity to learn the anatomy of a lawsuit inside out." Reaching for a thin manila folder on his desk, he withdrew a copy of a letter written on Ashworth & Palmer stationery and addressed to the Corporation Counsel of the City of New York. "Here! Take a look."

> Dear Sirs,
>
> On May 26 of this year at approximately 6:30 P.M., I was descending the stairs at the Wall Street Station of the Lexington Avenue IRT subway. When I reached platform level, I noticed that there was a considerable amount of yellow paint on my suit. Retracing my steps, I found a transit worker engaged in painting the handrailing by the stairs bright yellow.
>
> No warning sign had been posted. When I sought to discuss the matter with the painter (who identified himself as Anthony Pisano), he became loud and abusive. My suit, which was purchased this spring at a cost of four hundred dollars, has been ruined.
>
> I would very much appreciate prompt receipt of a check from you in the amount of four hundred dollars. In the event that payment is not forthcoming, legal proceedings will be instituted against you.
>
> Very truly yours,
> Lionel J. Hunker

"That was five weeks ago," Hunker announced. "This

morning, in the mail"—he reached for the manila folder and pulled out a second letter—"I received this. Read it."

Dear Mr. Hunker,

This is to acknowledge receipt of your May 27 letter.

The incident of which you complain was reported by Mr. Anthony Pisano on the evening of May 26. Thereafter, a Transit Authority investigator was dispatched to the scene. His report states that the area was properly cordoned off with appropriate warning signs in clear view and that perhaps you pushed through the barricade which closed off the stairwell, rather than walk one block to an unobstructed entrance. Mr. Pisano has been employed by the Metropolitan Transportation Authority for sixteen years, and no complaint of loud or abusive language has ever been registered against him. Moreover, given rush hour conditions at our Wall Street station, one would think that an inadequate warning sign would have resulted in far more than one soiled suit, yet yours is the only complaint we have received.

I regret that we are unable to comply with your request for payment.

Sincerely,
Abraham Waltuck
Staff Attorney

"This," Hunker declared, "is a matter of principle. Someone is going to pay for that suit, and it won't be me. I want the two of you to take a look at the statutes and find out what has to be done to sue the city. Cover every angle—which court to sue in, punitive damages, and anything else that's relevant."

"How much time do you want us to spend?" Ed queried.

"I want you to do the job right. Treat this as you would

any other firm matter. Charge your time to Office General. And remember, this is a priority item. I expect some answers from the two of you by Friday at the latest."

"Do you believe it?" Hardesty asked as we walked back to my office.

"Not quite," I said. "But frankly, I'd rather work on Hunker's paint case than stick red dots on documents for the Union Construction Company. At least this way maybe we'll learn something about litigation."

"I doubt it, but where do we begin?"

"Since neither of us has any idea how to sue the city, I suggest we start in the firm library."

Which was what we did. And for the first time since coming to Ashworth & Palmer, I began to feel as though I was unraveling the complexities of the law. Actually, the City of New York wasn't the proper party to sue. Rather, Hunker's complaint appeared to be against the Metropolitan Transportation Authority—a wholly independent organization which operates New York's mass transit system. For the better part of Monday, Ed and I sat in the library, leafing through black-bound volumes trying to determine whom to sue and where to sue them. At day's end, I returned to my desk where a blue envelope marked "Thomas Henderson—Personal" lay unopened. Inside, I found a sheet of lined yellow paper:

> Dear Tom,
>
> Sorry I couldn't talk this morning. Would you like to come for dinner Friday night?
>
> Beth

"Yes," I penned in reply. "But no lima beans or carrots."

Then I joined Hardesty for dinner. "You know," he said over drinks in a Chinese restaurant, "you shouldn't take

Beth Anders too lightly. She might turn out to be more than you bargained for."

"What do you mean by that?"

"I'm not sure," he mused. "It's just my normal stream of consciousness. But you seem to think of her as a secretary first and as Beth Anders second, and that could be a serious error."

"How's your love life?" I asked, refocusing the subject.

"Lousy. I'm much better at giving advice than living it. At present, I'm still lavishing my thoughts on the bitch from last semester's pottery class."

We ordered wonton soup, shredded beef Szechuan style, and hot spicy shrimp.

"This might seem like a silly question," I asked, "but if she's such a bitch, why are you still in pursuit after six months of absolute failure?"

"I didn't say I was in pursuit. I said I think about her—largely because she's gorgeous and I'm weak. Like I said, I'm better at giving advice than living it."

The waiter placed our soup in front of us. Ed sprinkled some noodles in his bowl. "You still want to make partner at Ashworth & Palmer, don't you?"

"Yes."

"Why?"

"Because it's the best law firm in the country, and I like to accomplish what I set out to do."

"Does Lonnie Hunker strike you as the cream of America's legal crop?"

"Not really," I answered, "but Hunker's atypical. He's a weak link in the partnership chain, and everyone knows it. My guess is that people like James Moffitt and George Witherell are much better lawyers and also far nicer as human beings."

"Maybe."

We split the beef and shrimp into two portions, and began

wrestling with the chopsticks. "Why do you stay at Ashworth & Palmer if you have such negative feelings about it?"

"For a couple of reasons," Ed answered. "The money is good. I like working in an office that functions well and surrounds me with bright people. I assume I'm learning something, and it would look bad on my résumé to leave before two years are up. Plus, I have no idea what I'd do if I left. There are thousands of legal jobs, but I'm not sure which are worth having and which aren't. I don't want to make a mistake twice." Suddenly his eyes brightened. "Hey! The two of us could quit law altogether and go into business. We could market an inflatable Anthony Perkins doll for women to take into the shower."

"That," I explained, "is why you have trouble getting dates."

Tuesday, Wednesday, and Thursday, my time was divided equally between *United States* v. *Union Construction Company* and *Hunker's Yellow Paint*. Twice, I passed Beth Anders in the corridor, but the first time I was on my way to a UCC team meeting and the second she was with Jordan. Our only conversation occurred on Wednesday night and was brief since I had the audacity to call while she was watching an old Humphrey Bogart movie on television. Friday afternoon, Ed and I met with Hunker to discuss *the* case.

"What have you got?" The Hunk demanded.

I took the lead in discussing our findings. "First," I explained, "we're talking about a lawsuit against the Metropolitan Transportation Authority, not the city. As far as procedure is concerned, the case appears similar to most negligence actions, with one exception. Prior to suit, you'll have to file a Notice of Claim against the MTA."

"When does the notice have to be filed?"

"Within ninety days of the incident."

"This is going to be a pain in the ass," Hunker muttered.

"Local bureaucracies are all the same. They never settle. They never give an inch. They're so pigheaded, they'll fight this case forever."

"What about Small Claims Court?" Ed suggested. "That would give you a quick adjudication."

Inside Hunker's head, the wheels were turning. "We'll sue the Wop," he blurted out.

"Pardon?"

"That's it!" he bellowed. "We'll sue the Wop. He's the bastard in this, anyway. If we sue the city or the MTA, they'll assign a half dozen lawyers to the case. But if we sue the Wop, he's on his own. Don't you see? I'll allege in the complaint that he was acting outside the scope of his authority by not setting up proper signs before painting, and as a civic-minded New Yorker, I don't expect the taxpayers to pay for *his* error. I'll sue *him* personally. That way, either he gives in, or he has to shell out to hire a lawyer."

A decidedly queasy feeling was working its way down toward the pit of my stomach.

"Federal court," Hunker was saying. "If we could sue there, he'd never find his way around without a lawyer, but New York State Supreme Court is just as good. I want the two of you to find out where this fellow lives. Then draw up a complaint for twenty thousand dollars—four hundred for the suit, a couple of thousand for loud, abusive language, and the rest for punitive damages. Anthony Pisano will come crawling on his knees to settle this case before we're through."

Back in my office, Hardesty and I conducted the inevitable post mortem.

"The whole thing stinks," Ed said.

"Maybe it really did happen the way Hunker claims."

"Maybe, but given the Lonnie Hunker I've come to know and love, I doubt it. I know who I'm rooting for."

"Me too," I admitted.

"The same person?"

"I think so."

The door opened, and a honey-colored head popped in. "Sorry," Beth apologized. "I didn't know you had company."

"It's okay," I assured her. "In a world of friends and foes, Ed is a friend. Have the two of you met?"

She shook her head, and I introduced them.

"Charmed," Hardesty announced in his finest Elizabethan manner.

Beth curtsied and smiled. "About dinner tonight," she began with a trace of awkwardness. "Is eight o'clock all right?"

After work I went home, changed into a pair of blue jeans, and went shopping for a bottle of wine. Red or white? I'd forgotten to ask what we were having for dinner, although as far as my palate was concerned, the color of the wine didn't matter. A connoisseur might view mixing burgundy and fish with the same horror as pouring ketchup on chocolate mousse, but I'm not a connoisseur. After due deliberation, I opted for red and took the subway down to Beth's apartment.

The Bleecker Street area where she lived was vintage Greenwich Village—narrow sidewalks, small shops, and residential buildings, with enough trees on each block to remind me that, even in New York City, nature did exist. Beth lived on the third floor of a four-story brownstone near the corner of Bleecker and Charles Street. When I arrived, she was dressed in jeans and a snug-fitting T-shirt.

Her apartment was smaller than mine, but decorated in extremely good taste. The living room was maybe ten by twelve feet long with a highly polished parquet floor, stone fireplace, pine bookshelves, and refinished walnut furniture. Streams of ivy climbed the walls. Tiny baskets, vases, and assorted bric-a-brac added character. The bedroom was similar in decor, only slightly smaller. A kitchen alcove with neatly organized cabinets and shelves stood just off the front door.

"Very nice," I told her.

"I've always felt that women have more of an eye for decorating than men."

I cast a challenging look in her direction.

"Really," she added. "The average woman is far better able to appreciate subtlety and art than the average man."

"Well, as a hatchet-wielding man who just last week ripped up a painting by Leonardo da Vinci at the Metropolitan Museum of Art, I'm impressed."

"Touché," she said.

We returned to the living room, and I settled on the sofa. "How was your day?"

"Boring," she groaned. "This morning, I typed twelve pages of statistics. This afternoon, I spent two hours at the copying machine because Jordan had an emergency copying and collating job."

"Is he as good a lawyer as people say?"

"As a legal secretary not admitted to the bar, I'm hardly in a position to judge. But Moffitt likes him. I know that."

"What happens to you if Jordan becomes a partner?"

"I guess I become secretary to a partner."

"Is that a big thing?"

"Some people think so. My salary will go up fifty dollars a week, and there's an element of prestige involved. But that's two years off, and I haven't thought that far ahead. I like what I'm doing now. I'll worry about the future later."

"Doesn't the thought of being a secretary for the next umpteen years bother you?"

I was treading on dangerous territory.

"You're starting right in, aren't you?" she said. "No preliminaries or anything. Just 'let's talk down to the stupid secretary.' "

"I didn't mean it that way. To the contrary, all I'm saying is that you're too smart for your job."

"I happen to like my job."

"But you're in a rut."

"So are a lot of lawyers."

"At least they have upward mobility," I pressed.

"And how many jobs with upward mobility do you know of that are available for a woman with a high school diploma?"

"You could go to college."

"Sure, if someone gave me twenty thousand dollars."

"What about part-time classes?"

"That sounds marvelous. How would you like to put in eight hours at work each day and then go to school and study for tests on weekends plus four nights a week for the next eight years?"

"Okay," I said. "Maybe I should go out the door and try coming in again on a different note."

"Don't bother. Just open the wine. Dinner's ready."

One of the things I've noticed in recent years is that fewer and fewer women know how to cook. That's not to say anyone should spend all of her or his time in the kitchen, but many women don't cook for friends or themselves anymore. They're dependent on eating out or warming up fast foods and, in truth, oftentimes cook less well than men. Beth was a first-rate cook. We had boneless chicken breasts in white wine and mushroom sauce with broccoli on the side.

"What do you do with your free time?" I asked midway through dinner.

"Lots of things."

"Like what?"

"I read, go to movies, window-shop, have dinner with friends. Every Thursday night, I go to an old-age home in Queens."

"What for?"

"To visit an eighty-year-old man named Robert Grissom. He used to tend bar with my father. Then he contracted Parkinson's disease and his wife died. After that, his children put him in the home. My father visits two afternoons a week. I go Thursdays after work. We're his only regular visitors."

"What about his children?" I asked.

"They're not so hot."

Dinner ended, and I stood up to help clear the table.

"The kitchen is kind of small," Beth said. "It would be easier if you let me clean up alone."

Relieved of the obligation to be a "good guest," I returned to the living room and began scanning the bookshelf titles. "Hey," I called out, reaching for a volume that caught my eye. "Is it all right if I look at your high school yearbook?"

"Sure."

With Beth still in the kitchen, I started leafing through the senior class portraits—hundreds of smiling, clean-scrubbed faces, each one accompanied by a brief biography . . . Johnny Abruzzo . . . David Ambrose . . . Beth Anders . . . She was dressed in a pastel-shaded sweater with a single strand of pearls. Even then, she was dazzling. "Beth has been one of Ridgewood's most popular students," read the biography. "A member of the National Honor Society and Forum Club, she was elected class Vice President in both her junior and senior years. Favorite subject—English; career goal—to be a writer; favorite saying—'Get off my back, Louie.' "

"Who's Louie?" I called out.

"Some idiot who kept asking me out and telling everyone how much he loved me."

"Did you ever go out with him?"

"No."

"So how come your name is linked with his in the yearbook?"

"The editor-in-chief was Louie's girlfriend. She wanted to embarrass both of us."

Beth finished washing dishes and returned to the living room to join me.

"What happened to your career goal?" I asked. "Once upon a time, you wanted to be a writer."

"Give me a break, okay?"

"No, really! According to this yearbook—"

"I know what it says in the yearbook. It's something stupid I put down on a form when I was seventeen years old."

"It's not stupid."

"What's Ed Hardesty like?" she asked, changing the subject.

The question caught me slightly off guard. "He's nice," I answered. "Very solid. He might not have the intellectual aggressiveness that Ashworth & Palmer looks for in its lawyers, but I like him."

"Did you tell him about us?"

"What makes you ask?"

"Because I'd like to know the answer." She had a very straightforward way of staring a person down with those big blue eyes (which, incidentally, contained more than a trace of steel).

"Yes," I admitted, "but he's the only one."

"You don't have to apologize. Everyone needs a confidant."

"Who's yours?"

"Coreen McDermott—who, in case you're wondering, is the woman I usually have lunch with when I eat in the firm cafeteria."

"Does she have a big mouth?"

"I'm not sure I like that question. My friends are just as discreet as yours, probably more so. And for your information, I'm no more anxious to become a page-one gossip item at Ashworth & Palmer than you are. So you can change the subject by telling me about that nice Edwin Hardesty who, by the way, is the only lawyer in the office who says hello to the unattractive secretaries as well as the good-looking ones. Are you close friends?"

"Not yet, but we seem to be getting there. Our present bond is mutual shame over an impending onslaught against a New York City transit worker named Anthony Pisano."

"Who's Anthony Pisano?"

I told her about the yellow paint and Hunker's plan of attack. "When all is said and done," I added, "it's incredible. Ed and I spent twenty hours each on the case this week. That's over two thousand dollars worth of billable time, and we've only just begun."

"What happens next?"

"I'm hoping Hunker will come to his senses and forget the whole thing."

"And if he doesn't?"

"Then Ed and I will represent him the same way we would any other client. That's the morality of the law. Lonnie Hunker is entitled to counsel just like any other litigant."

"Aren't you a little embarrassed at the thought of three Ashworth & Palmer lawyers ganging up on Anthony Pisano?"

"The answer to that question is yes, but it's my job. And if Jordan were assigned to the case, you'd type the briefs because that's your job, right?"

She nodded. "I suppose so."

"Look! One of the things I've learned is that the law is not a gentlemanly institution. To the contrary, in some ways it's as much a question of power and brute force as war.

The United States government sent people to jail during the Vietnam era for burning draft cards. Eighteen-year-old kids still get locked up for smoking marijuana. Large corporations do pretty much what they please so long as they don't step on the toes of other large corporations. In *Hunker v. Pisano*, Hunker has the power and he'll use it."

"And if you refuse to work on the case?"

"I'd probably be fired. At the very least, it would end my chances of making partner."

There was some wine left over from dinner, but I didn't want it. "You're awfully quiet all of a sudden," Beth said as we settled on the sofa.

"I guess I'm a little depressed."

"How come?"

I shrugged. "I don't know. Maybe I'm confused, that's all. Last Friday night, there was magic between us. I came here tonight hoping for a repeat performance, but instead all we've done is argue and debate. I like you; I really do. But somehow I seem to be saying everything wrong, and it's all the harder because our relationship is so undefined. I don't know what you expect from me or vice versa. I have no idea whether you'll invite me to spend the night this evening or what. I'm not an easy person to know. I realize that. I have very few confidants and fewer friends. I'd like you to be one of them, but I have a sense of foreboding that something is going to come between us, if it hasn't already."

"What do you want from this relationship?"

"Something more than just going to bed together."

"So do I," she answered.

"But that shouldn't rule out going to bed."

"Then let's."

"When?"

"How about now?"

We took off the first of our clothes together, piling shirts, shoes, and jeans by the living-room sofa.

"Not bad," she said, stepping back to look at my body, "but I'm better."

"I can't argue with that. At the risk of diverting attention from your other charms, you're about to pop out of your bra."

"Then take it off me. I dare you."

"That's a non sequitur."

"Do you care?"

"No."

Shortly thereafter, we climbed naked beneath the quilted spread that covered Beth's bed. "On your stomach," she ordered.

"How come?"

"Just do what I tell you to do."

I did.

"All right," she announced. "You now have a choice between a back scratch and a back rub."

"Which do you do better?"

"The rub."

"I'll take it."

Effortlessly, her hands began to glide across my shoulders, up and down my spine, working their way inside my body where they eased every knot and point of tension.

"You know something," I told her. "I remember the first time I saw you. It was at the end of my first day at Ashworth & Palmer. Ed Hardesty had just gotten a check from Moffitt for one thousand dollars, and I was going back to my desk to get mine. You were wearing a blue knit dress, and I could hardly take my eyes off you. God! I was scared that day. I kept trying to feel important, but everything was all so new to me."

"I remember, too," she said. "Jordan came back from

lunch and told me the firm had hired someone from the University of Nebraska. I asked what you were like, and he said you seemed nice and bright—in that order. For some reason, I wondered what you looked like. Then when we passed in the corridor, I knew it was you."

I turned on my side and pulled her close.

"How are you doing?" she asked.

"Fine."

"Can we make love?"

"All night if you want."

"You're too old for that," she told me. "I'll settle for half an hour."

"Anything you say, but there's something I want to ask you first."

"Okay."

"This might sound silly, but last week we saw each other for dinner on Friday. And this week you invited me for the same night. Is there someone you see regularly on Saturday night? And if not, could I see you again tomorrow?"

"The answer to your first question is no. The answer to your second question is I'd love to."

Saturday night we had hamburgers for dinner and went to a Woody Allen movie afterwards. It was a lovely evening—until the movie ended. That was when I noticed we were on the receiving end of a look that could kill from a fellow sitting two rows behind us—Jordan Caine.

"The cat's out of the bag," I announced glumly as we walked from the theater.

For all her free and easy spirit, Beth didn't look too pleased with the development either.

IX

Early Monday afternoon, I was wrestling with the complexities of sewage treatment technology when Beth made a rare appearance in my office.

"Am I disturbing anything?" she asked.

"Only a very tedious review of biochemical oxygen demand."

"What's that?"

"The amount of oxygen required for decomposition of organic matter in waste water. You're more than welcome to have a seat."

Brushing a strand of hair from her cheek, she accepted the offer. "I got bawled out by Jordan this morning," she announced. "In case you're wondering, that's b-a-w-l as in yell, not b-a-l-l as in fuck."

"What happened?"

"Right after I got to work, he called me into his office

and said that he had chanced to see us at the movies on Saturday night. Then he asked if I liked Woody Allen. I told him 'yes,' after which I got The Speech."

"What's the speech?"

"The speech goes roughly as follows: 'Dear Beth—I don't mean to pry into your personal affairs, but, as the associate to whom you are assigned, I think it best for me to offer a few words of advice. Ashworth & Palmer is a strange place, and certain things are frowned upon by the partners. As you well know, dating within the office is one of them.' " There was anger in her voice as she went on. " 'Now I realize that you're a mature young woman, but at age twenty-two you're likely to be unduly impressed by the thought of going out with a Wall Street lawyer. Thus, I urge you to remember that three careers are at stake—Tom's, because the partners will question his maturity and judgment if this leaks out; yours, because the partners might come to regard you as a potential source of scandal; and mine, because as your boss I'm at least partially responsible for your conduct. Thus, for your own good as well as the good of others, I strongly suggest that you reconsider your actions.' "

"What did you say?"

"I told him that I was fully cognizant of everyone's position within the firm, and that I would do my best to conduct myself in a mature, responsible manner."

"Then what happened?"

"He started reading his mail, which was my signal to leave."

"That's quite something."

"I thought so, too," she said, "and I didn't like it. My dentist screams at me because I don't use dental floss. My hairdresser nags because the ends of my hair are split. I don't need Jordan Caine complaining about who I date. And speaking of Jordan, he's due back from lunch any minute, so I'd better get back to my desk. I just thought you'd like a rundown on the news."

She got up to leave, then stopped just short of the door. "Hey, Tom, can I ask you something?"

"Sure."

"Would you have invited me for dinner that first night if I wasn't good-looking?"

"Probably not," I admitted.

She wasn't quite out the door. "Are we going anywhere in this relationship?"

"I hope so," I said.

Jordan's warning augured ill. He had already tattled once to Moffitt—when Jim Britt got drunk at lunch—and his latest discovery would certainly work its way on high when convenient to his purposes. I was about to consult Hardesty for advice and moral support when the telephone rang.

"Mr. Hunker would like to see you in his office," a secretary said.

The walk upstairs was a long one. "Young man," I envisioned The Hunk saying, "two weeks ago, in open court, you called me a liar. Last week you were seen fornicating with a secretary at the movies. What's on your schedule for this Friday?"

Contrary to my expectations, Hunker was in a relatively congenial mood when I arrived. "Tom," he began, motioning me toward a chair, "the UCC case is not going exactly as I had planned. Everyone here is doing a splendid job, but the facts need more development. So far, we've been dealing with sewage treatment technology and general industry trends. Now it's time to get down to specifics." Reaching for a pile of papers on his desk, he pulled out a twenty-page memorandum. "This is a list of the five hundred top management, sales, and engineering personnel at the Union Construction Company. It's my considered judgment that the time has come for Ashworth & Palmer to interview every one of them in depth."

"That would take five lawyers almost a full year," I said.

"Precisely, and I do expect some company resistance. Like most corporations, UCC is keeping closer tabs on its legal fees these days, and the cost of this interview project could run high. Tomorrow night, I'm flying to Unger. Wednesday morning at nine A.M., I have an appointment with the Chairman of the Board of UCC. At that time, I expect to convince him of the necessity for this project. I'd like you to come along in case it becomes necessary to discuss the specifics of document review or sewage treatment technology."

That, in a nutshell, is how I came to find myself in the Unger Inn cocktail lounge on a Tuesday night waiting for Lonnie Hunker to freshen up in his room so we could have dinner. In truth, I was somewhat pleased to have been chosen as his traveling companion. With ten associates on the case, there had been other, more likely choices. For whatever reason, I was on Hunker's good side and, in terms of my future within the firm, that was a plus.

"Would you like a drink?" the waitress asked.

"No thanks. I'll wait."

The lounge was maybe thirty feet long with red carpeting and small, square polyurethaned tables. Except for the bartender and waitress, the room was virtually empty. For a couple of minutes, I stared at the walls and fiddled with a black plastic ashtray on the table in front of me. Waiting in a hotel bar for Lonnie Hunker wasn't the most exciting thing in the world to do. Then I began to run a song through my mind and was just starting to enjoy the melody when Hunker arrived.

"Let's have a drink to loosen up," he said. "Then we can go in for dinner."

I ordered a Tom Collins, Hunker a double vodka martini, which he drank as if the waitress was going to grab the glass out of his hand if he didn't hurry. Then we went into the dining room, where he ordered another round for both of us. "Christ," he muttered, perusing the menu. "Even in Unger, a shrimp cocktail costs three dollars. That must be why Jews don't eat shrimp." He laughed at his own joke, adding, "Don't worry. You should know by now that the client pays for everything."

We ordered dinner, and I started to feel the second drink. I never could hold my liquor, and on two Tom Collinses I get extremely high. Not screaming, roaring drunk, but decidedly fuzzy. As Hunker and I sat there, I was aware of the fact that my motor skills were dropping below par, and I was starting to wonder what in hell I was doing sitting in the Unger Inn drinking with Lonnie Hunker when I could have been home in bed with Beth Anders.

"You're pretty up to date on this sewage treatment technology, aren't you?" Hunker asked.

"I think so."

"That's what I figured. Word is that you're a real go-getter. Do you want to explain to me the differences between the three stages of sewage treatment, just in case the subject comes up tomorrow?"

For a moment, I thought he was joking. After almost three years as the partner in charge of the UCC case, he was asking about the most fundamental technological concept in the entire litigation. Hardesty and I had mastered it our first week on the job.

"Primary treatment is the first stage," I began. "That's the separation of solid materials from waste water through the use of screens or settling tanks. Sometimes the process is aided by flocculation."

"What's that?"

"The combination of small particles to form larger ones."

"Go on."

"Primary treatment eliminates about sixty percent of all solids from sewage. The next stage is secondary treatment, which entails oxidizing and dissolving organic material. That's accomplished by the use of filters, aeration, and passing the sewage through bacteria-activated sludge. Secondary treatment removes about ninety percent of all organic material from waste water."

He nodded to connote understanding, but I had the distinct feeling that I was beginning to lose him. "Tertiary treatment is everything which follows," I added, trying to make the rest of my explanation as simple as possible. "It's designed to further purify the water and make it drinkable again. Meanwhile, the extracted waste material is dried and incinerated, used for landfill, converted to fertilizer, or dumped into the ocean."

"Very interesting," he said.

It was as though he had just heard the explanation for the first time.

"Arlen Cohen wrote some very good memoranda on the subject," I told him.

"Oh, yes! I remember."

The waitress brought our dinner—steak for Hunker, stuffed filet of sole for me. We ate in silence (if one considered Hunker's belching and slurping to be silence). "Be in the lobby at eight o'clock tomorrow morning," he instructed when the meal ended.

As expected, the next day UCC agreed, albeit reluctantly, to the interview project. "I'll need more manpower," Hunker told James Moffitt when we returned to New York. Soon, three new associates were assigned to the case, freeing Ed Hardesty, Arlen Cohen, and Richard Watkins to work exclusively on interviews. Carole Shiner was assigned to full-time document coordination ("the red-dot lady," we began calling her), and

Harris Boyd was instructed to prepare a report on the possible impact of environmental legislation on the case. All other assignments remained the same, except for yours truly. "Tom," Hunker announced, "I'm putting you in charge of the technological aspects of the litigation. From now on, if anyone wants to know anything about sewage treatment technology, they should come to you."

"Golly," Hardesty said when I told him the news. "That's almost as exciting as sticking red dots on documents."

Unable to think of a rejoinder other than, "Fuck you, Ed," I chose not to answer.

Hunker went on vacation in mid-July, the courts shut down, and despite Judge McAleer's warning that sloughing off during the summer would not be tolerated, work on the UCC case slowed. Frequently, I found myself sitting at my desk, knowing I should apply myself more, yet letting my mind wander. More often than not, the focus of my thoughts was Beth Anders. Despite Jordan's cautionary note, we continued to see each other, usually on Friday and Saturday nights, always "discreetly." The discretion was my idea.

"We're not doing anything wrong," Beth said indignantly one night. "I don't understand why you're hiding me."

"I'm not hiding you," I answered. "I just don't see the need to make a big deal about it."

Grudgingly, she acceded to my concept of "discretion." In late July, Moffitt gave a party for all litigation associates, their spouses, and dates. I went alone. Outside of Hardesty (on my side) and Coreen McDermott (on Beth's), we refrained from discussing our relationship within the office. Whenever we spent the night together, it was at my apartment. Except for several occasions when Ed joined us, we dated alone. Once, on a "work day," we lunched together at a Greek restaurant near the office. At my suggestion, we met in the lobby by the elevators.

"If you were so afraid people would see us," Beth said sarcastically as we returned from lunch, "why didn't you suggest we meet on the corner of Broadway and Wall Street?"

"I didn't think of it," I answered.

"If you had any class," Hardesty told me later, "you'd take her to lunch in the firm cafeteria."

"You're the one who's free of the partnership mystique," I countered. "Why don't you do it?"

"I might," he said.

Meanwhile, it was clear that, if anyone at Ashworth & Palmer lived in a goldfish bowl, it was Beth. Secretaries have very little privacy to begin with. Unlike "bosses," they can't go into an office and shut the door behind them. Nor can they take breaks when they want to. Even when no work is at hand, they're expected to sit at their desks and wait in case a letter has to be typed, a phone call made, or a cup of coffee fetched. Beth was chained to her desk eight hours a day, on display for any associate who chose to examine her.

"Did you see Beth Anders today?"

The question was posed by Richard Watkins. Through a series of unfortunate circumstances, I was having lunch in the firm cafeteria with him, Harris Boyd, and a pretentious snot whose name I've long since mercifully forgotten.

"Not yet," the snot answered. "How does she look?"

"Big tits. She's wearing that tight blue leotard top."

"What size bra do you think she wears?" Harris inquired.

"I don't know," Watkins said, "but her cup runneth over."

"It sure does," the snot volunteered. "She's bigger than Texas."

Guffaws all around.

"Let's go down after lunch and check her out," Watkins suggested. "I could use another look."

All of which gave unwarranted significance to an otherwise minor event which occurred on August 6th—Beth's twenty-third birthday. That morning, I wandered by her desk.

"Mr. Hardesty and I request the pleasure of your company for lunch," I announced. "After due deliberation, we have decided to formally celebrate the anniversary of your birth."

"Where are we going?" she asked, looking up from her typewriter.

"The firm cafeteria."

There was a long pause. "Does this mean we're going public?"

"I think so."

The three of us met in the reception area shortly before 1 P.M.

"We might all get killed doing this," Beth said. "I hope you realize that."

"You're not having second thoughts, are you?" I chided.

"Not really, but I am scared stiff."

"Don't worry," Hardesty interjected. "The partners never eat in the firm cafeteria."

"I know," she said. "But they talk with the people who do."

The sixty-fourth-floor corridor leading to the cafeteria seemed narrower than usual and considerably darker.

"I wonder if there's such a thing as reincarnation," Ed mused. "Then I could come back in my next life as a crown prince or head of state, and I wouldn't have to worry about things like getting yelled at by a partner."

"It's possible," Beth speculated. "In fact, for all you know, in an earlier life you might have been Napoleon or Louis the Fourteenth."

"I doubt it," Ed said. "I can't speak French."

As we entered the cafeteria, a half dozen heads turned —the normal sign of Beth's arrival. It was still unclear to most observers that we had come as a threesome. To the unsuspecting, Henderson and Hardesty were simply having lunch together, and Beth Anders had happened to arrive at the same time. Seasoned Anders-watchers might have noticed the absence of Coreen McDermott, Beth's usual lunch companion, but that was the only clue to our revolutionary intentions.

"Hot turkey sandwiches," Ed noted, looking up at the menu taped to the serving-area wall. "Did you know that the price of turkey has gone up to ninety cents a pound?"

"At that rate, you'd cost one hundred sixty-six dollars and fifty cents," I offered.

"Very funny," he said. "Within the hour, we could be dead, and you're telling jokes."

The lunch line moved slowly. Beth and Ed bought turkey sandwiches. I opted for chicken salad on rye. Trays in hand, we paid the cashier and emerged from the serving area in search of an empty table. Since Beth looked particularly good (she was wearing a yellow sweater and brown slacks just a shade darker than her hair), the number of associates watching had swelled to about a dozen.

There was an empty table for four by a corner window. Beth and I sat on one side, Hardesty on the other. Around the room, the murmurs began.

"Tell the truth," Beth said, looking me square in the eye. "Would you have had the courage to do this without Ed?"

"Probably not," I admitted.

"But in fairness to Tom," Ed added, "I wouldn't have done it on my own either. When all is said and done, Ashworth & Palmer is a pretty intimidating place. And associates do not have lunch with secretaries."

The cafeteria ceiling was still in place. Outside, the sky had not yet fallen, although a fair amount of attention was being lavished on our little corner.

"What's that?" Beth asked, pointing to a brown-paper bag I had carried with me through the lunch line.

"Something for you," I said, reaching in and pulling out a small bouquet of violets. "Happy birthday."

X

Hunker returned from vacation in mid-August. Shortly thereafter, the Summons and Complaint against Anthony Pisano was served and filed. Drafted by good soldiers Henderson and Hardesty, it recounted Hunker's version of events as follows:

> On May 26 of this year at approximately 6:30 P.M., plaintiff Hunker was descending the stairs at the Wall Street station of the Lexington Avenue IRT subway. When he reached platform level, he noticed that there was a considerable amount of yellow paint on his gray pinstripe suit. Retracing his steps, he found defendant Pisano engaged in painting the hand railing by the stairs bright yellow.
>
> No warning of wet paint had been posted in the vicinity of the stairs.
>
> When plaintiff Hunker sought to discuss the matter with defendant Pisano, the defendant became loud and

abusive. Among other things, he called plaintiff a "ton of blubber" and threatened to dump the remaining paint on plaintiff's head.

As per our instructions, the complaint went on to allege that Hunker had been "placed in fear of imminent bodily harm and suffered severe emotional distress," and closed with a flourish:

WHEREFORE, plaintiff Lionel J. Hunker demands judgment as follows:

(1) Four hundred dollars in compensation for damage to his gray pinstripe suit.
(2) An additional four thousand six hundred dollars in damages for assault.
(3) Fifteen thousand dollars in punitive damages as a consequence of defendant's conduct as described above.
(4) Costs, reasonable attorneys' fees, and such other and further relief as this court deems just and proper.

Messrs. Ashworth & Palmer
Ten Wall Street
65th Floor
New York, N.Y. 10005

Ten days later, Hardesty and I were summoned to Hunker's office. "The battle is joined," The Hunk announced, reaching for the manila folder now labeled *Hunker v. Pisano*. "This letter came in the mail today. I assume a copy has been filed with the court":

Dear Judges of the Court and Mr. Ashworth and Mr. Palmer,

Someone from the lawyers, he gave me the complaint.

But I didn't do nothing wrong and what it says it's not true. Please tell me when I should come to court so I shouldn't pay the money. I didn't do nothing wrong and I don't have much money.

Your friend

Anthony Pisano

"I thought he'd ignore the complaint, and we could file for a default judgment," Hunker growled. "But I suppose that in a rough sort of way this letter constitutes an answer and general denial. I'm not quite sure what to do next."

"Why don't you go fuck yourself?" I considered saying.

"How about a subpoena for documents?" I suggested. "The letter you received from the city in response to your original demand indicated that at least one report was prepared on the incident."

"That's right," Ed added. "We could get all the documents and stick red dots on the bad ones."

Hunker was too deep in thought to acknowledge Hardesty's comment. "A subpoena for documents," he murmured thoughtfully, stroking his chin. "That's a good idea. If there's any dirt on this Pisano character, that's the way to find it. Tom, Ed, draw me up a subpoena for documents."

That was how August ended. September started with a bang.

On Wall Street, Labor Day marks the close of the summer season. Partners return from vacation, courts reopen, and eager young associates arrive fresh out of Harvard and Yale. At Ashworth & Palmer, the "new year" had been marked for decades by the annual firm outing.

The outing was no small matter. Held at the posh Thousand Oaks Country Club on the day after Labor Day, it was twelve hours of eating, drinking, fun and games. The facilities were, to say the least, impressive. Thousand Oaks covered ninety acres of choice land in upstate New York, including an eighteen-hole golf course, twelve tennis courts, two softball diamonds, an Olympic-size swimming pool, and a clubhouse which rivaled Buckingham Palace in grandeur. The firm rented the club for the day. From 10 A.M. until dinner, partners and associates were free to roam the grounds using whatever facilities they chose. In the event of hunger, a buffet lunch with lobster salad, fresh shrimp, and assorted cold cuts, cheeses, and fruits was available. There was an open bar, and all charges were paid by the firm. An evening banquet concluded the festivities. Secretaries, messengers, and other nonlegal staff were not invited. Attendance by attorneys was compulsory.

As viewed by the partners, the outing served two purposes. One, it celebrated the fact that everyone was about to buckle down to hard work after the summer lull, and two, it showed incoming associates (most of whom arrived at Ashworth & Palmer circa September 1) that the rewards of hard work were plentiful. Invariably, the competitive highlight of the day was the firm softball tournament. Shortly after lunch, eight partners acting as captains chose up teams from the eighty or so lawyers who volunteered to play. Then the teams —each of which bore the name of its captain—engaged in an elimination tournament to determine the firm champion. As befitting Ashworth & Palmer, every member of the winning team was handed a one-hundred-dollar bill as prize money at the evening banquet.

Hardesty and I were both chosen by Lloyd Kemper, a corporate partner, who assigned Ed to play shortstop and yours truly to third base. In game number one, we edged a squad captained by Ellis Slattery and then, in the semifinals, walloped "The Moffitts" twelve to three. In the final contest, we were matched appropriately enough against "The Hunkers."

As far as I was concerned, except for the hundred dollars, the game didn't matter. Ed had a slightly different view. "I owe Two-F a little something," he told me just before the game began.

"Who's Two-F?" I inquired.

"The captain of The Hunkers."

"And what, may I ask, does Two-F stand for?"

"Fat fuck."

It was a good game. Ed scored twice, and I got two hits, including a bases-loaded triple. In the bottom of the ninth inning, we were leading seven to six with two men out when Lonnie Hunker stepped to the plate. On the first pitch, he lined a fast ball to left center field and lumbered around first base heading for second. Arlen Cohen, playing in center, cut the ball off and threw to Hardesty who had moved over to cover the play. The ball arrived while Hunker was still a good ten feet away from second base, and the only question in the minds of most observers was whether Lonnie would slide and be tagged out, or slide, break his ankle, and be tagged out. But there was a third possibility that none of us (except maybe Hardesty) had considered. As Hunker charged closer to second base and showed no sign of sliding or slowing down, it suddenly became quite apparent that he was going to ram full speed into Ed and try to knock the ball loose. Given those circumstances, Hardesty did what any normally aggressive, red-blooded American who hates his boss would do—he cradled the ball in his glove, put his right hand across the glove pocket to hold the ball in place, braced himself, and as Hunker came charging in, crammed the ball as far down his throat as possible. There was an extremely loud crash, after which the umpire called Hunker out and we won the ball game seven to six. The next day, Hunker showed up at the office with a fabulous fat lip.

"I had no choice," Ed said later. "It was him or me; he or I; or however it should be put grammatically."

One week later, Hunker exacted his revenge by sending Ed to inspect sewage treatment plants in Helena, Montana, and Bismarck, North Dakota. "I really don't want to take this trip," Ed grumbled the day before he left. "It gets cold early in the great American Northwest, and I don't like landing at rinky-dink airports in the snow."

"Take a boat," I suggested.

"You're a big help. What this place really needs is a union. If the associates unionized, we could put an end to all this crap."

"The partners would crush a union in a minute," I said.

"Hey!" he continued, chattering away merrily. "I've got an even better idea. Do you think it would hurt my long-range professional aspirations if I cut Hunker's head off with a meat cleaver?"

"Probably," I told him. "I think you'd be better off trying to form a union."

"I can't," he answered. "They'd crush us in a minute. You just said so yourself."

The first-year associates who started in September were as naive and wet behind the ears as Ed and I had been twelve months earlier. Three of them—John Spencer, Frank Haviland, and Ira Kamenstein—were assigned to the UCC case and, on Ed's return from exile, he and I were instructed to take Kamenstein to lunch for an orientation session. In a moment of nostalgia, I suggested we dine at Lindemann's—the site of my initiation by Jordan Caine and Jim Britt one year earlier.

Ira was five feet ten inches tall and skinny, with wire-rimmed glasses and curly black hair. He wanted to know everything about Ashworth & Palmer, and began bombarding us with questions the moment we were seated. In due course, we discussed salaries, diary cards, billable hours, and assorted other topics. "The firm is extremely liberal in letting associates use their expense accounts," Ed explained, "probably because the charges are passed on to the client. If you work past seven-thirty at night, you're allowed to bill dinner. Ditto for a cab instead of the subway if you stay until eight."

"What are the partners like?" Ira asked.

"After you," Ed said with a wave in my direction.

"That's a hard question," I waffled. "I suppose the first thing to say is the most obvious. They vary from one another just like any other class of people. Most of them are extremely bright. All of them are driven men. Some like what they do. Others seem locked into their jobs by their success."

"Do they take a personal interest in the associates who work for them?"

"Not really. As a general rule, partners are available if you want to make an appointment but, with the possible exception of George Witherell, I've never known one to show a genuine interest in an associate's problems."

"I'll go you one better," Ed said. "Ashworth & Palmer partners and Ashworth & Palmer associates are in an adversary relationship. There's quite a bit of talk around here about team spirit, but in truth we're labor and they're management. Every so often a laborer works his way up to the top but, when someone makes partner, it means a smaller slice of the pie for the rest of them. So very few associates make partner."

"Do you two want to be partners?"

"There's a split of opinion on that," I said. "I do. Ed doesn't."

Ira looked toward Hardesty. "Why not?"

"One, I don't want to spend my life doing the kind of work that's done at Ashworth & Palmer. Two, I don't want to spend my life working that hard. And three, I don't want to be like them."

"Meaning?"

"Partners here are in a world of their own. They consider

themselves to be such good lawyers that things like personality and manners don't matter. They reinforce one another in the view that their defects as human beings are unimportant. In some ways, it's the ultimate escape from reality."

"If Tom becomes a partner," Kamenstein pressed, "will he become like them?"

"I don't know," Ed answered. "He hasn't made it yet, and I'm not sure which has to come first—the chicken or the egg."

Several days later, Ira, John Spencer, and Frank Haviland weighed anchor for a two-week orientation session in Unger. "I was never in the army," Ira told me just before he left, "but the rookie year at Ashworth & Palmer strikes me as being very much like boot camp."

"So are years two through eight," I answered.

Meanwhile, Beth and I continued on an even keel. After our experiment in cafeteria integration, we lunched together publicly at least once a week—sometimes with Ed, sometimes alone. Not until late September, when Coreen McDermott dared to join us, did another party hurdle the class barrier.

Coreen was black, married, and in her late twenties with no children. Her husband was an air force veteran enrolled in an Eastern Airlines management-training program. "Now I know what it felt like to march in Selma," was her sole comment as we waited together on the cafeteria lunch line. Half an hour later, she was somewhat more at ease. "Have you taken your vacation yet?" she asked me over dessert.

"Not yet," I answered. "I figured it would be smart to stick around during the summer months in case something important came up. That way I could pick up brownie points and extra experience."

"And did it pay off?"

"I'm the senior associate on a lawsuit against a penniless mass transit worker named Anthony Pisano."

Having made the judgment that this twist in my life was

not worth pursuing, Coreen turned to Beth. "What about you? When are you going on vacation?"

"I'm waiting for someone to ask me," Beth answered, at which point one of them (I'm not sure which because I was concentrating on my strawberry yogurt) kicked me hard in the ankle.

"Why can't we go away together?" Beth asked on the telephone that night.

"I didn't say we couldn't."

"Then let's do it. I'll be good. I'll pay for myself. There won't be any hassles. We'll just go away for a week, have a nice time, and come back."

"Where to?"

"How about Cape Cod? It's the last week of September, so the tourists will be gone. The water might be a little cold for swimming, but the beaches will be nice."

"What if someone kicks sand in my face?"

"Don't worry," she said, "I'll handle him, or her, as the case might be."

So we went to Cape Cod. Hunker agreed to the time off, and Jordan, after quizzing Beth on her destination (but not her traveling companion), did the same. The last Saturday in September, we rented a car and drove from New York to Provincetown at the far end of the Cape. The next eight days were among the best in my life. The weather was sunny and warm, the daytime sky particularly blue. Beth brought two bathing suits—a gold bikini that she just about fit into and a black one-piece. Most days we goofed around in T-shirts and jeans, Beth with her hair pulled back. We jogged on the beach, climbed sand dunes, visited a half dozen historical sites of minor interest, and made castles in the sand. Each night, we went to a different restaurant before retiring to a tiny inn near the ocean's edge. It was one of the few times in our relationship that we forgot about Ashworth & Palmer and abandoned the "lawyer-secretary" labels. Our last night in Provinceton, bundled in sweaters, we went walking along the beach.

"That's Venus," Beth said, pointing to a spot in the star-studded sky.

"How do you know?"

"It has a big V on it."

"Very scientific."

The tide was starting to deposit shells and pieces of driftwood on the sand. Bending over, I picked up a smooth piece of jasper.

"Have you had many girlfriends?" Beth asked.

"That's an odd question."

"Not really."

I sent the jasper skipping across the water. "Three or four," I answered.

"What sort of relationships were they?"

"They varied."

"Who ended them?"

"I did."

"Each time?"

"Yes."

We walked hand in hand with the waves breaking beside us. "Tell me about them," she said.

"All right. The first was with a girl named Celia Tuttle. She was a freshman at the University of Nebraska when I was a sophomore. Two years later, I dated another student—Karen Greany. My second year of law school, I went out with a nurse named Bonnie Wade."

"Were they all good-looking?"

"Karen and Bonnie were. Celia Tuttle was kind of cute, but not very."

"Why did the relationships end?"

"I got tired of them. Things always reached the point where I felt I wasn't growing. And, even in Nebraska, there are lots of unattached women." Up ahead, an abandoned lighthouse loomed to our left. "How come you're asking all this?"

"Maybe I want to be next on the list," she said, "or the one and only in an entirely new category." She stopped walking and turned to face me. "But there's a problem. I've never felt that I had to shine brighter than other people. And my goals are personal, not professional. I'm not sure you can accept either of those qualities in me."

"Of course I can."

"That's not the answer I want. You said it much too quickly. I want you to think about us, not just tonight but for a long time. It could be important."

The next morning we drove back to New York, where I learned that circumstances at Ashworth & Palmer had changed. After eight years of litigation, the American Steel controversy appeared firmly enough in hand that James Moffitt had agreed to relinquish one of his top associates to a more beleaguered partner. The new senior associate on the UCC case was Jordan Caine. Something in the pit of my stomach suggested I might be better off running away with Beth to become a sewage treatment mechanic in Bismarck, North Dakota.

XI

Several days after Beth and I returned to New York, good soldiers Henderson and Hardesty followed up on Hunker's order to prepare a document demand for service on the Metropolitan Transportation Authority. Drafted in impeccable Ashworth & Palmer style, it subpoenaed every conceivable scrap of paper relating to the yellow paint incident. One week after we sent it to Hunker for approval, I was summoned to his office.

"Sit down," he instructed. The document demand was on his desk. "This is more than satisfactory," he said. "You've closed up all the loopholes and done a good job."

"Thank you."

"But there's something else I want to discuss."

I waited.

"As you know, one of the most important things we do here at Ashworth & Palmer is make partners. Our selection process is carried out with utmost care, and each associate remains under scrutiny from the day he starts with the firm until a decision on his future is made."

I nodded, and Hunker went on. "Your performance to date has been excellent. In the course of a year, you've mastered the facts of the UCC case, and very shortly you'll be assigned further responsibilities with regard to legal strategy. Your billable hours aren't what mine were when I was an associate, but fifty-five hours a week—which is what you average—is acceptable. As you probably know, the key to victory in any lawsuit is staffing, and I'm delighted you're on my team. Your future at Ashworth & Palmer is bright, but one disturbing matter has surfaced."

He paused for effect, then came to the point. "It has come to my attention that you've been sleeping with a young lady employed by the firm. It is also my understanding that the two of you recently went off together on a junket. For your own good, I suggest you put considerably more distance between yourself and the office staff."

There was silence between us. "I'm not sure I see the problem," I said at last. "The junket you're referring to was my vacation. And I would think that who I date is a personal matter."

"Not if it affects your professional performance."

"With all due respect, I don't see how it does. The people at UCC aren't interested in my social life. And who I date is hardly a matter of concern to the courts."

"It's a matter of concern to people at Ashworth & Palmer, and that's enough. It affects your professional performance."

"How? The messengers still deliver my mail. The telephone operators still put through my telephone calls. The only people who seem to care are—"

"Tom," he interrupted, cutting me off with a wave of his hand. "I want to tell you something about power. And I'll put it in terms that someone from your generation can understand. When the Beatles first came to America, their hair was too long and their music was unorthodox. They stood for a new order, but a sizeable segment within the power structure figured they could make money off them. Record company executives saw big dollar signs. Newspapers and television reporters liked them because they were good copy. Parents tolerated them at the urging of their children. So the power structure let the Beatles in. American society was invaded with the consent of its own institutions. Eventually, the Beatles' hair got longer, and their lyrics changed from 'I Want to Hold Your Hand' to songs about revolution and drugs. But by the time the power structure realized what was happening, it was too late for the mischief to be halted. That sort of thing will never happen at Ashworth & Palmer. If you expect to become a partner here, you'll have to do things our way. In sum, you would be well advised to follow the time-honored axiom, 'Don't love where you work.' Or more crudely put, 'Don't get your meat where you get your bread.'

"Think about it," he said, his voice softening. "Maybe I'm being unduly harsh, but I doubt it. I'm honestly trying to put your interests first, both inside the firm and out of it. Beth Anders is an extremely attractive young woman. I'm well aware of that. I've seen her around the office for five years. But she's a secretary with a secretary's mentality, and you have one of the finest legal minds in the country as evidenced by the fact that you're an attorney with Ashworth & Palmer." An almost benign look crossed his face. "I won't mention the matter again. Do what you think is best."

Beth was sitting at her desk, filing her nails, when I walked by. "You look cheerful," she gibed.

"I just heard from Hunker on the subject of dating within the office."

"And?"

"He's opposed to the idea."

"So?"

"So we'd better have a talk."

"Right now?"

"It's as good a time as any."

"I can't stay away from my desk too long," she warned, following me to my office. "Jordan will have a fit."

"It won't take long," I told her, closing the door behind us. "Do you want a seat?"

"I'll stand, thank you." Her look was more befuddled than anything else.

"Don't worry," I assured her. "There's no crisis. I like you as much as ever. All I'm about to suggest is that we cool things publicly for the time being."

"What does that mean?"

"That we not have lunch together in the firm cafeteria, and maybe be a little more discreet."

"I thought we'd gone beyond that point."

"So did I. We were both wrong." The confusion in her eyes was turning to anger, and I tried to stem the tide. "Look. You work for Jordan, who doesn't like us as a couple. I work for Hunker, who's even more opposed to intra-office dating. And to further complicate matters, Jordan has been reassigned to the UCC case, so he works for Hunker and with me. All I'm suggesting is that, for the time being, we cool it."

"Why?"

"As a matter of survival."

"Whose survival?"

"Mine."

"That's what I figured," she snapped. "It was okay for us to be good buddies when Jordan was threatening *my* job, but now that Hunker is coming down on you, it's a different story."

"I'm not saying that things between us should change. I'm simply suggesting that, for the time being, we adopt a low profile. This is a critical juncture in my career at Ashworth & Palmer. Hunker is my boss. He can make me look very good or very bad. I've got one year left with him before reassignment, and I need him on my side. My future is at stake. Yours isn't."

Her face was a collage of emotions. At any moment, I sensed, she could break out in tears or strike out in anger. "Look," I said, reaching an arm around her shoulders—

"Take your hands off me."

"Beth—"

"Take them off or I'll scream and you'll have every partner in this place outside your office."

"Calm down, please. I just want you to see my point of view. It's only temporary. Once I get a little more established, what Hunker thinks won't matter. And in the meantime, we can keep seeing each other on the outside like we did when we first met. Don't you understand?"

"I understand perfectly. It's okay for the two of us to go to bed together as long as I'm perceived by the rest of the office as a little extra on the side. But the moment we get serious, that's the end of it because I should know my place, and my place is opening mail and typing letters. I'm not a hotshot lawyer."

"That's not what I'm saying."

"Then what are you saying? That there's no sex in the office? Because if you are, that's hogwash. I've been propositioned in one way or another by almost every man in this place, and now that people know you're getting into my pants, it happens more than ever. Don't you think Hunker would take me to a hotel if he had the chance? Every time he passes me in the hall, he stares at my chest. And don't you think I hear the comments about me that the lawyers make? The only man in this entire office who wouldn't ball me is Ed Hardesty, and that's because he's your friend."

"You're overreacting."

"To the contrary, I'm reacting just fine. I understand your world a lot better now. You only have allies, never friends. Hunker's your ally, and that's the way to success. Well, you don't have to worry about my hurting your chances of making partner because I'm calling a halt to this relationship now."

"Will you calm down for a minute."

"I'm quite calm, quite cool, and quite collected. Now, if you'll excuse me, I have to get back to my desk where some menial secretarial chores await me."

"I'm sorry," I said on the telephone that night, "I was wrong, and you were right. I apologize."

"Don't you see how you make me feel?" Beth said. "I know the pressures you're under. I've watched Jordan for five years. And I realize that dating inside the office is a danger. I try to be discreet, honest I do. I've never embarrassed you in public or anywhere else. I always wait for you to invite me to lunch, rather than the other way around. I haven't even mentioned your name to anyone except Coreen McDermott. What upsets me isn't how you treat me when we're at work. It's how you think of me inside the office and out. I'm one level beneath you because you're a lawyer and I'm a secretary, and I can't handle that."

"I've got a proposition for you," I said.

"What is it?"

"It's now the beginning of October. Every November the firm has a formal dinner dance in the Grand Ballroom of the Waldorf Astoria. Attendance is mandatory—two hundred thirty lawyers, their spouses, dates, and concubines. Last year Hardesty and I missed it because we were in Unger studying sewage treatment technology. This year, like it or not, we have to go."

"So?"

"So, in admittedly half-assed fashion, I'm inviting you to the Ashworth & Palmer Prom. For the next six weeks, despite your hatred of the word, let's be 'discreet'—just so Hunker doesn't think I'm going out of my way to defy him. Then we'll go public. What do you say?"

There was a long pause. "I'm thinking," she said at last.

"Well?"

"It's a date—unless, of course, I get a better offer for the same night."

On that note, Beth and I returned to our old ways. More and more, though, I began to respect her. More and more, I saw her in a different light. One day we took an IQ test I had found in an old magazine. She scored four points higher than I did. "It's no big thing," she said afterwards, "but it serves you right."

She had a strong ethical character and was far from shy about voicing judgments—about the Pisano case ("It stinks! You and Ed should be ashamed of yourselves."); Lonnie Hunker ("You're right! He's a slob."); and anything else that crossed her mind ("Ashworth & Palmer is a wonderful institution," she told me one night. "It keeps some very dangerous, very greedy, exceedingly power-hungry people out of government service.").

She never cut corners. Both at work and in personal dealings, she did things aboveboard and well. "Would your parents have liked me?" she asked one afternoon as we walked in the park. It was hard to imagine otherwise. That's how decent and good a person she was, and I told her so.

"Thanks," she said, holding my hand a little tighter.

The second Saturday in October, I went to the nursing home to meet Robert Grissom. Normally, Beth made the trip on Thursday nights and, since I worked considerably later than she did, my going along had never been feasible. But in the fifteen weeks we'd known each other, I'd grown curious about "the other man."

"I'm renting a car tomorrow," she told me one day at work.

"How come?"

"Robert wants to see the autumn leaves, so this week I'm going on Saturday afternoon instead of Thursday night. Want to come?"

"Sure."

Beth paid for the car (she insisted) and drove ("It's my show," she said.). "Robert hasn't been able to walk for several months," she explained as we neared the nursing home. "And except for two visits to the hospital, this will be his first trip outdoors since early spring. But he's mentally alert and wants to do this. Every year as far back as he can remember, he's driven through the countryside in October, and he's afraid this is his last autumn."

The nursing-home parking lot was full so we double-parked on the street. I waited by the car while Beth went inside. Ten minutes later, she returned pushing a wheelchair that seated a thin white-haired man. Robert was wearing a red and black plaid shirt, pleated brown pants, and a brown beret. He looked his age, which was eighty. An orderly walked with them and, when they reached the car, Beth introduced me as "my friend, Tom, from work." Then the orderly helped Robert into the front seat, and I climbed in back next to the folded-up wheelchair.

"I shaved today," Robert announced as Beth began to drive. "Usually they shave me on Sunday and Thursday. Sunday because it's Sunday, and Thursday because that's when you visit. But this week I asked for a shave on Saturday so I'd look clean for you."

"You look wonderful," she said.

I considered concurring but decided to wait until spoken to. Beth was the one bit of glory left in Robert's life, and the less I said, the less my presence would be resented.

"How are your parents?" Robert asked as Beth turned the car onto the Brooklyn-Queens Expressway.

"They're both fine," she told him.

"Your father came to visit yesterday. He says things at the bar are still the same."

"That's what I hear. But the guys all miss you."

He smiled and looked out the window. "I hope we get to the country soon. I want to see the leaves."

It took about thirty minutes to drive through the city and across the George Washington Bridge onto the Palisades Parkway in New Jersey. The fall colors were at their peak and, after an hour of viewing, Robert began to include me in the conversation. By day's end, he even seemed to like me. All he appeared to want out of life was that something happen on any given day to make the living of that day worthwhile.

"You're a good person," he told Beth when the day ended. "You make me very happy."

"He'll be dead soon," she told me as we drove home that night. "And every time I leave him, I wonder how I'll feel when I'm seventy or eighty years old and see someone fifty years younger."

Meanwhile, the UCC case dragged on. Ed Hardesty, Richard Watkins, and Arlen Cohen interviewed scores of company employees. Carole Shiner kept putting red dots on documents with the help of John Spencer and Frank Haviland. Harris Boyd continued to research environmental law, while Ira Kamenstein was assigned to assist me on the subject of sewage treatment technology. Three more associates —Dennis Hayes, Rupert Thorpe, and Glenn Maxwell—were assigned to miscellaneous tasks. All totaled, there were fourteen lawyers on the case. Twelve regular associates, Lonnie Hunker, and Jordan Caine.

Jordan's position was something of an anomaly. Clearly, he was different from the other associates. His orientation session in Unger was a one-man show hosted by a UCC vice president. Moreover, he appeared to have no set daily responsibilities and spent most of his time reviewing what the rest of us did. The only constant in his routine occurred at the end of each day, when he met alone with Hunker to discuss the case.

In truth, Jordan's command of the litigation was extremely impressive. Almost overnight, he appeared to have mastered the facts of the sewage treatment industry as well if not better than any of us. Indeed, his performance was so good that rumors soon began to spread. One story had it that he had been given a twenty-thousand-dollar bonus as a token of the firm's appreciation after being transferred from the American Steel litigation. Another report (equally unsubstantiated but more intriguing) was that the firm had arranged for Hunker to be eased into a federal judgeship one year hence, and that Jordan would be made a partner and placed in charge of the UCC case. Whatever the truth of these and other rumors, Jordan kept his own counsel. While carefully putting some distance between himself and the other associates, he was always extremely deferential to Hunker and gave no indication that he was anything other than a good soldier in the service of the Lord.

Meanwhile, the Lord forged ahead in his battle against Anthony Pisano. In mid-October, the New York State Supreme Court approved our subpoena, and the Metropolitan Transportation Authority was ordered to deliver all relevant documents to Ashworth & Palmer. Ten days later, as I was sitting at my desk contemplating what to eat for lunch (it was only 10 A.M., so I had a while to wait), the telephone rang.

"I've got a job for you," Hunker said. "The receptionist just told me that Abraham Waltuck is in the reception area."

"Waltuck?"

"Right! He's the city attorney who refused my claim for damages. Apparently, he's brought the documents—says he wants to deliver them to me personally, but I'd rather not deal with him face to face. I want you and Hardesty to talk with him. Get the documents, and find out what he's up to."

"What makes you think he's up to something?"

"I've never known a Jewish lawyer who wasn't," Hunker chuckled.

"Was that comment necessary?"

"Look, Tom. I really don't have time to get into a debate over human rights, but I doubt very much that any lawyer would hand-deliver documents which could be sent just as easily by mail if he wasn't up to something. Now, please go down to the reception area and check him out."

"How do you know he's Jewish?"

"Do you know any Abrahams who aren't?"

"Abraham Lincoln," I said.

"Look, just do what I tell you to do. I'm very busy."

Abraham Waltuck was standing in the alcove off the reception area where I had waited for Katherine Whittle one year earlier.

"Nice office you have here," he said as Hardesty and I introduced ourselves. "The Statue of Liberty looks very nice." He was short and heavyset, maybe fifty years old and twenty pounds overweight. His suit was frayed at the lapels; his face was gentle but somewhat dour.

"Real nice office," he said again. "I suppose I could have put the documents in the mail, but I've always wanted to see what Ashworth & Palmer looked like. You wouldn't have time to show me around, would you?"

"I don't see why not," Ed answered. "Come on, we'll give you a tour."

Somehow, half an hour later, the three of us wound up in my office. Waltuck looked approvingly at the neat piles of memoranda around the room and took a seat by the file cabinet. Ed perched on his customary spot near the edge of my credenza, and I settled behind the desk.

"Here are the documents," Waltuck said, handing a nine-by-twelve-inch brown envelope to Hardesty. "There isn't much—a report on the incident from an MTA investigator, Anthony Pisano's job application filed seventeen years ago, and sixteen annual supervisory evaluations of Pisano's performance. That, and now Lionel Hunker's complaint. It's a real shame to ruin a spotless record."

"It's a real shame to ruin a spotless suit," Ed countered.

The joke fell flat. "Tell the truth," Waltuck said. "Aren't you two a little ashamed to be working on this case? I mean, really! I might not be a high-powered lawyer like the two of you, but it doesn't take much in the way of smarts to figure this one out. Your boss pushed through a barricade because he was too lazy to walk an extra block. Then, when he got yellow paint on his suit, he tried to pin the blame on an Italian immigrant who's been doing his job for sixteen years. Sixteen years Anthony Pisano has been employed by the MTA. In sixteen years, he's missed a grand total of nine days' work. Until this incident, no one had ever filed a complaint against him. People like that are the salt of the earth, and what do you do to him? You don't even have the guts to sue the MTA because your case is so weak that a shlock lawyer like me could beat you. So you sue Anthony Pisano instead, knowing full well that he's too poor to hire a lawyer."

"Why don't you handle the case for him?" I asked.

"Because lawyers on the public payroll aren't allowed to take on private clients. You knew that when you filed the complaint."

"You can't be sure that Lonnie Hunker's story is false."

"Bullshit," Waltuck snapped. "I know it, and what's more important, the two of you know it, too. People like you are a disgrace to the legal profession. You hide behind platitudes like 'everyone is entitled to a lawyer,' and then you distort the legal process for your own selfish ends. You do things on behalf of clients that you'd be ashamed to do for yourselves, and you justify everything on grounds that by participating in the legal process you're only helping the system work. Well, I think this case stinks, and I think you stink along with it. You can tell your boss that I said all three of you will be dead in ten years. By then, you'll have eaten everybody up and burst."

"That's uncalled for," I said.

"Is it? Let me know how you feel after you've met Anthony Pisano."

That night, Hardesty and I went drinking. "I'm hungry," Ed said. "Can we go some place where they have peanuts?"

"Sure! I'll take you to the zoo."

"The zoo's closed," he deadpanned. "It's after six."

"All right. I'll buy you a pizza instead."

We went to a dive on upper Broadway, where they sell cheap Italian food and forty-cent beer. Both of us were pretty quiet.

"Waltuck's right," Ed said at last. "You know that, don't you?"

"I suppose so. But is representing Hunker really any different from defending a guilty criminal client? Legal Aid lawyers do that all the time."

"I've never thought of the Legal Aid Society as being particularly moral," he answered. "In fact, I'm beginning to think the entire practice of law is built on amorality."

"Does that make lawyering worse than any other profession?"

"Not really, but I grew up with the naive notion that the law was populated with men like Louis Brandeis and Oliver Wendell Holmes. What an illusion that was! Now I see negligence lawyers traveling to state capitals to lobby against no-fault automobile insurance because new laws would cost them business. Judges ignore two-year case backlogs to take three-month summer vacations, which suits Wall Street just fine since most corporations have a vested interest in slowing the legal process down. I'm starting to wonder if I want to be a lawyer at all."

"So what are you going to do?"

"I don't know," Ed confessed. "Right now, I'm just trying to survive one day at a time. My most immediate problem is finding someone I can invite to the firm dinner dance at the Waldorf Astoria. . . . And stop laughing, goddamn it! It's a serious problem. We've been *instructed* to attend this gala happening, and I have no one to attend with."

"Can't you invite one of the women you've gone out with during the past month?"

"No."

"Why not?"

"Because there's something wrong with each of them. This might sound silly, but I feel as if I have to bring the right kind of date to the Prom. There will be two hundred thirty Ashworth & Palmer lawyers there, and every one of them will judge me on the basis of my date. Is she stupid? Is she good-looking? Did she spill her wine at dinner? I know that sounds insecure, but it's how I feel, and I have no one to go with."

"It's too bad I'm going with Beth. Otherwise, I'd be glad to go as your date in drag."

"You're not helping," he said.

"That's because I have my own problems. When Hunker finds out what my Prom plans are, he'll have a fit. Or have you forgotten the firm's attitude toward intra-office dating?"

"Which is why you couldn't go as my date in drag even if you wanted to. Meanwhile, I'm on the verge of inviting my married sister and asking her to come under an assumed name."

"Don't panic. Who are the other possibilities?"

"There aren't any."

"There have to be."

"There aren't."

"Who have you dated recently?"

"Do you really want to know?"

"Yes."

"All right. Three weeks ago, I was fixed up on a blind date with a woman named Stella Pottios. Early in the evening, I thought Stella was unfriendly, but actually she's just quite stupid and unable to carry on a conversation. Stella has the intellect of a defensive tackle for the Cleveland Browns and the unlined face of one whose brow has never furrowed in thought. When I soap myself up in the shower each morning, I don't think of Stella. In fact, on the night we met, after five or six beers and two joints, she still looked awful.

"Next, there's Harriet Shaspeth. Harriet is what is known in the trade as a princess. She only dates men who are rich. I was a clerical error. Once, many years ago, Harriet accidentally went out with a man who was poor. She scrutinized him the way an eight-year-old would scrutinize smoked octopus before eating it. My date with Harriet almost ended after fifteen minutes, when she refused to go to the movies by bus. Then, after the movie, we went to dinner and she complained when I took a sip of her wine. Can you believe that? Here I was buying her dinner, and she complained when I took a sip of her wine. She wanted me to buy my own. In all fairness, Harriet is moderately attractive and would make a relatively good impression on those with values similar to her own, which encompasses most of Ashworth & Palmer. However, she makes me sick, and I refuse to give her the satisfaction of attending a formal dinner dance in the Grand Ballroom of the Waldorf Astoria. Also, I never want to see her again."

"Okay," I said. "We've ruled out numbers one and two. Is there a third candidate?"

"Candidate number three is my sister."

"Oh."

"Oh is right. Look, you're sitting pretty. You'll catch a little flak for bringing Beth, but she's a winner and everyone knows it. Ninety-nine percent of the complaints you get about her will be based on sheer envy. I, on the other hand, have a real problem."

"Why don't you invite the bitch from last semester's pottery class?"

"Be serious."

"I am being serious. Try it."

"She'd never come. Besides, I'd be embarrassed to ask her. I haven't seen her since the course ended, and she didn't like me then anyway."

"Maybe you came on too strong. Do you like her, or is she really a bitch?"

"Both."

"What's her name?"

"Susan."

"Susan what?"

"Susan Tryon."

There was a hesitancy in his voice which indicated that my idea had not been completely rejected.

"What have you got to lose?" I pressed.

"Nothing."

"So call her. Try the honest approach. The worst she can do is say no."

Excerpted Transcript of the Telephone Conversation Between Mr. Edwin Hardesty and Ms. Susan Tryon (as reported by Edwin Hardesty)

(Telephone rings)

SUSAN: Hello.

ED: Hello, Susan? This is Ed Hardesty—the guy from your pottery class. How are you?

SUSAN: Fine.

ED: How's your cat? (Chuckle, chuckle)

SUSAN: It died two months ago.
(Long pause)

ED: I'm sorry to hear that.
(Another long pause)

ED: Listen, I'll be honest with you. I have two problems, and I thought you might be able to help me with both of them. Problem number one is that I like you, but you won't go out with me. That alone would not have occasioned this telephone call, but a second problem of even more monumental proportions has now arisen. Are you with me so far?

SUSAN: I'm not sure, but keep going.

ED: All right. Remember the law firm I told you about —the one I work for?

SUSAN: Yes.

ED: Good, because that's my second problem. You see, every year on the Saturday night before Thanksgiving, the firm has a formal dinner dance in the Grand Ballroom of the Waldorf Astoria. All two hundred thirty lawyers are required to attend, and if I don't show up, I'll be in trouble. In and of itself, those simple facts would not create a crisis, but I have no one to go with. Please, will you go with me to the Ashworth & Palmer Prom?

SUSAN: Are you serious?

ED: Serious isn't the word for it. I'm desperate.

SUSAN: Good lord! You are serious, aren't you?

ED: Yes!

SUSAN: I don't know what to say.

ED: Say yes, please. Do you realize how hard it was for me to make this telephone call?

"That," I will someday tell my grandchildren, "is how Ed Hardesty got his date for the Ashworth & Palmer Prom."

XII

The first Monday in November, Hardesty and I were called into James Moffitt's office and informed that our salaries had been increased from thirty to thirty-three thousand dollars. "That's a substantial raise," Moffitt told us, "and it reflects our high regard for your performance. Moreover," he added, handing each of us an envelope, "based on your work to date, you're entitled to the enclosed bonuses."

With great solemnity, we thanked him and left. The three-thousand-dollar raise was standard for associates starting their second year at Ashworth & Palmer. By contrast, the bonuses were our report cards. The greater the amount, the better our chances of making partner.

"How much did you get?" Ed asked as we opened our envelopes in the privacy of my office.

"*Six thousand.* How about you?"

A look of discomfort crossed his face. "Fifteen hundred, and I think they suck. Moffitt didn't have to give us our envelopes together. He just wanted you to taste my blood."

Later in the day, I learned that Jordan was the only associate on the UCC case who had received a bonus larger than mine. That news, coupled with the fact that six thousand dollars buys a lot of pizza, made the drudgery of sewage treatment technology more palatable—for me. Others had a slightly different view. Carole Shiner, Frank Haviland, and John Spencer were getting increasingly sick of sticking red dots on documents. Dennis Hayes, Rupert Thorpe, and Glenn Maxwell had found that their "legal duties" consisted largely of indexing previously written memoranda. Harris Boyd was reaching the conclusion that his environmental study was a monumental waste of time, while Richard Watkins, Arlen Cohen, and Hardesty were learning that most of the interviewees on their list of five hundred UCC personnel had no knowledge relevant to the case. Ira Kamenstein claimed that studying sewage treatment technology was the most painful experience known to man. ("I disagree," Ed told him. "Obviously, you've never been kicked in the testicles on a football field with twenty thousand people watching.")

In sum, dissension was spreading and, as The Team grew more disenchanted, Hunker became more aloof than ever. On occasion, I was summoned upstairs to meet with him but, for the most part, our assignments were funneled with increasing regularity through Jordan. "Lonnie would like you to do this," Jordan would tell us. "Lonnie asked me to advise you that . . ." Hunker, of course, had never been a pleasure to deal with but, at least in the past when a job was well done, the performing associate had picked up brownie points. Now even that benefit was lost, since Jordan generally hoarded credit for himself whenever good work was produced.

"Most of the associates don't have a vested interest in the case," Arlen Cohen complained to me one afternoon. "Only

Jordan does—and maybe you. The odds are that the rest of us will be passed over for partner, and in the meantime, we're not even learning how to be lawyers. I've never negotiated a contract or drawn up a will. I have no idea how to argue a case in front of a jury. For the past four years, I've been nothing but a small cog in a big machine and, when I wear out, the firm will simply find another cog to replace me. Now, on top of all that, I'm not even getting credit for the work I do."

Later that afternoon, Arlen spoke his piece at one of Hunker's increasingly rare team meetings. "We're not paying you to like it," Hunker responded. "We're paying you to do it."

"I realize that," Arlen said. "But my not liking the work is only half the problem. I also question whether this case is being run in the best interests of the client."

The unspeakable had been spoken.

"What do you mean by that?" Hunker demanded.

"Look at the record," Arlen answered. "We've been working on an interview project for four months, and most of the people we've talked with don't know anything even remotely related to the case; or if they do, it's duplicative of something somebody else told us months ago. The project isn't helping UCC's defense one bit, but it keeps going on and on."

"What do you suggest," Hunker snapped, "that I go back to Unger and tell UCC's board of directors that we've decided to scrap the project after wasting a half million dollars of their money?"

"Isn't that better than wasting another million?"

Benignly, Hunker shook his head. "Arlen, let's suppose for a minute that the interview project is a mistake. Do you honestly believe we should tell that to our client?"

"Why not?"

"Because this is the real world, and none of us are children. Suppose, hypothetically, you're not feeling well, and you visit a doctor who diagnoses your illness as the flu. Then, two weeks later when your symptoms haven't changed, you revisit the same doctor, and he realizes his first diagnosis was wrong—that all along you were suffering from a kidney infection. You know full well the doctor won't say, 'Sorry, I goofed.' Instead, he'll tell you, 'The virus has developed into kidney trouble.' Do you understand my point?"

Arlen nodded with moderately veiled contempt.

"Don't worry about the client," Hunker assured him. "The history of antitrust enforcement in the United States is hardly cause for alarm. UCC will make out all right. Besides, the money comes from the shareholders, and they have plenty of it."

After the meeting ended, we caucused—minus Hunker and Jordan.

"I wonder if Hunker's partners know how bad he is," Hardesty asked.

"I doubt it," Arlen said. "The way this place operates, every partner is a king. The only way they'd learn about Hunker is if . . ."

"Finish the sentence," Ed prompted.

"The only way they'd learn about Hunker is if Jordan is Moffitt's spy, and the real reason he's been assigned to the UCC case is to check up on Lonnie Hunker."

The idea of espionage was intriguing enough for me to run it through Beth on the telephone that night.

"I don't know," she said. "It's possible, but that's not the sort of thing Jordan would confide in me."

"Why not?"

"Because if word leaked out, Moffitt would have a fit, and Jordan doesn't take risks. He also doesn't trust me very much anymore."

"Does he talk with you at all about Hunker?"

"No."

"How about the case in general?"

"You missed my point. I told you, Jordan doesn't trust me. He figures you'll pump me and I'll pass along anything he says. Judging from this conversation, he's at least half right."

On that note, the inquisition ended, and I was left to ponder Jordan's role at Ashworth & Palmer. Certainly, he was the quintessential company man—diligent, always following orders, working long hours, never speaking ill of his superiors. Yet something about him rang false, maybe the fact that he was the type of person one partner would recruit to spy on another. He struck me as being totally amoral and ruthlessly efficient, someone who controlled his environment as completely as possible and inevitably got what he wanted. Among other things, I was afraid of him.

As autumn moved toward winter, Beth and I spent an increasing amount of time together. Once we double-dated with Coreen McDermott and her husband, another time with Hardesty and a friend. Mostly, though, we did things alone—museums, movies, long walks. By mid-November, she was familiar enough with my place to know where I kept spare light bulbs, the location of every pot and pan, how much I watered my plants, and which doormen were on duty at what hours. More important, though, we were becoming comfortable as a couple. The only cloud on our horizon was the Ashworth & Palmer Prom, which loomed ever closer.

"Boy oh boy," Ira Kamenstein declared. "I guess the shit's really going to hit the fan!"

The occasion for this cheerful remark was distribution throughout the office of seating arrangements for the Prom. On the third Friday in November at 3 P.M., the messengers handed out a mimeographed list of seating assignments for the following night. Twenty seconds later, Ira was in my office, pointing to the relevant page:

Table 27

Mr. and Mrs. George Witherell
Mr. and Mrs. Lionel Hunker
Mr. and Mrs. Jordan Caine
Mr. and Mrs. Richard Watkins
Mr. Thomas Henderson and Ms. Elizabeth Anders
Mr. Edwin Hardesty and Ms. Susan Tryon

"You certainly are a big morale booster," I told him. "Do you have any more helpful comments?"

"Not really. I just want to say that I'd heard rumors you were dating Beth Anders, I'm very jealous, I think that bringing her to the prom is an exceptionally courageous act, and I hope Hunker doesn't kill you because the last thing I want is to be elevated to the role of number one expert in the field of sewage treatment technology."

The door to my office opened, and Hardesty wandered in. "Have you been fired yet?"

"No, you asshole, I haven't been fired."

"Don't get touchy about it," he admonished. "Besides, you could be fired at any minute, or haven't you noticed, we're assigned to the same table as Lonnie Hunker?"

"I noticed, thank you. Obviously, prom seating is based on case assignments."

"So it is. But how come George Witherell is with us?"

"Because he's eighty-five years old and isn't assigned to any case."

"You certainly have this place figured out," Ed told me with what was fast becoming identifiable as mock respect. "I'll miss you after you're fired."

By Saturday night, I was pretty nervous. The cummerbund on my rented tuxedo was too tight, and it occurred to me that I didn't know how to ballroom dance (although, having attended numerous sock hops and proms in my youth,

I was confident I could fake it). Of greater concern was the fact that Beth and I would be seated with the two most ardent opponents of our union. One gaffe by either of us and Hunker, Jordan, or both of them would have our heads. By the time I arrived at Beth's apartment, my emotional state was somewhat tumultuous.

"I have bad news," Beth announced as I stepped inside. "I'm very nervous and need reassurance, so you'll have to hold my hand a lot tonight in front of the partners."

Her gown was black silk, simply tailored and tapered to the waist, sleeveless with a scoop neck. The single gold chain she always wore hung around her neck, matched by a gold bangle bracelet. Her hair flowed several inches beneath her shoulders, and there was just a touch of makeup on her face. Like the dress, her sandals were black silk. She was stunning.

"You look incredible," I told her.

"Do you really think so?"

"Yes."

"That makes me feel better," she said. "Sometimes it helps to have something to fall back on." I helped her into her coat. "Any final words of advice?"

"Not that I can think of."

"There must be something," she pressed.

"Just the standard rules of conduct. Be careful what you say to a partner because anything you say might be held against you. Even though partners can get drunk in public, the same does not hold true for secretaries or associates. And don't drink wine while you're chewing gum."

"Not even bubble gum?"

"Not even bubble gum."

"All right," she said. "But one more thing. I don't want to dance with Lonnie Hunker."

"Neither do I."

"Be serious," she prompted. "If Hunker asks me to dance, I'm going to say 'no'. Is that permissible?"

"How about 'no thank you'?"

"Fair enough. Also, you should be warned in advance that Jordan is pissed."

"How do you know?"

"Yesterday afternoon, right before I left work, I couldn't resist sticking my head inside his office and telling him, 'See you Saturday night.'"

"Wonderful! What did he say?"

"He said, 'Grumble, hrumpf.'"

"What happens if Jordan asks you to dance?"

"I haven't made up my mind yet. He's good-looking, but not very sexy."

We took a cab up Park Avenue and arrived at the Waldorf Astoria a little before seven. Then, threading our way past the hotel shops, we rode to the third floor where the Prom Cocktail Hour was already underway in an area adjacent to the Grand Ballroom. Two huge bars ten yards apart were surrounded by tuxedoed attorneys queuing up for drinks. Waiters in blue dinner jackets scurried back and forth, carrying platters of shrimp, cold salmon, champagne, and assorted hors d'oeuvres. A dozen tables were available for those who chose not to mingle, but the majority of guests stood clustered in small groups around the room. Hardesty and Carole Shiner were together against the far wall, and we walked toward them. "In four years of college football," Ed was saying, "I touched the ball twice. Once I recovered a fumble against Dartmouth and once I intercepted a pass against Yale."

I tapped him on the shoulder and said hello.

"This," he announced with a flourish, pointing to the woman standing next to him, "is Susan Tryon."

I introduced Beth, and Carole presented her husband. Despite the buildup she had received, Susan Tryon (a/k/a "The Bitch from my pottery class") was rather pleasant. She and Beth established a fairly quick rapport, and before long

Susan was talking about her job as a model ("It's not all that great"), her former husband ("I was nineteen and very naive"), and Ed ("This might sound strange, but I could get to like him"). For the record, Susan was Beth's height, a little on the skinny side, and one of the better-looking women in attendance. After twenty minutes of conversation and three glasses of champagne, I felt confident enough to suggest to Beth that we mingle more widely. She agreed, and we had just begun to march across the room toward Ira Kamenstein when Ellis Slattery, one of the firm's top corporate partners, blocked our way.

"Just wanted to take a look," he slobbered, glass in hand. "Gorgeous young creature."

A fairly large number of partners and associates were looking in our direction, but none came over to talk. A tall white-haired man passed on his way to the bar. "That's William Montgomery," I said. "He's the firm's senior tax partner."

"I know," Beth told me. "He has quite a reputation among the secretaries."

"How come?"

"In 1948, just after he made partner, Montgomery gave his secretary a thirty-five-dollar bonus for Christmas. That equaled one week of her salary, and every year since he's given her the same thirty-five dollars for Christmas. In the interim, his own salary has gone up to three hundred thousand dollars."

"That's very funny," I said.

"Yeah! Unless you happen to be William Montgomery's secretary."

I nodded in the direction of an equally distinguished-looking partner. "That's James Coville. He was a Special Assistant to Henry Kissinger during the Ford Administration. His primary accomplishment was administering a program which distributed powdered milk to drought-stricken countries in Northern Africa. The natives used it to fill potholes in their only major highway."

Arlen Cohen, Ira Kamenstein, and their wives chatted with us warmly. Richard Watkins made a point of ignoring us. "Dinner should be fun," Beth said, "especially with Hunker, Jordan, and Watkins all at our table."

The ballroom doors opened wide, and a bell sounded summoning us to dinner. Grabbing a final glass of champagne, I led Beth inside. The room was immense. Eighteen crystal chandeliers hung from the fifty-foot-high blue and gold ceiling. Small reflecting mirrors dotted the walls, which were blue and red with gold trim. Forty tables with gold napkins and tablecloths spread across the floor. At the west end of the room, a twelve-man orchestra was making music.

Five-by-seven-inch numbered cardboard markers on the center of each table pointed the way to our destination (table twenty-seven). Hardesty and Susan Tryon arrived the same time we did.

"Where do we sit?" Ed asked.

"Try looking at the placecards," I suggested.

"You think of everything, don't you?"

The seating was arranged so that dates sat next to one another but husbands and wives were separated. Our table was set as follows:

Lionel Hunker

Gloria Watkins — Barbara Caine

Jordan Caine — Edwin Hardesty

Elvira Witherell — Susan Tryon

Richard Watkins — George Witherell

Jane Hunker — Elizabeth Anders

Thomas Henderson

"You women are in for a real treat," Ed told Susan and Beth. "You've never seen Lonnie Hunker chew his food before, have you?"

Before they could answer, Jordan and Barbara Caine arrived, followed by Richard and Gloria Watkins. Much to my surprise, Jordan greeted us rather warmly and thrust his wife forward with the sobriquet, "This is my better half." Indeed, Barbara Caine appeared to be just that. She was about Beth's height and not unattractive with long brown hair and hazel eyes, but her most redeeming feature was a wonderfully warm smile. "I'm glad to meet you," she told Beth. "My husband says you're invaluable."

Watkins introduced his wife to the Caines and, without approaching further in our direction, told us, "This is Gloria." Then Hunker arrived. "I think I know almost everyone here," Lonnie announced, circling the table and shaking hands. "Jordan . . . Barbara, good to see you again. . . . Ed . . . you must be Susan Tryon; I'm Lonnie Hunker. . . . Ms. Anders (with a nod) . . . Tom (with a glare) . . . Dick, Gloria, good to see you, too."

Having made the rounds, Hunker settled at what had just become the head of the table. The plain-looking woman in the brown cocktail dress who accompanied him but had not been introduced took a seat to my left. "I guess I sit here," she said, peering at the placecard. "I'm Jane Hunker." Her hair was short and straight, her figure nonexistent.

"I'm Tom Henderson," I said, extending my right hand. "And this is Beth Anders."

"What a beautiful young lady," Mrs. Hunker told us.

George Witherell appeared and helped his wife, Elvira, into her chair. "I'm quite satisfied with the seating arrangements," he announced, after taking his own seat between Susan and Beth. "Without meaning to slight the pulchritude of the other ladies in attendance, it's clear that I have been placed between the two most glamorous women at the entire ball. I only wish I could reduce my internal clock by ten years and be seventy-four again."

"Ten years would make you seventy-five, dear," Elvira corrected. "You just had a birthday."

As soup was served, Beth and I journeyed to the dance floor.

"So far, so good," I told her.

"Just keep an eye on Jane Hunker," she said.

"How come?"

"I think she's soused."

"Speaking of the Hunkers," I queried, "how come Lonnie Hunker keeps glaring at me but not you?"

"I guess he figures I'm a secretary who can't be expected to know her place, and that my being here is your fault. Or maybe he's just jealous."

As dinner progressed, our table broke down into several groups. Seated between two partners' wives, Richard Watkins obsequiously tried to ingratiate himself with both. Hunker was flanked by Barbara Caine and Gloria Watkins, both of whom had obviously been instructed to do anything short of performing oral sex to keep him happy. Jordan tried as politically as possible to make sure that Barbara said the right things to Hunker. That left an enclave of five—Ed, Susan, Beth, yours truly, and George Witherell—over which Witherell held sway. "I like these parties," he told us. "They remind me of my wedding in Boston back in 1927. Prohibition was still the law so we had a separate room in back for drinking. My cousin Arthur brought the whiskey. It was bad, and nine guests, my father-in-law included, passed out, but the rest of us kept on drinking and dancing."

"I'll tell you how to solve the graffiti problem," I heard Hunker say from across the table. "Don't let black teenagers ride the city subways."

"Your generation never learned how to ballroom dance,"

George Witherell continued. "That's a shame. Whirling around the floor is really quite glamorous. Of course, at my age, I don't do much whirling. Also, you young people don't read enough. When I was young, I read all the classics—Dickens, Tolstoy, all of Shakespeare's plays. Nowadays, people pay homage to great writers, but they don't read them."

The orchestra was playing "I'm Gonna Sit Right Down and Write Myself a Letter."

"Several years ago," Witherell went on, "it occurred to me that I had never read *Origin of the Species.* My grandson was at Columbia, and at my request he borrowed the book for me from the university library. Charles Darwin's most precious thoughts had been on file in that library for over fifty years. Not once had they been properly read. Half a dozen pages in the copy I borrowed had been accidentally joined together by the printing process. After more than half a century, I split the pages on Columbia University's copy of *Origin of the Species.*"

Hunker and Barbara Caine went off to dance, followed by Ed and Susan Tryon. With a certain amount of effort, George Witherell rose and escorted Elvira to the floor. Still seated, Beth turned in my direction. "You never took dancing lessons, did you?" she asked.

"What makes you say that?"

"Because you don't know how to dance. Whatever they play, you just lurch around very slowly at the same pace."

As expected, dinner was quite good—watercress soup, filet mignon, scalloped potatoes, asparagus with hollandaise sauce, salad, and baked alaska.

"It's really interesting to watch Hunker eat," Beth whispered as the object of her admiration sucked up a stalk of asparagus. "Have you noticed?"

"Many times," I said.

"I'd like to go to law school," Barbara Caine told Susan,

"but Jordan thinks the idea is silly. He wants me to take tennis lessons instead."

Hunker reached into his tuxedo jacket pocket for a match and pulled out a mothball.

"How do you like working for my chubby hubby?" Jane Hunker called across the table to Hardesty.

Hunker glowered.

"Chubby hubby," she said again. "I thought that was clever. Like this pile of wash is definitely brighter, or this cola tastes more flavorful. I have a good imagination."

"Would you like to dance, dear," Hunker ordered. They took to the floor together for the first and only time that night, returning to their respective seats several minutes later.

"Lonnie told me to keep my trap shut," Jane announced in my direction. "But I'll say whatever I want to."

"How did you and Lonnie meet?" I asked, starting to feel a little embarrassed and seeking to turn the conversation to happier times.

"In college. Lonnie was at Harvard, and I was at a lesser school in Boston. We weren't lovers, just friends. Then the years passed, and no one came along for either of us. On my twenty-eighth birthday, we agreed that if we were both single at age thirty, we'd get married. It was marvelously practical."

"And unique," I added.

"Not really. Since then, we've made all the textbook mistakes. When the marriage started to sour, we had two children because we thought they would bring us closer together. After that, we tried sex therapy because Lonnie fucks like he eats. Nothing worked. Do you know what happened in bed the other night? Lonnie and I were fucking when all of a sudden he announced, 'Sorry, but I have to cut one loose.' Then he farted."

Hunker stood up from his chair and worked his way

around the table toward Beth. "You've tried an associate," he said. "Now, would you like to dance with a partner?"

"No thank you," she answered.

A little after midnight, we left. Back at my apartment, Beth disrobed and hung her gown in the closet.

"Two hundred thirty penguins with dates," I said. "That's what we all looked like tonight."

Beth reached into her purse and withdrew her souvenir of the evening—a small white placecard with the name "Elizabeth Anders" penned in ink. "This is my half of the bed," she announced, laying the card on her pillow.

Together, we climbed beneath the covers, lights out, Beth resting her head on my shoulder. "I had a wonderful time," she said. "I really did."

"Me too."

"Did I say the right things?"

"Yes."

"Was I really all right?"

"You were perfect."

"For sure?"

"For sure."

She giggled.

"What's so funny?" I asked.

"I feel just like Eliza Doolittle in *My Fair Lady*," she said.

XIII

Monday morning at nine-thirty, Ira Kamenstein and Arlen Cohen came by for a postmortem on the Prom. At ten-ten, Julie Swerzbinski (my secretary) inquired with a particularly knowing smile whether I had enjoyed myself on Saturday night. The last of the curious (Carole Shiner) departed my office circa ten-thirty, whereupon Hardesty entered.

"I'm very unhappy," he announced.

"How come?"

"I'll tell you, but you have to promise not to breathe a word to anyone."

"All right."

"And you have to promise not to kid me about it."

"Fair enough."

Taking his customary seat on the edge of my credenza, he stared downward. "Premature ejaculation," he whispered.

"Pardon?"

"Premature ejaculation. Saturday night, after the Prom, with Susan at her apartment."

I started laughing.

"You're a big help," he said.

"Sorry," I apologized, "but I happen to think it's funny. How can you call ejaculation premature if you've waited ten months for it?"

"A real friend, that's what you are."

"Be honest! Don't you see the humor in it?"

"It would be funnier if it had happened to someone else."

"How did Susan react?"

"She thought it was funny, too. You'd get along great with each other. You could sit around and have orgasms together in your underwear."

The telephone rang, ending round one. I picked up the receiver and was greeted by the voice of Lionel J. Hunker. "Tom, I'd like you and Jordan to go to San Francisco next week. You'll be leaving here Monday morning and flying home on Friday. Jordan will explain everything to you on the plane. It's a two-man mission."

"Some people have all the luck," Ed groused after I had hung up. "I traveled on expense account to Bismarck, North Dakota. You get to go to San Francisco. Hunker must think you're hot stuff."

"I wouldn't know," I answered. "I haven't checked his pants lately."

The rest of the week passed without incident. Twice I met with Hunker to discuss details of UCC's marketing system and Jordan worked daily with Beth, but intra-office dating was not discussed. At one point, I even theorized that the firm's social taboo might be less real than imagined, but Ira Kamenstein did his best to scuttle that notion. "They're just waiting until you come up for partner seven years from now," he advised. "Then they'll get even."

Jordan and I rendezvoused Monday morning at Kennedy Airport. "We should have shared a cab," I said as we stood on line preparatory to boarding American Airlines flight 901 to San Francisco. "It would have saved the client twenty dollars."

Jordan shrugged.

"Really," I persisted. "The cab from my apartment to the airport cost twenty dollars. The per capita income for all of Kenya is only three times that amount for an entire year."

"I guess that explains why so few Masai warriors take cabs from midtown Manhattan to Kennedy Airport," he answered.

In due course, we were seated in the first-class cabin, and Jordan flipped his briefcase open. "Let me tell you what this trip is about," he said. "The people at UCC headquarters in Unger are unhappy with the pace of the litigation. Rightly or wrongly, they feel we've done all the work we have to and that Lonnie's interview project is simply a means for running up an extra two million dollars in legal fees. Needless to say, if that attitude were to prevail, it would not help the reputation of Ashworth & Palmer."

"Or the reputation of Lionel J. Hunker," I added.

"True," Jordan acknowledged. "However, getting back to the interview project, UCC's Vice President in Charge of Legal Matters has selected three names from our list of five hundred prospective interviewees. Each of the three is stationed at the company's West Coast regional headquarters in San Francisco. Our job is to interview them and find out what they can add to our knowledge of the case. If our stay in San Francisco produces new data, UCC will be satisfied, the interview project will continue, and Lonnie Hunker will be very happy with both of us. If on the other hand we come home empty-handed, the project will end, UCC will be convinced that Ashworth & Palmer has been churning legal fees, and Lonnie will be very sad. Our job is to show that the interview project works."

"And if the facts don't justify that conclusion?"

"Then we find new facts."

A UCC sales representative named Harry Barnes met us at the airport in San Francisco and drove us to our hotel. "The interviews are set," he told us. "Donald Brewer on Tuesday, Oliver Forbes on Wednesday, and Thursday you get Sam Burchelle. That's one Regional Sales Manager, one Vice President in Charge of Marketing, and one Senior Engineer. I'll pick you up in the hotel lobby at nine o'clock each morning and bring you home each night. Whatever you want—theater tickets, restaurant reservations—let me know. I can handle it."

Traveling first-class on expense account in San Francisco isn't bad. Like most modern giants, our hotel had a lobby that looked like a cross between a shopping mall, an indoor basketball arena, and an airplane hangar. But our rooms were comfortable and the breakfasts quite good. Each night, with Harry Barnes as our host, we dined at a different three-star restaurant. Like Bud Daley, who had been our guide in Unger, Harry was destined for less than greatness. Short and squat, a twenty-four-year veteran of UCC's sales force, he smoked smelly cigars and wore the same red and yellow plaid sports jacket four days running. His sense of importance (such as it was) came largely from hobnobbing whenever possible with higher management, and he was under the mistaken impression that, by chauffeuring us around for four days, he would gain access to a wealth of inside information about *the case*. Also, his role as host allowed him to shake hands on consecutive days with Donald Brewer, Oliver Forbes, and Sam Burchelle, all of whom patted him on the back, said, "Good to see you again, Harry," and congratulated him on transporting us from the hotel to regional headquarters without a traffic accident.

By contrast, Brewer, Forbes, and Burchelle were higher management. They knew precisely why we had come to San Francisco and were extremely well versed in the case.

"I don't know why you're asking me that," Brewer responded when Jordan posed a question about UCC's limited warranty protection plan. "That was answered for you people three years ago when your boss went to Unger for the first time. I read the minutes of the meeting myself. Our own Chairman of the Board told Lonnie Hunker all about it."

Oliver Forbes was more direct. "Sometimes I think we'd be better off using political muscle instead of lawyers to handle this case."

"I understand you tried that before the complaint was filed," Jordan shot back. "And it didn't work."

"Maybe we should have tried a little harder," Forbes said.

So it went, day after day. Virtually every fact we elicited had already been recorded in a previous Ashworth & Palmer memorandum or told to and then forgotten by Lonnie Hunker. The only significant item we picked up came on the third day. "There would have been a considerable operating-cost saving to our customers if UCC had installed rotating biological contractors in our secondary treatment process," Sam Burchelle told us. "But it would have cost UCC money and there wasn't any competition so we didn't bother. I guess that kind of hurts our legal position, doesn't it?"

It did. But one piece of information, good or bad, hardly justified a week-long trip to San Francisco by two lawyers whose time was being billed at a combined total of close to two hundred dollars per hour.

Our meeting with Sam Burchelle ended just before six o'clock on Thursday night, after which Harry Barnes escorted us to dinner and then back to the hotel. It was too late for a movie and too early for bed.

"Do you want a drink?" Jordan asked.

"Sure."

We wandered into the hotel bar and sat at a corner table. A waitress came over to take our order. Two couples sitting several yards away were laughing loudly, almost shouting to one another. A lone guitarist was making noise at the far end of the room.

"Can I ask you something?"

"Go ahead," Jordan said.

"What were you and Forbes talking about the other day when he mentioned political muscle?"

Jordan fiddled with his swizzle stick, then looked up. "By the time this case is over, UCC will have spent between ten and fifteen million dollars in legal fees. You can win quite a few Presidential primaries for that amount. According to Moffitt, they spent a bundle trying to keep the Justice Department from filing the complaint in the first place. But they weren't very subtle about it, and they left too many footprints."

"Will they try again?"

"Maybe, but I doubt it. At this stage, it would be too risky for UCC to do anything without the guidance of its lawyers, and Lonnie Hunker has never been particularly adept at dealing with the centers of power."

I looked up from my drink. "If UCC's prices are too high, why haven't there been more complaints? Any municipality in the country could have filed suit."

"The company does its best to keep local officials happy. It wines them and dines them pretty lavishly. Then, if someone is still inclined to make a fuss, there are ways to sweeten the offering—college scholarships for children, low-interest mortgages, things like that. Occasionally, headquarters might even cut the price of a sewage treatment plant. Or, as we'll say in court, there are no complaints because our prices are fair and reasonable."

For a while, we sat in silence. "It hasn't been a very successful trip, has it?" Jordan said at last.

"I guess not. How do you suggest we present it to Hunker?"

"Very carefully," he answered.

"Meaning?"

"First, I'd better give him an oral report. Then we'll see whether he wants it in writing. I think it would be best if I handled things alone."

"You're the boss," I told him. "You have been, ever since you came on the case."

An odd sort of smile crossed his face. "I know," he said.

We finished our drinks around eleven, and I went upstairs where I was in the closing stages of brushing my teeth when two knocks on the door sounded. "Coming," I hollered, spitting a mouthful of toothpaste into the sink. After rinsing quickly, I opened the door and was greeted by an absolutely gorgeous willowy green-eyed blonde dressed in an emerald pants suit.

"Hi," she said. "Harry Barnes sent me. I'm yours for the next hour."

Not quite comprehending, I backed into the room and she followed. "Don't worry," she purred. "I'm free. Harry took it out of petty cash."

She was stunning.

"Mind if I sit down?" she asked.

"Actually . . ." I stammered, "I sort of do . . . I do mind, that is."

"Oh."

"You see . . ." I felt tongue-tied and foolish. "You see, I've never slept with a prostitute. And while you're absolutely beautiful and, I'm sure, very nice, I'd feel funny about it. Also, I've got a friend back home, and I'd hate . . . what I mean is, even though she and I haven't discussed my sleeping with other women . . . or her sleeping with other men—"

"It's okay," the blonde interrupted. "You don't have to explain. I get paid for trying. Have a good night."

Then she left, and I went to bed pondering the extent of my loyalty to Beth. Was it conscious choice or a simple reflex reaction? What if I had met the same woman in the hotel lobby and been told that she was a visiting model from Los Angeles instead of a hooker? I fell asleep, my questions unanswered.

The next morning, I shaved, showered, dressed, and packed—all by seven-thirty. I was in the process of paying my bill at the cashier's desk downstairs in the hotel lobby when Jordan exited from the elevator—the green-eyed blonde at his side. Given the lobby layout, the three of us came face to face. No words were spoken.

Later in the day, midway through our plane ride home, Jordan looked up from the copy of the *Wall Street Journal* he was reading and turned toward me. "I assume you'll be discreet about this morning," he said.

"More so than you," I answered. "But do me one favor. No more lectures about my going out with Beth."

That night, I told Hardesty about the incident. Needless to say, he was ecstatic. "What a hypocrite!" he shouted. "What a goddamn hypocrite! We ought to put an orgy sign-up sheet on the bulletin board outside Moffitt's office. I'll bet Jordan Caine would be the first person to scrawl his John Hancock." Later, though, Ed was somewhat subdued. "Even Harry Barnes bowed to the pecking order," he moaned. "You were only scheduled to get the blonde for an hour. Jordan had her for the entire night."

"Maybe so," I answered. "But if she wasn't planning to take a bath in between, going first would have had its advantages." Beth, when apprised of the situation, concurred with my judgment.

Several days after Jordan and I returned to New York, Lonnie Hunker sent the following letter to UCC's Board of Directors:

> Dear Sirs,
>
> At your request, Ashworth & Palmer has carefully reviewed the gains to be had in continuing the antitrust interview project begun last July in conjunction with the United States government's lawsuit against the Union Construction Company. Our steadfast belief is that, despite its cost, the project must continue.
>
> As you know, two of our associates recently visited

your regional headquarters in San Francisco and conducted interviews with three UCC employees. Let's take one of those interviews as an example. On their last day in San Francisco, Mr. Caine and Mr. Henderson spoke with Sam Burchelle. At that time, Mr. Burchelle told them there would have been a considerable operating-cost saving to UCC's customers had UCC installed rotating biological contractors in its secondary treatment process but that UCC had refused to do so, apparently because there was an absence of competitive pressure.

The dangers inherent in facts such as these are obvious. If the reality of the marketplace is such that UCC can refuse to provide its customers with cost-saving devices simply because there is no competitor around who will step into the breach, then we have a very serious claim of unlawful monopolization on our hands. In order to properly litigate this case, it is imperative for us to root out *every* potentially damaging fact and then analyze these facts one by one in order to rebut them. Despite its cost, the interview project is an essential tool in this process. Should it be discontinued, UCC will be forced to trial with a less than comprehensive defense, and in the end, it is your own shareholders who will suffer.

Very truly yours,
Lionel J. Hunker

Shortly thereafter, UCC's Board of Directors authorized continuation of the interview project. Hunker called a team meeting to break the news. "Jordan and Tom deserve particular credit," he told us. "They're the ones who gathered the crucial evidence from Sam Burchelle."

Arlen Cohen offered his congratulations when the meeting ended. "You two are the new Gold Dust Twins," he said.

Beth subsequently reported that Jordan seemed "very pleased" with the development, but in truth her thoughts were elsewhere. I had been invited home to meet her parents for dinner the following Saturday night.

We made the journey by subway. "Are you nervous?" I asked as the train jostled its way toward Metropolitan Avenue in Queens.

"A little," she admitted. "I don't bring friends home very often."

"What made you do it now?"

"I want you to meet my parents, and they want to meet you."

Pursuant to instructions, I had dressed in slacks and a sport shirt. ("Don't wear a suit," Beth had said.) She was wearing thick-ribbed black corduroy pants and a blue cotton blouse. The ride took over an hour. We arrived at Metropolitan Avenue just after dusk, and Beth led me along a shabby street to a four-story walk-up building with grimy brick walls where her parents had lived for thirty years.

"Which apartment?" I asked.

"Two B."

"Or not to be," I added.

"Huh?"

"Forget it. It was Shakespeare."

We climbed the stairs, and her father met us on the second-floor landing. He was a large, barrel-chested man of about sixty, red-faced with thick white hair, dressed in a plaid flannel shirt and baggy pants. "Good to meet you," he said, pumping my hand. "Beth has told us a great deal about you." Then, after giving his daughter a bearlike hug, he led us inside. Mama Anders was next on the receiving line. For some reason, I had pictured her as being short and Italian-looking with brown eyes and dark hair. Don't ask me why. Instead, she looked like an older (albeit less ravishing) version of Beth—about the same height with blue eyes and graying blond hair.

Beth's father took our coats, and Mrs. Anders led us to the

living room. The furniture was worn but spotless. "Can I offer you a drink?" she asked.

"I'd like a beer if you have one."

"Light or dark?"

"Light."

Beth asked for a glass of wine. Mr. Anders ("Call me Ben," he said) joined me for a beer. "Beth's brother, Roger, is out tonight," Mrs. Anders told us. "But he would have liked to meet you."

"Maybe I'll get to see him another time," I answered, knowing full well that the last thing any seventeen-year-old boy wanted was to meet his older sister's lover. Parents, it suddenly occurred to me, might feel awkward about it too.

"Beth told us about your job," Mrs. Anders said. "You must be very proud of being a lawyer at a firm like Ashworth & Palmer."

"It's a nice place to work."

"I would think so. Beth has been happy there for almost six years. Six years and she's always had the same boss. That must be some kind of record."

Throughout dinner, the conversation was dominated by references to Ashworth & Palmer. "I've heard how hard you lawyers work," Ben said. "Beth tells me about some of the partners and this Jordan fellow she works for. Seems like a shame. A man's work should be a building block to happiness, not his entire life. Beth says they're all hung up on this partnership mystery."

"Mystique," Beth corrected.

"Pardon?"

"Mystique! Partnership mystique."

"That's right," Ben said, turning away from his daughter and back toward me. "Anyway, what I was saying is you seem like a nice young man, and I hope you keep things in perspective."

I assured him I would.

"That's good," he said. "There are times I think the only thing worse than a lawyer is a landlord or a politician, but Beth tells me that some of you fellows are all right."

After dinner, the family photo album came out, and the evolution of Beth Anders was recreated before my eyes— "Skinny Legs" Anders, age four, in a bathing suit at Coney Island with Proud Papa looking on; Beth, age six, with her newborn brother; Beth, age ten, in a green Girl Scout uniform.

"Did Beth tell you about the time she broke the record for selling Girl Scout cookies?" Mrs. Anders inquired.

"Not that I remember."

The story followed. Ben had been a bartender for thirty-five years. In her childhood, every Saturday afternoon, Beth had accompanied him to work to play with the pinball machine and watch the color television behind the bar. The practice began when she was six and ended half a dozen years later, when she began to attract more than fatherly attention from Ben's customers. At age ten, Beth had enrolled in the Girl Scouts and, like her contemporaries, been co-opted into selling Girl Scout cookies. Rather than go door-to-door with her product, she simply brought several cartons (not boxes, cartons) to the bar and sold them to the regulars, who had known her for years and couldn't very well refuse to buy a box of cookies from Ben Anders' daughter. Beth had sold more cookies than any other five girls in her troop put together. She was also expelled from the Girl Scouts for selling cookies in "a disreputable establishment."

"I had a good head for business," she explained when her father had finished telling the story.

There were photos of Beth in junior high school when she began to fill out and several years later when she began to look like a goddess. Her report cards from grades seven through twelve were bunched together toward the back of the album. Slipping them out of their envelopes, Ben examined them one by one and murmured his approval. "Almost all nineties. She was a good student, never any trouble."

We left about eleven—any later and the subways would be dangerous. "Did they like me?" I asked on the ride home.

"I think so," Beth answered. "My father said you seemed like a nice young man—a little on the stuffy side, but he attributed that to your being nervous."

We rode a while longer in silence. "What did *you* think?" she asked at last.

"They're nice people."

"Is that all you have to say?"

"I liked them. Really, I did."

"They've accomplished quite a lot," she said. "What they have might not seem like much to you, but to them it's everything. My father was one of seven brothers and sisters who grew up in a tenement in Brooklyn. My grandfather died when all seven of them were children. My grandmother raised them alone. Sometimes, on Saturday nights when everyone else was cooking dinner, there wasn't any food at home. My grandmother was a proud woman. She'd take an onion, put it in a pot of boiling water, and leave the door open so all the neighbors would smell it and think she was cooking dinner. Now my father has a decent home, enough to eat, and three children. I'm a legal secretary who makes fourteen thousand dollars a year and hangs out with a Wall Street lawyer; my sister is a registered nurse; next autumn, my brother will be a freshman in college. My father is quite pleased with himself."

"He should be," I said. "He did a good job with you." As the subway roared underground through Queens, I leaned over and kissed her—on the cheek.

"Hey, Tom," she said. "I want this story to have a happy ending. All right?"

"I'll try," I promised.

XIV

Some of my best thinking is done in the shower. Generally, I'm in a zombielike state when I wake up in the morning. Then I drink a large glass of orange juice and shave (nicking myself and spilling blood all over the place). After that, I shower. Without hot water pouring down on my head, it's doubtful my brain cells would start.

The idea came while I was in the shower. Christmas and New Year's had just passed, the January blahs were setting in, and I was feeling kind of lonely. I raised the subject with Ed in my office that morning.

"Have you ever lived with anyone?"

"Sure," he answered. "My parents, my brother and sister, and a dozen roommates."

"That's not what I had in mind. Have you ever lived with a woman?"

"Once."

"How was it?"

"So-so."

"What made you do it?"

"I didn't have much say in the deliberations. I was dating this girl during my senior year of college, and one night she showed up at my apartment with two large suitcases. When I asked what they were for, she told me, 'I'm moving in. We can get the rest of my stuff tomorrow.'"

"Did it work?"

"Not really. We stayed together until the end of the school year. Then she split. Basically, she just wanted to live with somebody, and I figured what the hell. The world was younger then."

The door to my office opened. A messenger came in, deposited several memos on my desk, and left.

"Why the interest in co-ed living?" Ed asked.

"Because I'm thinking of living with Beth."

"No kidding! Her idea or yours?"

"Mine. She doesn't know about it yet."

"Oh!"

"Oh, what?"

"Oh, don't you think it would be wise to include her in the decision-making process?"

There were times when Hardesty was a fountain of wisdom.

"I suppose so," I answered. "But first I have to make a threshold decision of my own. Right now, I'm trying to sort out my feelings on the subject."

"Do you love her?"

"I can't answer that. I've never been quite sure of the distinction between loving someone and being in love. The first seems to imply a sense of permanence. The second is so unpredictable and erratic that it's hard for me to envision it as more than a transitional stage. But I trust Beth. I like it when we're together, and I sleep better when she's next to me in bed."

"How does she feel about you?"

"We might find out very shortly."

The look cast in my direction indicated that my answers were less than satisfactory. "Let me ask you something," Hardesty pressed. "How often do you consider Beth as a person apart from her admittedly phenomenal looks?"

"A lot."

"Are you sure?"

"I think so."

"Ten years from now, when she looks less like a goddess and more like an average human being, will you still want her?"

"Yes."

"Then good luck. It's worth a try. I'd live with her in a minute, but for reasons I don't fully comprehend, she appears to prefer you."

That weekend, I raised the subject with Beth. Like Ed, she had remarkable faith in my instincts.

"How much of this is for the sake of convenience?" was her initial response.

"What is that supposed to mean?"

"I'm just wondering if it isn't too simple. We've been seeing each other for seven months. I know when to talk and when to leave you alone, where the dishes are, and what you like to do in bed. I haven't done anything really wrong, and since you envision my moving into your place, you won't suffer any dislocation at all. It's not that I'm unalterably opposed to the idea, but I do have some doubts. I'm not quite sure why you want to do it."

"Because I'm happier when we're together. And you are too."

"Maybe," she conceded, "but we're still very different from one another. Your goals are professional, and I'm personally oriented. You want to be a superstar. I never cared about shining brighter than anyone else. Maybe we could blend together, maybe not. It would take a lot of tolerance and hard work from both of us."

"We could do it."
"That depends on several unknowns."
"Such as?"
"Your ability to build bridges and maintain a relationship. I don't know if you're capable of doing it. Except for Ed Hardesty, you don't have a friend in New York. Ed and I are the only two people you even see outside the office. In the seven months I've known you, not one person has visited from Nebraska. You've torn up all your old roots without planting new ones."
"Then help me plant them."
"I'll think about it."
"If it doesn't work, we can always get out of it."
"That's the wrong attitude," she cautioned. "If we do this, it will be because it *will* work."
Two weeks and many conferences later, Beth arrived at my apartment with a dozen roses.
"Why the flowers?"
"We're celebrating," she told me. "I've decided to move in."

For such a big step, once the decision was made, it was remarkably easy to orchestrate. Beth sublet her apartment. Her parents, while not ecstatic, accepted the arrangement. I agreed to pay two-thirds of our rent, with other expenses to be split on a less formal basis. We decided to keep half of my furniture and exchange the rest for hers. All the other mechanics of moving—packing, giving the post office a forwarding address, and so on—fell into place. Two movers agreed to haul everything for three hundred dollars. Hardesty promised to help unpack on the day of the move.
The gala event came to pass on the last Saturday in February—eight months after Beth and I had shared our first night. The moving men came on time, the weather was sunny, and miraculously nothing went wrong. With Ed's help, we rearranged the furniture in my (strike that—) *our*

bedroom to provide space for a second dresser. Two of Beth's bookshelves went into the living room along with her sofa. While she and I hung clothes in the closet, Ed began unpacking books.

"How do you want these organized?" he called out.

"Just put them on the bookshelves anyway you want," Beth answered. "I'll rearrange them later."

"How about if I put all the red books on one shelf and all the green ones on another?"

"How about trying it by subject matter?"

"All right," he told her. "I'll put all the sex guides and cookbooks together on a 'How to Catch a Man' shelf."

After an hour of unpacking and shelving books, Hardesty was exhausted. "You're out of shape," Beth snickered.

"Not everyone can have a body like yours," he shot back. "Besides" (and here he grabbed his stomach) "this isn't flab; it's dislocated muscle."

"If you were ten pounds lighter," she told him, "I might have fallen for you instead of Tom."

"I'll never eat again." Twenty minutes later, the vow was rescinded. "What's for lunch?" Ed wanted to know.

"There are bagels, cheese, and apples in the refrigerator," I told him.

"Instead of food?"

"What are you talking about?"

"Be serious, cheese and apples aren't filling, and bagels are nothing but an excuse to eat cream cheese and lox. Don't you have anything good like jelly doughnuts or brownies?" Whereupon the man who was never going to eat again disappeared out the front door and returned half an hour later with a large pizza. "I was going to get one with sausage on it," he explained, "but Beth thinks I should lose ten pounds so I got one with mushrooms instead. Want a piece?"

"No, thanks," I told him. "I'm a rocketarian."

"Huh?"

"A rocketarian. I can't stand the thought of eating animals, animal products, or poor little plants so I only eat rocks. . . . Yes, you dummy. Of course I want a piece!"

After lunch, the heavy cleaning began. Ed dusted, I vacuumed, and Beth wandered off to scrub the bathroom floor. "There's no need to do the tub," I called after her. "I put water in it every day."

"So I've noticed," she shouted back. "And you wash the floor once every six months whether it's dirty or not." Minutes later, she returned to the living room with a dead roach in hand. "There's wildlife in the bathtub," she announced.

Inexorably, the apartment grew cleaner. Walls and corners began to look spotless. The last packing cartons were thrown away. New posters went up in place of old ones.

"I'm getting very tired," Ed groused as the day neared an end. "I haven't worked this hard since football practice five years ago."

"Back to work," Coach Anders ordered.

"Wait! I have a question."

"No stalling."

"This is for real." He had a slightly giddy look about him. "What happens if you put six ducks in a box?"

"I give up," Beth answered. "What?"

"You have a box of quackers."

"Go back to work."

"No! Wait! I have a better one. How many psychiatrists does it take to change a light bulb?"

"I don't know. How many?"

"Only one, but the light bulb really has to want to change."

"That's all."

"Not yet, please!"

"I've had enough."

"Just one more."

"Back to work, now."

By early evening, the job was done, and the three of us went out for dinner. "What's kwishee?" Ed asked, examining the menu in the restaurant.

"Huh?"

"Right here," he said, pointing to the second entry under "Appetizers."

"That's quiche," I told him.

"Oh!"

"Sometimes I think you're stupid on purpose."

"Of course. It livens the party."

Somehow we muddled through the meal, after which Ed departed ("To go home and take a bubble bath with dishwasher soap," he insisted). "You won't ever replace Johnny Carson," I shouted after him as he disappeared down the street.

"Or Ed McMahon," Beth added.

Then we returned home, where a battered brown teddy bear sat waiting at the foot of our bed. "That's Gideon," Beth told me. "He was my best friend for a long time. He shared my secrets, held me at night when I was scared, and consoled me when I cried. He always listened to my problems and laughed at my jokes. Now that I've moved in, I have two of you."

There was a very large bottle of champagne I had put on ice in the refrigerator for the occasion. Together we popped the cork and began to celebrate. We talked and laughed and drank, and for the first time in a long time, I felt there was someone who cared.

"I'm glad you're here," I told her as the bottle ran dry. "I really am."

"Me too," Beth answered.

Around midnight, just before we went to sleep, I looked up at the pictures of my parents on the wall above our bed. My mother seemed a little nonplussed, but my father was smiling.

PART THREE

XV

There's an old adage, "You don't know someone until you've lived with them." Well, it's true. And you can add to that, "You don't know yourself until you've lived with someone else." I'd always assumed that someday I'd find a partner, but assuming and experiencing can be radically different from one another. To be honest, I wasn't prepared for the intrusion of another person in my life on a day-to-day, hour-by-hour basis.

For twenty years, every morning when I brushed my hair, I'd left the brush bristles up. Beth (who preferred my brush to her own) left it bristles down. I'd always folded bath towels and left them on the rack with the label facing toward the wall. Beth sort of crumpled them up and left them dangling any which way. Unimportant? Sure! But I noticed. Beth slept with the windows open; I liked them closed. She watched sitcoms on television; I liked ball games. Both of us were willing to market; neither of us liked doing the laundry.

Fortunately, the "little things" turned out not to matter. Beth grew accustomed to my preference for all-news radio ("But I still refuse to make love listening to it," she said), and I adjusted to having three kinds of shampoo on the bathroom shelf ("How often do you wash your hair?" I once asked. "Every four hours," she told me). She stocked half the refrigerator with lettuce and cottage cheese. I bought a thirty-two-ounce jar of crunchy peanut butter ("Nobody buys a jar that large," she wailed, "not even the United States Army."). Both of us, it turned out, liked sardine sandwiches (skinless and boneless mixed with mayonnaise on white bread with lettuce and pepper). And we each preferred reorganization to disorganization. It wasn't a bad union on the little things.

The big things were harder. All my life, I'd enjoyed a zone of privacy, and suddenly it had been invaded.

"How many women have you slept with?" Beth wanted to know.

"I never kept count."

"About how many?"

"I don't know."

"That's bullshit," she said. "Everybody knows approximately how many people they've slept with."

"Do you?"

"Sure! Fifteen—an average of two point five a year for six years. Do you want to hear about them?"

"Not particularly."

"Okay, I just thought maybe you'd like to learn a little more about me."

There were pockets in my psyche that I had never discovered. Beth found them. There were experiences I had never fully come to terms with, and she probed. "Is there anything about yourself so embarrassing that you've never told anyone?" she asked. "And if so, what is it?"

There was no place to hide, no subject that was taboo.

"You're not a very open person," she told me. "You have to work at this relationship."

Somehow, we got by, and slowly we began to develop a routine of our own. Every night before bed, we lay on the carpet and did pushups, sit-ups, and leg-lifts together. We divided up household chores and compromised through negotiation where necessary.

"My pants are torn along the seam," I told her one Sunday afternoon. "Will you sew them for me?"

"Sure, for five dollars an hour."

"That's outrageous."

"No, it isn't. I also work for four dollars an hour, but my four-dollar hours include lots of breaks and daydreams. You'd be better off paying me five."

"No deal."

"Okay, how about a different arrangement? I'll sew your pants if you take me out to dinner."

"How hungry are you?"

"Very."

"Forget it. I'll fix them with Scotch tape. Or better yet, I'll sew them myself."

We started talking more openly than either of us had before. We began to understand each other. One night, I couldn't sleep. Beth sat up and watched television with me until morning.

We goofed off together. That was important. And we accumulated a store of memories (large and small) to look back on. Once I heated up apple cider for the two of us and mixed in curry powder instead of cinnamon by mistake. Another time, I brought home two coloring books and a box of crayons.

"How come you always get the red crayon first?" I asked several coloring sessions later.

"Because my hands are quicker," Beth advised me.

She was working on a smiling circus clown in polka-dot

garb. I was trying to fill in the colors on a locomotive. "Besides," she added, "you don't need the red crayon. There's no such thing as a red locomotive."

"I have a good imagination," I told her. "And I want the red crayon."

"Tough."

"It's not fair. How come you always get the red crayon?"

"That's the law."

"Why?"

"Because possession is nine-tenths of the law, and the red crayon happens to be in my possession."

On other occasions, long-range thoughts came to mind.

"Can we get a dog?" Beth asked one evening.

"No!"

"Please! Wouldn't it be nice—a cute little cocker spaniel?"

"I don't want a dog."

"Why not?"

"They're a nuisance."

"But this would be a nice dog."

"They're a pain to walk, and they mess up an apartment."

"But they're cute, especially little cocker spaniels."

"If we're going to go to all that trouble, I'd rather have a child. I like children."

"For real?" she asked with excitement.

"For real—not now, but maybe in a couple of years if everything works out right between us."

"Should we have a boy or a girl?"

"It doesn't matter. I like them both."

"Suppose we had a little boy. Wouldn't he be adorable?"

"Naturally."

"Then we could buy him a cocker spaniel."

Word of our living together spread throughout the office, but most people left us alone. Occasionally, on a day when Beth looked particularly good, some asshole would come over and pat me on the back or shake my hand, but by and large people were "discreet." Hunker was mute on the issue. Jordan had nothing to say either, although one slightly chilling note did crop up in early April when an updated version of the office directory was distributed throughout the firm. Without either of us requesting the change, Beth's address and telephone number had been conformed to mine. "Big Brother is watching," Beth told me after the booklets had been distributed. "And obviously he likes his office directory to be accurate."

Meanwhile, the UCC case continued with no change in strategy, and the interview project dragged on. Poor Ed (at times like this, we referred to him as Poor Ed) was shipped off to regional sales offices in Casper, Wyoming, and Baton Rouge, Louisiana, after which he got to spend a week in Trenton, New Jersey.

"The week in Trenton was especially fun," he told us in recounting his journey. "The television set in my motel room didn't work, but who needs TV when there's live music coming through the floor directly beneath your bed from the cocktail lounge below?"

"Did anything good happen anywhere?" Beth wanted to know.

"Yes," Ed answered, "but I'm a little embarrassed about it. In Baton Rouge, I met an absolutely gorgeous waitress. She was very dumb. We had no possible future together, and both of us knew it. Nor was there any pretense about what either of us wanted. She was looking to hit the sack with a lawyer from New York who was twenty-seven years old and wearing a three-piece suit. And I saw this absolutely luscious, voluptuous eighteen-year-old staring at me. Need I say anymore?"

"I hope you get crabs," Beth told him.

In late April, there was a flurry of excitement in the office when the Justice Department announced an end to the American Steel litigation. Technically, the case was "settled" pursuant to a consent decree by which American Steel agreed "not to violate the antitrust laws of the United States" in the future. However, the company admitted no past wrongdoing (indeed, the decree specifically recorded its claim of righteous behavior), and no penalties were imposed. The result was an enormous triumph for James Moffitt (who had defended the company from the case's inception) and a major boost for the firm. One of the largest antitrust cases in history, involving hundreds of millions of dollars, had been disposed of for the cost of legal fees and a hollow promise by American Steel to obey the laws of the United States (which every corporation is obligated to do, anyway). It was the type of victory that had made Ashworth & Palmer famous, and American Steel showed its appreciation by presenting Moffitt with a thirty-thousand-dollar Rolls-Royce. Then Moffitt did something remarkable. Rather than keep the car for himself, he took sixty pieces of paper, each one bearing the name of an associate who had worked on the case during the preceding seven years, put them in a black silk top hat, and conducted a drawing. The winner (a former associate who wasn't even with the firm anymore) was awarded the Rolls. It was an uncanny display of noblesse oblige, and Moffitt's stock among associates throughout the office soared. Even Hardesty admitted to being impressed.

Shortly thereafter, Hunker had an opportunity to demonstrate his own class. Six months earlier, Abraham Waltuck had appeared in our office to deliver a sheaf of documents relating to the infamous yellow paint litigation (a/k/a *Hunker* v. *Pisano*). Since then, the case had lain dormant, and both Ed and I had grown optimistic that it would be abandoned. Indeed, on several occasions I had been tempted to ask Hunker whether I should close my file on the matter but decided against it on the theory that sleeping dogs should be allowed to lie. Then, in early May, a form letter from the Clerk of the New York State Supreme Court arrived at Ashworth & Palmer:

> Dear Sirs,
>
> In an effort to clear our docket of unprosecuted litigation and expedite the handling of active matters, the Administrative Judge has asked for a status report on all cases presently pending before the Supreme Court of the State of New York, County of New York.
>
> You are listed as counsel for plaintiff in:
>
> *Hunker* v. *Pisano*
>
> Please check the appropriate box below and return this form to the Office of the Clerk, 60 Centre Street, New York, N.Y.
>
> ☐ Case discontinued.
> ☐ Pretrial discovery underway.
> ☐ Request a conference with the Court re settlement or other matters.
> ☐ Ready for trial.

The form was delivered to Hunker, who returned it to the Clerk's office after placing an "X" in the box marked "Ready for trial."

On June 1, the annual partners' meeting was held behind closed doors and the fate of twenty eighth-year associates resolved. Thereafter, each of the twenty was called separately into James Moffitt's office for sentencing.

"I'm sorry," Moffitt told a senior associate named Richard Burke. "I think you're a good lawyer, but there just wasn't sufficient enthusiasm among my partners for your work. You will not be made a partner."

"I'm afraid the decision on your future has been made in the negative," Catherine Fairly, the firm's senior female litigator, was advised. "Everyone had nice things to say about you, but no one was really pushing on your behalf. You had no godfather, so to speak."

One by one, the executions proceeded. David Austin, a summa cum laude from Harvard Law School and former law clerk to United States Supreme Court Justice William Brennan, had worked for Moffitt on the American Steel case for eight years. "This is one of the hardest things I've ever had to do," Moffitt told him, "but it's my sad obligation to report that you will not be made a partner. I supported you in our deliberations but, as you know, decisions on partnership must be unanimous. I have no complaints about your work. You've done a first-rate job at Ashworth & Palmer, but there are a number of partnership-quality associates coming up for consideration in the next year or two and not everyone can be made a partner. We have to take a long-range view."

"That's not fair," Austin said.

"Life is unfair," Moffitt told him. "It doesn't always work the way we want it to."

The "June 1 Massacre" (as it became known throughout the firm) produced no new partners. Rumor had it, though, that the day after David Austin was passed over, Jordan Caine was called to Moffitt's office and told, "Don't worry. We're saving room for you."

Later that week, George Witherell not so accidentally bumped into me in the corridor and invited me into his office. "I'm worried," Witherell said when we were seated. "Today is a bright, sunny day, but I brought my umbrella to work. I'm not quite sure why I did it."

I looked up at the painting of Russian nobility on the wall behind him.

"Maybe I'm getting senile," Witherell went on. "After all, I'm eighty-something. Do you think that might be the answer?"

"You're more alert than ninety percent of the people here," I responded. "It just looked like rain when you left home this morning."

"I don't think so," he said. "And I don't remember making a conscious decision to bring the umbrella. I just had it with me when I arrived at the office. I'm definitely worried."

"Senile people don't know they're senile," I suggested. "So that can't be it."

"Maybe not, but the past twenty-four hours have been very troubling. Last night, I couldn't sleep, and when I looked at the clock, it was two-thirty. I didn't want to wake my wife so I lay in bed and played *Die Walküre* through in my mind. Have you ever listened to *Die Walküre*?"

"No," I admitted.

"Well, it's a great opera. Wagner wrote it. I've seen it performed forty-seven times. From beginning to end, it takes almost four hours. Last night, I performed it in two hours and forty minutes. I think I left something out."

He looked at me and waited for an answer.

"How many acts did you perform?" I asked.

"Three."

"With or without intermissions?"

"Without," he said, and his eyes brightened. "That accounts for almost all of the missing hour."

"And isn't it possible that you performed at a slightly upbeat tempo?"

"I believe you're right," he answered, "although your musical vocabulary leaves something to be desired."

There was a moment of silence between us; then Witherell spoke again. "Anyway, let me get to my reason for calling you here. Your name came up at our annual partnership meeting earlier this week. I thought you should know that, for a second-year associate who breaks all the rules of social conduct, you received a great deal of favorable comment."

XVI

"There are two kinds of associates at Ashworth & Palmer."

The author of the above statement was Lonnie Hunker, and sooner or later he repeated it to every associate who worked for him. Almost always, the statement was followed by a question: "Do you know what those two kinds are?"

For the uninitiated, there were an infinite number of possible answers. Associates can be smart or stupid; tactful or brusque; hard-working or lazy; black or white; male or female; fat or thin; and so on down the line. But to Hunker, the answer was simple: There are associates who want to make partner and those who don't. And to really "want" it, you have to "want it bad."

I wanted it. Maybe I wasn't as company-oriented as Jordan. And certainly my living with Beth had raised more than one set of eyebrows. But all things considered, I fit the mold. My work quality was good, the partners who knew me liked me, and I had started to spend *long* hours at the office. Five days a week, I got in at nine (half an hour earlier than most people). Monday through Thursday, I stayed until ten at night. Generally, I worked half a day on Saturday. Discounting for lunch, I averaged sixty billable hours a week—not number one in the firm, but enough to make people sit up and notice. Beth noticed.

"We aren't spending much time together," she said one night when I arrived home just in time for the eleven o'clock news.

"Was there any mail today?"

"Did you hear what I said?"

"Huh? I'm sorry. I wasn't listening."

"We haven't spent much time together lately," she repeated.

At that particular moment, I had just spent the better part of twelve hours revising a strategy memo for Hunker, and I didn't want to be nagged.

"Let me take my suit off, okay? I just got in the door."

Beth followed me to the bedroom and watched as I stripped. She was already in her nightgown, her hair pulled back behind her head.

"We're almost never together anymore," she said as I began putting on my pajamas. "We take the same subway to work in the morning. Maybe we have an hour together at night. Saturday and Sunday are usually all right, but it's not enough."

"What do you want me to do?"

"I want you to invest as much time in me as you invest in Lonnie Hunker."

"We sleep next to each other every night. We wake up next to each other every morning."

"That's not enough."

It was after eleven, and another long day would start in eight hours. I really didn't want to have this particular conversation at that particular moment.

"You take me for granted," Beth pressed. "And you've spent even more time at the office since I moved in than you did before. Don't you understand? I get lonely sitting here by myself at night."

"Then make plans. Go to a movie. Read a book. Do something without me."

"No one makes you stay at the office until ten at night."

"Look," I told her (and I was starting to get pissed), "I have a job to do, and it happens to be time-consuming. Maybe that's hard for you to understand because your job consists of sitting at your desk and running errands for Jordan. But–"

"Don't start on my job," she warned.

"Why not? You're doing a number on mine."

"I have a good job," she cried. "A secretary is very important to her boss. I'm good at what I do."

"You're disposable," I told her. "You could leave Ashworth & Palmer tomorrow, and Jordan wouldn't notice you were gone once he found a replacement."

"That was unnecessary. Be careful or you'll go too far."

"I'm sorry," I said, backing off. "If it's any consolation, Hunker wouldn't notice my absence, either."

"Then why do you spend so much time down there?"

"Because I want to make partner."

"Why?"

"Because it's there."

"But that's not what life is about. You don't have to make it to the top in everything you do. You don't have to achieve everything just because it's there. Has it ever occurred to you–great superachiever–that you might not be happy as a partner at the most prestigious law firm in the United States?"

"I want it."

"Why?"

"It's something to hold onto."

"How about holding onto yourself? How about us?"

"Okay," I told her. "I'm wrong and you're right."

That seemed to be the easiest way to end the discussion and get to bed.

Two days later, Hunker announced that Jordan and I would be sent to UCC headquarters in Unger to conduct interviews with a dozen top management personnel. "These are big fish," Lonnie explained. "I can't trust the job to Hardesty or Arlen Cohen. It has to be handled by the two of you."

"How long will you be gone?" Beth asked when I told her that night.

"About ten days."

In truth, I didn't want to go. For starters, Unger was boring. More important, though, I *would* miss Beth and I told her so. "We'll get out of the rut we've been in when I come home. And I'll be more attentive. I promise."

As expected, Unger was a colossal bore. The interviews were unproductive, and Jordan, while cordial enough, wasn't the most exciting dinner companion in the world. Bud Daley, our host, added little in the way of merriment and, to top matters off, it rained seven of the ten days we were there.

The trip was significant, though, because it gave me some time to think. Four months had passed since Beth moved in, and during that period I hadn't had a chance to be alone. Ten days without sharing a bed let me set up some priorities.

Did I really want to become a partner at Ashworth & Palmer? Yes! What were my chances? Pretty good! How could I say that in light of all the associates who had been passed over? Easy! I was better than they were. And, equally important, I'd been checking out the competition in my age group. For whatever reason, the associates in my year, the year ahead, and the year behind weren't logging particularly long hours. Some of them were good lawyers, but I figured I could prevail in one-on-one combat against any of them. After all, Hunker was already an ally of sorts, George Witherell liked me, and even Jordan, who was on line for partnership, seemed acclimated to having me around. All I needed was some exposure to Moffitt, who was the kingpin in the firm's litigation department, and one or two other partners, after which I'd be set.

Relations with Beth were harder to figure. Over the preceding few months, every so often I'd gotten a flash that maybe she didn't understand me as well as I thought she did. And there were also times when her sense of fulfillment in typing other people's letters gnawed at my insides. On occasion, I even considered the possibility that Hunker had been right when he warned that an Ashworth & Palmer lawyer and a secretary from Queens with a high school diploma didn't have much in common. Take away Beth's looks and what did you have? "A lot," I told myself. And no amount of playing devil's advocate could change that. I could accept her for what she was, but she'd have to accept me in return.

"I'll try," I promised when I got back to New York. "But you have to try too."

"It's a deal," she said.

So we each tried a little harder. I couldn't cut down on my hours, but I started bringing work home at night instead of doing it at the office. That meant we could eat dinner together, and somehow having me around for the evening made Beth more content. I worked at the desk in our bedroom, and she would read sitting on the bed with her back against the wall.

There were moments when I envied her. Several months

earlier, Beth had made a list of twenty great books she'd never read—*War and Peace, The Grapes of Wrath,* and so on. One by one, she was knocking them off. "I got the idea from George Witherell at the Prom," she told me.

Initially, I was a little smug about her project. I'd already read eighteen of the books on the list. But in truth, most of what I'd read, I'd forgotten.

"Okay, Mr. Know-it-all," Beth asked one night. "Was Romeo a Montague or a Capulet? And if you guess, you'd better guess right, because if you're wrong you'll never hear the end of it."

"I'm not sure," I admitted.

"Ha! You really should read more," she gloated.

So it went. Beth read; I worked; and we shared. On the theory that knowledge would breed tolerance, at least once a week I tried to explain what I was doing at the office—not just by saying, "I'm writing a strategy memo," but by outlining for Beth what the memo was about and why our defense was structured the way it was. I told her how the case was organized and what the different associates did.

"I don't see why UCC is paying all that money to have Carole Shiner stick red dots on documents," Beth once responded. "I could do that. And given a two-week orientation session in Unger, I could probably interview salesmen and engineers just as well as Ed Hardesty."

"You might be right," I confessed. "But don't tell anyone, or you'll shake the foundations of the legal profession beyond repair."

We started jogging together and registered jointly for a course in Chinese cooking. We got out a little more often on weekends and saw a few more people than before. We tried some new things sexually and, the last weekend in June, celebrated the anniversary of our first night by renting a car and driving to Montauk Point on the tip of Long Island.

"I like it when we're away together," Beth said as we

walked along the beach Saturday night. "It's the only time I feel free of the office."

"You've worked at Ashworth & Palmer for six years. Why should it bother you now?"

"Because until I met you, it never intruded on my private life. It was a place where I worked from nine to five, and that was all. Now there are times when I feel as though everything I do is influenced by Ashworth & Palmer."

I held her hand as we walked. "Do you have fantasies?" I asked.

"Sure."

"Tell me about them."

A half smile flickered across her lips. "Coming from you, that's a very out-of-character question."

"Maybe, but it's the sort of question you ask all the time. If you can probe, so can I."

"What sort of fantasies did you have in mind?"

"All of them—family, career, anything that's relevant."

The beach was empty, no one else in sight.

"I guess I daydream about the things most women want. I want to be loved. I want a good marriage. I want children and a nice place to live. I want to travel a lot."

"If you could have any job in the world, what would it be?"

"A TV weatherman."

"Be serious," I pressed.

"Look, we've been through this before. I like my job just fine."

"Is that the truth?"

"Sort of."

"What don't you like about it?"

She shrugged. "The fact that I have to take orders from someone else; that the work can be boring; that it doesn't give me a chance to be creative. You should understand. That's the problem with your job too. You just get paid more money for it, and you have your own secretary. I'd like to have my own secretary. That way, when Jordan gave me something to type, I could simply hand it over to someone else and read a book."

A spiral-shaped shell lay where the tide had receded.

"In some ways, you scare me," Beth said.

"How come?"

"You're the only person I know who demands more of me than it's easy to give. I've coasted through life. I admit that. I do my job well; I'm nice to people; I've had it soft because of my ability and my looks. Now you come along and, for whatever reasons, suggest that what I do easily isn't good enough. On one level it's extremely flattering, but it also threatens my self-perception that as a person I'm already complete."

As was the case one year earlier, the office pace slackened in early July. Hunker departed on a two-week vacation, the UCC litigation slowed to a crawl, and things in general were pretty dead. On one particularly slow morning, George Witherell appeared in the doorway to my office and asked rhetorically if he could come in. Then without waiting for an answer, he entered and took a seat across from my desk.

"You're a bright young fellow," he said. "Maybe you can explain something to my satisfaction."

"I'll try."

"Good. It isn't a legal question, but they say legal training is the best background for most endeavors. Certainly, I've found that to be true in my own experience."

I nodded and waited for the question.

"Our icebox broke this morning," Witherell told me. "Although I guess it's been called a refrigerator for the past forty years. Did you know they used to call refrigerators iceboxes because they had ice in them?"

"Yes sir, I did."

There were times when I wasn't quite sure whether Witherell was losing his marbles or rambling for effect. This time he seemed dangerously close to the former.

"Anyway," he said, snapping back to the present, "let me get to my question. I've begun to think that in a previous life I was an African tribal chieftain. Every time my forehead touches an object, I remember tribal scars across my brow. And that's not all. More and more, I find myself chanting the same thing over and over again—'Gonna go foo foo.' That's what I say—not out loud, but to myself. 'Gonna go foo foo.' I say it again and again. Can you explain that?"

"No sir, I can't."

"Isn't it possible, though, that I was once an African chieftain?"

"I suppose so."

"Good."

Looking extremely satisfied, he relaxed in his chair, and I couldn't help feeling that he'd been pulling my leg; that with nothing better to do on a sunny summer morning, George Witherell had decided to play games with the hotshot associate from Nebraska.

"Henderson, do you like being a lawyer at Ashworth & Palmer?"

"Yes sir."

"You should. It's a wonderful job. Everything I set out to do here, I accomplished. I earned a lot of money. I made a name for myself. I tried cases my way. And I've watched the firm grow. I have only one regret."

"What's that?" I felt obligated to ask.

"I always wanted to go out on a sunny spring day in the middle of the week and play chess at one of those big stone chess tables in the park. I wanted to do that instead of going to work just once, and I never did. I'm sorry about that."

"We could do it today," I suggested.

"Today's a workday."

"I know, but that's the whole point." (Suddenly the idea

seemed very good, almost brilliant, to me.) "I'm willing to risk it. And you're a partner so you can do anything you want."

For maybe ten seconds, George Witherell sat in his chair, pondering the issue. "I guess we'd better not," he said at last. "There's work to do. And besides, I want to do it during the spring, and it's summer already."

"Maybe next year," I said.

"Maybe," he answered. "After all, I do enjoy the park. You young environmentalists think you're the only ones who appreciate trees. Old people like them too."

Ten days later, George Witherell was found urinating in a washbasin in the sixty-fifth-floor men's room. He was hospitalized for treatment of a stroke and died forty-eight hours later.

As expected, a crush of mourners attended his funeral. During more than sixty years of practice, Witherell had come to be regarded as a giant by his peers, and four hundred Ashworth & Palmer attorneys (past and present) joined with an equal number of lawyers from other firms to bid him farewell. Some of those present attended out of obligation, but a sizable number (Lonnie Hunker included) seemed genuinely moved by the occasion.

James Moffitt gave the eulogy and did a splendid job overall. Only once were his words trite. That was toward the end of his remarks when, in recounting a final moment with the deceased, Moffitt declared, "I was at George Witherell's bedside when he died. His last words were, 'I know my partners will take good care of my beloved wife, Elvira.' " (And at this point Moffitt looked directly at Elvira Witherell.) "Believe me, Elvira, we will."

No one, of course, believed the end had come that way. But Moffitt, in a conversation with several of his partners, later defended his remarks with the explanation, "What else could I say? How can I get up in front of eight hundred mourners, including Elvira Witherell, nine federal judges, and two United States Senators, and tell them that George Witherell's dying words were, 'Gonna go foo foo.' "

For my own part, I felt a little guilty that, in twenty months at Ashworth & Palmer, I had never taken the time to construct a legal argument, however spurious, against the insertion of blow-away cards in magazines.

XVII

July weather in New York is hot and muggy, which means a lot of women wear skimpy T-shirts, which, in turn, means their breasts seem larger and bouncier, which, in turn, I noticed. There were two reasons I didn't stray: (1) living with someone means not cheating; and (2) I figured that, if I cheated, Beth would too. The absence of a third reason (such as an already fulfilling relationship) was a pretty good clue that the Tom Henderson-Beth Anders alliance was in trouble.

The hostilities began over a ludicrous non-issue. Beth got her first credit card—a red and gold Master Charge from Bankers Trust.

"This piece of plastic says I'm an American citizen," she announced proudly when I came home from work. "It arrived in the mail this morning. I bought my first blouse with it at 6:14 P.M. Want to see it?"

"The card or the blouse?"

"The card, of course. I have dozens of blouses."

"Then why'd you buy another one?"

"Because I felt like it. I wanted to use the card."

I shot·my best that-doesn't-deserve-an-answer look her way.

"There's nothing wrong with my buying a blouse," Beth said. "You don't have to tell me how to manage money."

"I didn't say a word."

"No, but I know what you're thinking. Look, I have twelve hundred dollars in the bank. I can do what I want with it."

"Just don't spend it all in one place. On your salary, it will be hard to make it up." (It was a dumb thing to say, worse than dumb; I admit it.)

"Fuck you," Beth said.

"How many rounds is this fight scheduled for?" I asked, hoping to add a bit of levity to the proceedings.

"It's not funny, goddamn it. I'm tired of listening to you talk down to me. You pick and you pull and you scratch at everything. From the day we met, you've treated me like an intellectual and social inferior, and I'm sick of it."

"I'm sorry. It was a stupid thing to say about your salary, and I apologize."

"You know something? You have a rod up your ass about being a lawyer." (She was getting started now.) "And the funny thing is, your job isn't even so hot. Most Ashworth & Palmer lawyers hate their work. If salaries were cut in half, the firm wouldn't have an associate left."

"Since when are you an authority on lawyers?" (Now I was getting into the act.)

"Since six years ago when I started working at Ashworth & Palmer. And you want to know something? Snots like you don't even bother me anymore. You'll get your ass kicked all over the place just like the rest of them until you're passed over for partner. And if you do make it, chances are you'll wind up like Lonnie Hunker. I feel sorry for you."

"Are you finished?"

"Not yet," she said. "You've been at Ashworth & Palmer for less than two years, you have six years to go before you're even eligible to make partner, and you're already practicing for the coronation. Your only problem is that they haven't given you an associate to dump on, so you practice on the secretaries. Well, thank God I'm not your secretary because you must be a real prick to work for."

"I treat my secretary just fine."

"But you treat her like she's inferior, don't you?"

"You're being silly."

"And you're evading my question. You think she's inferior, don't you? And you treat her that way."

"I treat my secretary the same way you treat elevator men and checkout cashiers in the supermarket. I'm friendly, but you're right—I don't think she's my equal."

"And how about me?"

"How about you, what?"

"Am I your equal, or will you get tired of me someday and throw me back in the gutter where you found me?" Her voice, which had been rising steadily, suddenly broke. "I have feelings, and you treat me as if I had none. You never give me credit for anything. As far as you're concerned, I'm nothing but a piece of ass."

"That's not true."

"Yes, it is. You don't give a damn about anything but my looks. There isn't another thing about me that you admire."

"There isn't another thing about you that you rely on. You won't try for anything unless it comes easily, unless it's safe. Even I seemed safe. Out of all the lawyers at Ashworth & Palmer, you chose the one you figured wouldn't demand too much from you—the farm boy from Nebraska."

"Are you finished?"

"Not yet. First I want you to take a long look at yourself. There's more to life than a pretty smile and visiting Robert Grissom in a nursing home once a week. If you have trouble adjusting when I work nights, it's because you haven't learned to live with yourself."

"I did fine before I met you." And again her voice broke. "Isn't it enough that I love you?"

"I don't know," I told her. "Maybe not."

The next morning, I started to notice an unusual number of attractive women. They were in the park, on the street, waiting for buses, everywhere.

At Ashworth & Palmer, life went on. George Witherell might have been a firm institution, but he hadn't handled a client in ten years and he was hardly missed. Two days after he died, new stationery minus his name was circulated to the secretaries. One week later, James Moffitt moved his own belongings into what had once been Witherell's office. A few associates waxed nostalgically that when George Witherell was starting out at Ashworth & Palmer, Babe Ruth must have been playing right field for the New York Yankees, but in truth "the old man" was quickly forgotten. Indeed, his chief legacy was the rumor that the partners were disturbed about his death, not because they missed him, but because he had breached protocol by flipping out and urinating in the associates' rather than the partners' men's room.

Meanwhile, my bittersweet war with Beth continued. One night, we went to a party at Arlen Cohen's, left slightly drunk, and came home to bed. "Why did you grimace?" Beth demanded at the close of a particularly mechanical bit of lovemaking.

"I didn't grimace."

"Yes, you did."

I drummed my fingers on the pillow and said nothing.

"Why did you grimace?"

"Just forget it, okay!"

"We didn't even kiss. We just did it."

"I'm tired," I told her.

"That doesn't explain why you grimaced."

"You've said it three times now. Don't say it again."

"I watched you at the party tonight," she said. "You checked out every good-looking woman there."

"I'm glad to hear that. I was afraid I might have missed one."

"You're not funny."

"Don't worry. There might be a few women I'd like in addition to you, but none I'd like better."

"Be careful," she warned. "I'm more in demand than you are."

I hadn't realized there were so many things two people could fight about. One morning, Beth used up the orange juice, and I bitched when there wasn't any for me to drink. She threw a fit when one of her blouses tore while I was doing the laundry. I couldn't fall asleep on my side without hearing complaints that I was turning my back on her. Then she complained that I didn't take her seriously. ("You don't give me much credit. Whenever any man talks with me, you assume he's only interested in my body. I can carry on a conversation, too, you know.")

"Don't start," I told her one night. "I'm not going to sit here and listen to you tell me how awful I am."

The last Friday in July, Hardesty dropped by my office as I was getting ready to leave for home. "Want to join me for a drink?" he asked.

"Thanks. I'd like to, but I haven't spent much time with Beth lately and she'd have a fit."

"Actually, it was her idea."

"Pardon?"

"She wants us to talk," Ed said. "I had lunch with her today, and for some reason she thinks I might be able to save your living arrangement. She isn't quite sure why she puts up with you and neither am I, but I told her I'd try."

"Okay," I told him. "But let's walk instead of drink. I need the air."

"Fine."

We took the elevator down to street level and headed north on Nassau Street. Dressed in suits, carrying our attaché cases, we must have looked like ten thousand other lawyers, except we weren't talking about the Sherman Antitrust Act or stocks and bonds. Ed opened the conversation.

"First, let me say that I feel very awkward about this. You and Beth are two of my best friends, and I won't take sides between you. The only reason I'm doing this is to help patch things together, and I think the best way to do that is to identify the problem areas one at a time.

"Problem number one is that you're devoting too much time and energy to the office. Partly it's a question of hours, but really it goes beyond that. Beth feels that Ashworth & Palmer is more important to you than she is and, from what I've seen, she might be right.

"Problem number two is that Beth thinks you look down on her because she's a secretary and never went to college. Whether that's true is for the two of you to decide, but along those lines I will make several observations. One, you can't make people feel inferior and expect them to stay around. Two, you do have a touch of arrogance about you. And three, Beth is as smart as either of us, if not smarter. However, it happens that she doesn't have seven years of post-high-school education.

"Problem number three is more ambiguous than the first two, but in many ways it's the most important. Beth has serious doubts as to whether you're mature enough to carry on a successful relationship, not just with her but with anybody. Love is more than holding hands, and even loving someone isn't always enough to make a relationship work. Now I don't pretend to have any pat answers to your problems and, as I told you when we started this discussion, I'm not taking one side or the other. But that's what's on Beth's mind, and I'd like to know what you think."

"I'm not sure," I admitted. "There are times when I feel Beth and I are right for each other and other times when everything either one of us says and does is wrong. I know I spend long hours and a lot of energy at work, but that's not incompatible with a decent relationship. I'm not the first person in history to be ambitious."

The character of the neighborhood changed as we walked. The city's financial district gave way to rundown shops and lofts. "Maybe Beth and I aren't right for each other," I said. "I've begun to notice an awful lot of women lately—women who are writers and lawyers, teachers and analysts. I care about Beth—I really do. But sometimes I wonder if I might not have more in common with someone else."

"Why?"

"Because someone else might be more ambitious, more intellectually aggressive. I can't put my finger on it, but something *is* missing between Beth and me. Something both of us need isn't there."

"Want to know what I think?"

"Okay."

"I think you're afraid of commitment."

"That's not true."

"I think it is. Maybe I'm wrong, but I think you're afraid of making a commitment to any woman, and I think you're just as afraid of a woman making a commitment to you. Look, there are an infinite number of desirable women in New York. But a sane person can't spend his life thinking about every possible relationship with each of them. You have to concentrate on the relationship you *do* have and whether or not that person can make you happy. At the moment, that person is Beth."

"But there are degrees of happiness," I answered. "Suppose Beth and I get married, and a few weeks later I meet my perfect woman?"

"There's no such thing."

"There might be."

"Who? What? All this perfect woman would be is Beth Anders with a graduate degree in some arcane area of study. Realistically speaking, no one better than Beth is going to come along. She has a lot of growing up to do, and she knows it. You've asked things of her that no one else has ever asked before, and she's trying to meet your demands. But that's only half the battle. The other half is whether *you're* ready for the compromises that go with sharing a life with anyone. You're the only person who can decide that. But I think you have a lot to learn, about women and about yourself."

Beth was sitting on the bed reading *A Tale of Two Cities* when I arrived home. "How was your conversation with Ed?" she asked.

"Demoralizing," I told her, taking off my jacket and sitting on the edge of the bed beside her. "We're in trouble, aren't we?"

She nodded.

"I really don't know what to say," I confessed. "I'm trying the best I know how."

"Then you'll have to learn to try harder." There was nothing accusatory about her tone. The words were spoken as a soft, simple statement of fact. "You'll have to learn to consider what makes *me* happy and what *I* want because, the way things are going, I can't handle this relationship much longer. I wake up in the middle of the night and there are tears all over my face. I walk around during the day with a lump in my throat. Time is running out on the two of us."

Seeing her there sitting on the bed, I didn't want to lose her. "Can we make it work? If we both try?"

"I think so," she said.

"Okay! Let's give it the old college try."

"I can't," she told me. "I never went to college."

It was a nice weekend. All day Saturday, we wandered through Manhattan doing things I'd never done because I wasn't a native (and Beth hadn't done because she was) —climbing the Statue of Liberty, visiting the Empire State Building, picnicking at the Cloisters. Just after dark, on impulse, we checked into the Plaza Hotel for the night.

"This is the silliest thing we've ever done," I moaned after the bellhop escorted us to our room and departed.

"I think it's exciting," Beth answered. "I've always wondered what the Plaza was like."

"Seventy dollars a night is what it's like."

"Don't be so cheap. You make thirty-three thousand dollars a year plus a bonus, and you save a third on rent each month because we're living together. Besides, you're lucky we even got a room. A true romantic would have reserved the bridal suite in advance."

"Will you ever forgive me for such sloppy planning?"

"Only if you come up with a satisfactory form of reparations."

"How about if I order a large bottle of champagne from room service?"

"That would be satisfactory."

We talked pretty honestly about a lot of things that night, and I sensed that, once again, at least we were on the same side. "Maybe I have been afraid of commitment," I admitted as the champagne ran dry. "Thinking about all the things that lie ahead in life can be pretty scary. So far, I've had a childhood; I've gone to school; I've buried two parents; I'm working for a living. But I've really just begun to live, and there's so much ahead—marriage, the awesome responsibility of children, growing old. Maybe I'm not ready to face the rest of my life."

"But that's what this relationship was supposed to be for," Beth said, "to help us face those things together. I know the pressures you're under, and our working in the same office adds to them. But I feel pressure too, and you can't always leave me with the feeling that I'm second-rate. I wasn't going to tell you this," she added, "but a few days ago I cried at work. I was in Jordan's office taking dictation, when all of a sudden it seemed as though everything in life was wrong. I sat there trying to write down his words, and I started to cry."

"What did he do?"

"Nothing."

"How could he do nothing?"

"It was easy. He just sat at his desk looking uncomfortable, waiting for me to stop crying or leave. Finally, I stopped, he finished dictating his letter, and I left. In case you're wondering, it was extremely embarrassing to cry in front of my boss."

The following morning, we checked out of the Plaza and walked home. One week later, we celebrated Beth's birthday by taking seven days off and going camping in the Berkshire Mountains. Then we returned to New York, where the summer doldrums still held sway at Ashworth & Palmer, and for the first time since Beth had moved in we were able to spend ample time together. All totaled, the "honeymoon" lasted four weeks. Then, late one afternoon as I was studying a report on UCC's marketing system, I was summoned to meet with James Moffitt.

"Go right in," Katherine Whittle instructed when I arrived at her secretarial alcove. "Mr. Moffitt is expecting you."

Moffitt rose to greet me with a handshake as I stepped inside his office. "Have a seat," he ordered.

The room bore no trace of its prior occupant. All the deep greens and blues of the Witherell era had been replaced by chrome and glass.

"You are about to receive a promotion," Moffitt said. "As you know, the Ashworth & Palmer system is designed to give the broadest possible experience to our associates and train the most promising among them for partnership. This coming November first, you will have been on the UCC case for two years and, looking ahead, my partners and I feel it's time for a change."

I was about to escape from Lonnie Hunker.

"One of the firm's most valued clients," Moffitt continued, "is National Industries, Inc. As you are doubtless aware, National is the second largest defense contractor in the United States. The largest, of course, is General Arms, which is represented by the Kingsley firm in Washington, D.C. It's hardly an overstatement to say that these two companies form the backbone of our nation's military defense."

He paused to let the enormity of his remarks sink in, then went on. "For over a year, the Department of Justice and the Pentagon have been investigating an alleged price-fixing conspiracy between General Arms and National. The charge, quite simply, is that the two companies agreed to inflate prices on certain weapons and refrained from competing with one another in the manufacture of various other defense products. Sometime in the next three months—probably just before Thanksgiving—an antitrust suit will be filed by the government. It will allege price fixing and demand that each defendant pay in excess of one billion dollars in damages. As the firm's Chief of Litigation, I will be in charge of defending against the suit. I'm putting together a team of lawyers now, and I'd like you to be on it. Lonnie Hunker has agreed to relinquish your services as of November first, which will mark your second anniversary with the firm. I don't have to tell you how important this case is to your future. You'll be getting in on *the* major piece of litigation in the office, and you'll be getting in on the ground floor. Next to me, you'll be the most important man on it. Work hard, and you can ride this case straight to partnership."

There it was! Good-bye, Lonnie Hunker; hello, James Moffitt.

"The early stages of our defense will be particularly time consuming," Moffitt was saying. "But based on your record, I know you can handle it. You have a little more than two months to finish up with Hunker and get your personal life in order. *Then we'll be sending you to National's headquarters in Dayton, Ohio, for about six months to learn the business."*

"The choice is yours," Beth told me that night, "and it's a simple one—them or me."

"Be reasonable," I said.

"I'm being completely reasonable, and I have no intention of spending six months alone while you're in Dayton, Ohio. For over a year, I've made every effort to create a climate in which this relationship can succeed. But it's one thing to work at a relationship and quite another to suffer with it. I'm all used up. I have nothing left inside to give you."

"What do you want from me?"

"I want you to tell them 'no.' " There was an urgency in her voice I had never heard before. "I want you to tell James Moffitt that you're living with someone you love, and you aren't willing to leave her for six months to study guns and B-1 bombers."

"I can't do that. It would mean giving up my future."

"Only your future at Ashworth & Palmer. There are other law firms in New York and other cities in America. What is it about this place that makes it such an obsession with you?"

The words tumbled out of my mouth before I realized they were there: "Because I don't want anyone to say that James Moffitt or Lonnie Hunker or any of them were good enough to get something I couldn't get."

There was silence between us.

"Then you're just like them," Beth said at last. "And I can't live with that. In every person's life, there are turning points where they have to decide what sort of person they are and what sort of person they want to become. You're at a point like that now. I'm asking you for the last time, will you tell James Moffitt 'no'?"

"I can't do that."

"Then I really don't think the two of us can be happy together." Her voice was trembling, and it seemed only a matter of time before she'd cry. "Once upon a time, I thought I saw a warmth and sensitivity in you that was special. Obviously, I was wrong. Moving in with you was a mistake. I should never have done it."

One week later, she was gone. I helped her pack. Just before the movers came, Beth drew by my side. "In case you're interested," she said, "I'm also leaving Ashworth & Palmer. I have a new job with another firm starting September first. That way, we won't have to see each other around the office. It will be less awkward for both of us."

"I'd still like to see you," I told her.

"I know. But the feeling's not mutual."

The movers arrived and began carting Beth's belongings toward the door.

"Hey, Tom?" she said.

I looked toward her.

"There *was* magic between us that first night, wasn't there?"

I nodded.

"Where did it go?"

The lump in my throat was swelling, but I pushed it down. "Beats me," I answered.

For the next few nights, the apartment seemed very bare. More than once, I found myself lying in bed, pretending Beth was by my side. Occasionally, I reached out to hold her or rub the small of her back. About a week after the move, Jordan dropped by my office to offer an epitaph. "You cost me a good secretary," he said.

XVIII

September began in typical Ashworth & Palmer fashion. A flood of new associates arrived ripe for indoctrination in the ways of class struggle. The Firm Outing was held at Thousand Oaks Country Club. Jordan got a new secretary. Work on the UCC case picked up again. Most of my time was spent finishing up old projects and tutoring Ira Kamenstein in the nuances of sewage treatment technology. Lucky Ira had been designated by Hunker as my heir apparent effective November 1—the projected date of my reassignment to James Moffitt. Thereafter, he would be the new expert on technical matters. Everything seemed in order until a sunny day in mid-September when I returned from lunch and found a note on my desk:

> URGENT!!!
> Pick up Hardesty and see me as soon as possible.
>
> —L. J. Hunker

"We have a problem," Hunker announced as Ed and I

stepped into his office. Rummaging through the papers on his desk, he extracted a form letter and thrust it forward. This came in the mail today. Take a look":

> FROM: The Clerk of the New York State Supreme Court, County of New York
>
> TO: All Counsel in *Hunker* v. *Pisano*
>
> The above captioned case has been marked ready for trial by the Administrative Judge. You are hereby advised that, within the next thirty days, you will be called to trial on forty-eight hours' notice. No delay in the presentation of your case will be tolerated.

"The crunch is on," Hunker said. "I want the two of you to take the case file and examine it as thoroughly as possible. By nine A.M. tomorrow, I want a strategy memo outlining our strong points, weak areas, relevant issues of law, and a list of questions I can ask Pisano on cross-examination. Do it well. This is important."

"I have a question," Ed announced.

Hunker looked up inquiringly.

"Since the court clerk says we'll receive at least forty-eight hours' notice prior to trial, why does all this have to be done by nine A.M. tomorrow?"

"I don't understand your problem," Hunker said.

"It's almost three in the afternoon," Ed told him. "To do this job the way you want it means we'll have to work straight through until tomorrow morning."

"So?"

"So I want to go home and sleep tonight."

"Ed," Hunker snapped. "I'm not sure I like your attitude. Until I tell you otherwise, this is the most important case in the office. I want the job done by nine A.M. tomorrow."

Marching orders in hand, we retired to my office.

"Don't say a word," I warned. "I know it's ridiculous."

"It's more than ridiculous," Ed answered. "You and I have just witnessed a demonstration of idiocy unparalleled in the history of mankind. I don't mind all-nighters when there's a genuine crisis, but this is lunacy. The way Hunker is carrying on, you'd think it was the UCC case that had been marked ready for trial."

The door to my office opened, and a messenger entered. "Mr. Hunker asked me to give you this," he said, handing me an inch-thick folder. "It's some sort of case file."

"Thanks," I told him. "You've made my day."

He smiled and departed.

"Maybe your day, but not mine," Ed snorted. "I don't want anything to do with this."

"Be serious. You can't just not do an assignment."

"Want to bet?"

The telephone rang, and I picked up the receiver.

"Tom"—it was Hunker on the other end—"if you have a chance, find out whether this Pisano character is an illegal alien. If he did jump ship, it should help us with the jury." (Click.)

"Who was that?" Ed queried.

"Don't ask. Let's just get to work."

"I told you. I'm not going to do it."

"Look, if going home to bed means that much to you, you can leave at midnight and I'll do the rest. But at least give me a hand in getting started."

"It's not the sleep," Ed said. "Don't you have any pride in your work?"

"Sure! That's why I plan on doing this assignment as well as any other. Every job has its dirty side. We're professionals."

"Be honest! Are you concerned with professionalism or saving your ass?"

"Both," I admitted.

"And where does conscience fit in? How can you let yourself be pressed into service on something like this?"

"It's easy. We've been doing shitwork of questionable morality for UCC ever since we got to Ashworth & Palmer. Do you honestly see a difference?"

"Maybe not."

"Then, at the very least, keep me company while I do this. You don't even have to work. Just keep me company."

"Give me the goddamn file. We'll split it."

For the next few hours, we reviewed documents. There wasn't much—Hunker's letter to the MTA demanding four hundred dollars for his suit; Waltuck's written response; the summons and complaint demanding twenty thousand dollars in damages; Anthony Pisano's pathetic rejoinder ("Dear Judges of the Court and Mr. Ashworth and Mr. Palmer . . ."). Then we came to Pisano's job application —born in Genoa, Italy; immigrated to the United States at age twenty; eighth-grade education; naturalized American citizen. There were sixteen evaluation reports filled out by Pisano's supervisors. "My best worker," read one. "Conscientious, gets along well with fellow employees," proclaimed another. Waltuck had been right. According to the documents, in sixteen years of public service, Pisano had missed a total of nine days' work. The last item we came to was an MTA investigative report prepared on the night of the incident. It stated that the area had been properly cordoned off with appropriate warning signs in clear view. "Not conclusive," I scribbled in the margin. "Pisano could have posted the signs after the incident."

"If there were no signs," Ed pressed, "how come dozens of commuters didn't wind up with yellow paint on their suits?"

"Maybe they weren't as clumsy as Hunker. Or maybe they did and just didn't complain about it."

"Bullshit."

"Okay," I admitted. "It bothers me, too."

At 6 P.M., I called the steno pool to make sure there would be at least one secretary available throughout the night. "No problem," the steno head said. "We have twenty girls here now and a dozen more coming in at midnight." Then Ed retired to the library to research negligence and standards of proof, while I began listing the pluses and minuses of Hunker's case. Three hours later, we dispatched a messenger for sandwiches and coffee. By 4 A.M., a neatly typed twenty-page memorandum lay on my desk.

"Can we go home now?" Ed asked.

"Not yet. Hunker will want to see us at nine. If we leave now, we'll only get three hours' sleep before we're called back again. I'd just as soon wait and go home when everything is finished."

Glumly, Ed nodded his concurrence. "Let's stretch our legs," he suggested.

"Okay. Where to?"

"Outside, where there's fresh air."

Together we went downstairs and out onto Wall Street. The first rays of Friday morning's sun had begun to peer above the horizon. The sidewalk was wet, and I realized that for at least part of the night it had rained.

"It's been a good night," Ed said. "I got my priorities in order."

"Meaning what?"

"Meaning I'm tired of sitting at my desk being bored and working on cases that don't matter. My two years are almost up, and tonight was the last straw. I'm going to start looking for a new job next week."

"I'd hate to lose you. You're the best friend I have at Ashworth & Palmer."

"Thanks for the compliment, but you'll survive."

We walked a while longer in silence.

"Have you heard from Beth?" Ed asked at last.

"No."

"Do you miss her?"

"I suppose so."

"What does that mean?"

"It means 'yes.' I keep finding long honey-colored hair all over the apartment. I guess I'm not as self-sufficient as I thought."

"None of us are."

The sun broke fully above the horizon.

"I won't pry," Ed said. "But if you ever feel the need to talk about it, I'm available."

"Thanks."

We stopped at a greasy spoon diner for fried eggs and toast, then went back to the office. At nine o'clock, bleary-eyed and unshaven, we stood before Lonnie Hunker.

"Where's the memo?" he demanded.

"There are two memos," I told him.

"Why two?"

"This is the first," I said, handing over our twenty-page opus. "It outlines the pluses and minuses of your case, a possible cross-examination, and each of the legal issues involved."

"Fine," he said, reaching for the memo and thumbing through it. "What else is there?"

Ed and I looked toward each other.

"Look! The last thing I want is you two keeping secrets from me. If there's something else, I want it."

"There are certain things about this case which—"

"Get to the point," Hunker snapped.

"We typed this ourselves," I said, handing over a solitary piece of paper. "No one else has seen it."

Adjusting his glasses, Hunker began to read:

TO: Lionel J. Hunker
FROM: Thomas Henderson and Edwin Hardesty

We have carefully examined the file in *Hunker* v. *Pisano*. As attorneys, we recognize our obligation to perform to the best of our ability on your behalf. We have done so and will continue to do so. However, it is our belief that this case does not merit further prosecution, and we respectfully request that it be discontinued.

Finishing the memo, Hunker stared at us incredulously. "Is this the only copy?" he asked at last.

"Yes sir."

"Fine." Swiveling in his chair, he crumpled the paper into a tiny ball and dropped it in the wastepaper basket. "One of the nice things about my being a partner," he said, looking back toward us, "is that we do things my way."

The muscles in Ed's neck tightened. "I don't think I want to be a part of this case anymore."

"The work is done," Hunker said, leaning forward. "All that's left is one session in court, and you're going to be there whether you like it or not—both of you."

Battling against the flow of traffic, I made my way home and went to sleep. When I awoke nine hours later, it was night. The building I lived in had a half-dozen washing machines in the basement, and Friday was as good a time as any to use them.

"Laundry room," I told the elevator operator as I stepped on the car, lugging a bag of sheets, shirts, socks, and underwear. Downstairs, I found an empty machine and inserted two quarters in the appropriate slot. Next to me, a slender, dark-haired woman in her mid-twenties was emptying clothes from a dryer.

"Are you a new tenant?" I asked.

There was no response.

She was about five feet six inches tall, dressed in designer jeans with a blue and red plaid shirt. Her hair was straight and fell several inches beneath her shoulders. No wedding ring. She was quite pretty and looked like a bitch.

"What floor do you live on?" I asked.

As if to emphasize the burden inherent in responding, she sighed and turned toward me. "Is that any of your business?"

"Only if you want it to be."

"I don't."

"Fine."

I turned and stomped toward the door.

"Third," she said.

"Pardon?"

"I live on the third floor. My name is Laurie."

"My name is Tom. I live on eleven."

She looked me over from top to bottom. "I just paid sixty dollars to have two cavities filled, so my mood is rotten."

"You should get a job with better medical coverage."

She wasn't quite sharp enough to recognize sarcasm. "I didn't know there were any medical plans that covered cavities."

"Lots of unions have them," I said. "New York City teachers get free dental care. So do players in the National Football League."

"Maybe I should become a teacher."

"Or a middle linebacker for the Pittsburgh Steelers."

Again I got the top-to-bottom look. "When you finish your laundry, why don't you drop by my apartment?" she suggested.

An hour later, we were together in bed. By midnight, I was alone in my apartment, staring at the telephone. Slowly I lifted the receiver and dialed Beth's number. On the third ring, she answered.

"Hi," I announced. "It's Tom."

There was silence.

"I've been thinking about you a lot lately. How have you been?"

"Fine."

"How's your new job?"

"Pretty good."

"You're not very talkative."

"I really don't have much to say."

There were two hangnails on my right index finger. I bit them off.

"It's almost midnight," Beth said. "I really should hang up and go to bed."

"Couldn't we talk a little longer?"

"What for?"

"It would make me feel better."

"That's your problem, not mine."

"Could I see you sometime over the weekend, just for a cup of coffee?"

"I don't think I'd bring a very constructive attitude with me. If I change my mind, I'll let you know."

"I miss you."

"That's too bad. It might take longer than you'd like, but you'll get over it."

"We lived together for six months. Don't you think you owe me an hour of your time?"

"Tom, I don't owe you a thing. Please don't call again. Good night."

In the days ahead, more than ever, Hardesty became my confessor and friend. "You're not the only one with social problems," he said, seeking to buoy my spirits one night. "I had a date scheduled with Susan Tryon for last Saturday, and she broke it."

"How come?"

"She couldn't cope. It was the first anniversary of her cat's death."

"My situation is different. I'm really upset."

"I know," he said, turning serious. "But there's not much you can do about it."

"Could you call Beth? Maybe that would help."

"I'll try," he said, after a moment's deliberation, "but it won't do any good."

Two days later, Ed reported his findings: "I had dinner with Beth last night. I'm sorry, but she doesn't want to see you, period. She was quite vehement about it."

"Couldn't she see me just once to talk?"

"Apparently not. This is the best way she knows to protect herself. And incidentally, it might come as a surprise, but Beth's new job isn't secretarial. She took a two-thousand-dollar cut in pay to become a research assistant for NBC News."

Something inside me slipped. "I thought you needed a college degree for a job like that."

"So did I," Ed answered. "I guess she finagled it the same way you got your job at Ashworth & Palmer." He waited for my next question, but none came. "I'm your friend," he said at last, "and I'll be honest with you. I'm sorry it ended like this but, in my humble opinion, you deserve what you got."

For the next two weeks, I buried myself in my work. "Very impressive," James Moffitt told me after learning from the computer printout that I had billed one hundred sixty hours in a twelve-day period. "Obviously, I'm getting a real tiger on my team come November first."

Ed started actively looking for a new job.

I called "Laurie from the Third Floor" for another date. "Let's see," she told me. "Monday, I'm out for dinner; Tuesday, I'm going to theater; Wednesday and Thursday, I'm busy—Friday, I can make it."

All day Friday, it rained. Around seven, I called to finalize plans for the night. "I'll have to cancel out," Laurie said.

"How come?"

"I feel awkward about our first get-together."

"We don't have to go to bed again," I told her. "We can see a movie instead."

"It's raining much too hard to do that."

"Look! There's this fantastic new invention I want to tell you about. It's called an umbrella. It's a big round piece of nylon on a frame with a stick attached, and if you hold it over your head when you go out in the rain, it keeps you dry."

"Sorry, maybe another time," she said.

The women I'd noticed on the street all summer turned out to be not so desirable. When James Moffitt invited me to a dinner party at his Westchester mansion, I went alone. "Oh, Mr. Henderson," Mrs. Moffitt gushed on my arrival. "I'm so glad to meet you. My husband has told me so much about you. He's delighted you'll be on his team in November."

Most of the guests were Ashworth & Palmer associates who had worked for Moffitt at one time or another. For the better part of the evening, I listened to conversations about antitrust law and wished I was at home. "We have two paintings by Paul Klee," Mrs. Moffitt told me, noticing that I was outside the flow of conversation. "He was quite a prolific artist, but even so, it's extremely rare for anyone to have two of his works."

"I'm sure that's right," I answered. "Most people only have one."

Toward the end of the evening, James Moffitt pulled me aside. "Tom, you and I are about to embark on a great adventure. These are marvelous times to be a lawyer at Ashworth & Palmer. The firm has never been more powerful. Our cases are more challenging than ever. And thank God, with everything that's gone on in this country the past ten years, we still have the capacity to develop young lawyers like you."

I nodded.

"I've read your memos on the UCC case to see what kind of work you do," Moffitt continued. "They're very solid. The only criticism I have concerns your letters. The firm manual says you're supposed to sign them 'sincerely' or 'sincerely yours.' I've noticed that on occasion you close with 'best regards.' Try to correct that in the future."

"Yes sir. I will."

A little after midnight, I dialed Beth's number. "It's Tom," I told her. "Did I wake you?"

There was silence.

"I know you asked me not to call, but I have to see you."

"I don't see people on command."

"I'm lonely. I miss you."

Still no answer.

"I restructured my head so there'd be a spot for you in the center, and now you're gone."

"So you have an empty head. What else is new?"

"Please don't talk like that."

"You can hurt someone just so often, Tom. You'll have to learn that."

"I was wrong."

"Obviously, but what's done is done. Good night, and please don't call again."

"But you don't understand—"

A click followed by a dial tone sounded on the wire. "I really am in love with you," I whispered into the empty receiver. "I might not have been before, but I am now. I wish you could understand."

XIX

The New York Times; October 2–Anthony Pisano is a forty-six-year-old New York City transit worker who immigrated to the United States a quarter of a century ago. Lionel J. Hunker, a Harvard Law School graduate, is a partner in the prestigious Wall Street law firm of Ashworth & Palmer. At ten o'clock this morning, these two men will do battle before a jury of their peers at the New York State Courthouse at 60 Centre Street. Their struggle has all the overtones of a contest between David and Goliath.

According to documents filed with the court, the drama began in May of last year when Hunker, age forty-eight, brushed against a subway railing and came away with yellow paint on his four-hundred-dollar Brooks Brothers suit. At the time, Pisano was applying bright yellow paint to the railing at the Lexington

Avenue IRT station where Hunker was in transit. Hunker claims that no "wet paint" warning was ever posted. He also contends that, immediately after the incident, Pisano threatened him with bodily harm. All totaled, Hunker is suing Pisano for twenty thousand dollars.

Contacted at his office yesterday afternoon, Hunker emphasized that his lawsuit was not against the City of New York. "I don't want a single penny of the taxpayers' money," Hunker said. "My complaint is aimed solely at an individual who is on the public payroll and betrayed the public's trust."

Pisano vigorously disputes Hunker's version of events. Born in Genoa, Italy, and a transit worker for sixteen years, he maintains that the work area was properly cordoned off with appropriate warning signs in clear view. "I don't got no lawyer," Pisano said yesterday. "I'm gonna go to court and tell the judge what happened. Then, what the judge says I gotta do, I gotta do."

Pisano is married and has two children—Joseph, age twenty-four, and Stefanie Marie, age twenty-two. His oldest child, Anthony Jr., was killed in Vietnam in 1972, Judge Leonard Fulcher will preside at trial.

The New York State Courthouse in downtown Manhattan is a solid granite structure five stories high. Thirty steps lead to the main door. Sixteen massive columns, each one fifty feet high, bolster a facade which bears the inscription, "The True Administration of Justice is the Firmest Pillar of Good Government."

Inside, the building loses its grandeur. Once-spacious courtrooms have been partitioned into smaller tribunals one-third their original size. The entire building has fallen into disrepair. At 9:30 A.M. on October 2, I entered the squat, ugly box of a room where *Hunker* v. *Pisano* would be tried. Hardesty was already there.

"Did you see this morning's *New York Times*?" he queried.
"Yup."
"What do you think?"
"Maybe Hunker will become a household word like Scotch tape or Kleenex."
"Drano would be more like it," Ed answered.
The courtroom walls were yellowish gray, the floor well-scuffed linoleum. The windows were so dirty that the glare of the onrushing sun made it impossible to see through them. What little furniture there was seemed crammed together. Two small tables for counsel and their clients stood in the center of the room with three chairs beside them. A jury box for six jurors and two alternates was located to our left. Two spectator pews hugged the back wall. The Judge's bench stood in front. Ed, myself, and one other person were present.
"Are you attorneys?" the third man asked.
"Yes, sir."
"I thought so. You're dressed like Wall Street fellows—fancy suits, attaché cases, and all that. I'm the court clerk. I guess I don't have to ask which side of *Hunker* v. *Pisano* you're on."
"I guess not," Ed said.
The courtroom door swung open, and Hunker lumbered in. "Did you see that shit in the *New York Times*?" he demanded.
I nodded.
"David versus Goliath, my ass." He laid his briefcase on the counsel table and sat down heavily. A court stenographer came in and began setting up a recorder. A security guard took his position by the door.
"Are you Mr. Hunker?" the clerk inquired.
"That's right."
"And who are these young fellows with you?"
"Thomas Henderson and Edwin Hardesty. They're my associates."

"Will you be calling any witnesses?"

"Just myself."

A young woman carrying a reporter's notepad slid into the spectator pew directly behind us. In a matter of minutes, a half dozen more onlookers had gathered.

"It's almost ten o'clock," the clerk announced. "Does anyone here know where the defendant Anthony Pisano is?"

A short balding man dressed in brown pleated pants, a gray sport jacket, and white shirt open at the collar stood up in the spectator pew nearest the door. "That's-a me," he said. "I'm Pisano."

Hunker turned around and nodded grimly. "Good to see you again, Mr. Pisano."

"For me it's not so good," the little man answered.

"Mr. Pisano?" the court clerk queried. "Do you have a lawyer?"

"I don't."

"Did you try to get one?"

"I'm-a try, but they cost too much."

"Very well. If you'll come up and take a seat at the counsel table to your left, I'll notify Judge Fulcher that we're ready to begin."

Leonard Fulcher was a man whose best days, such as they might have been, were long behind him. A product of the Democratic party machine that had ruled city politics for decades, he had served without distinction on the bench for twenty years. Large and balding with red cheeks and gray hair, he seemed moderately impressed by the fact that three Ashworth & Palmer lawyers were arrayed before him but too old and tired to really care.

"Are you Pisano?" he asked the little man seated at the counsel table nearest the door.

"Yes sir."

"Why don't you have a lawyer?"

"It's-a the cost. I don't got much money."

"You understand, don't you, that if you lose this lawsuit, you might be required to pay a great deal of money to Mr. Hunker—much more than the cost of a lawyer?"

"Yes sir. But I didn't do nothing wrong, so I let the jury decide."

"Very well," Fulcher said. "Are you familiar with the mechanics of selecting a jury?"

"I do what you tell me to, Judge."

The woman reporter was scribbling notes furiously directly behind us. She had been joined by a rival whose notepad bore the insignia of the *New York Daily News.*

"You're probably familiar with twelve-men juries," Fulcher told Pisano. "But in the New York courts on civil cases such as this, we use juries of six. Is that satisfactory?"

"Yes, Judge."

"Very good. Will the court clerk please call down to the jury room for a panel of jurors?"

In less than an hour, four men and two women had been seated as jurors. "Ladies and gentlemen," Fulcher told them. "This is a case involving allegations of negligence and assault. The plaintiff is Lionel J. Hunker. Mr. Hunker, will you please rise so the jurors can identify you?" Hunker stood up and smiled. "The defendant is Anthony Pisano." Pisano rose, but without the smile. "I expect this to be a short trial since there will be only one witness for each side. Your duty as jurors will be to decide whether or not the defendant was negligent, and whether he acted improperly thereafter so as to place Mr. Hunker in fear of imminent bodily harm. In the interest of time, we will dispense with the opening statements. Mr. Hunker, why don't you take the witness stand and begin your testimony?"

Dressed in a three-piece, navy blue pinstripe suit with a white shirt and maroon tie, Hunker mounted the witness stand.

"Raise your right hand," the court clerk instructed.

Hunker complied.

"Do you promise to tell the truth, the whole truth, and nothing but the truth so help you God?"

"I do."

"State your name and address for the record."

"Lionel J. Hunker; 1009 Park Avenue, New York, New York."

Leaning forward, Judge Fulcher addressed the witness. "Mr. Hunker, will you be questioned by one of your associates, or do you plan to conduct this examination yourself?"

"I'll do it myself, Your Honor."

Anthony Pisano stared silently at his accuser. Hardesty looked down at the tops of his shoes.

"Mr. Pisano," the Judge explained. "At the close of Mr. Hunker's testimony, you will have the opportunity to pose questions of your own on cross-examination, so I urge you to listen carefully."

The defendant nodded.

"Would you like a pad and pencil to take notes?"

"No thank you, Judge."

"Very well," Fulcher said, nodding toward Hunker. "You may begin."

Suddenly, I had to go to the bathroom. It wasn't psychological or anything like that, and it wasn't just the feeling you get when you're washing your hands before lunch and someone says, "Never pass up a chance to go to the head." My bladder or my ureter or whatever it was had started to throb.

"Ladies and gentlemen of the jury," Hunker was saying. "This is a very unusual position I find myself in this morning. Never before have I testified on my own behalf in court. Why am I here? The answer to that question is simple. I'm here because the conduct of the defendant Anthony Pisano poses a danger to the personal safety and property rights of every resident of this city. In effect, I'm suing on your behalf. Let's take a look at what happened. . . ."

The aching in my bladder and/or ureter was getting worse.

"Like most New Yorkers, I take the subway to and from work. On May twenty-sixth of last year, at approximately six-thirty P.M., I was on my way home when . . ."

I got up from my seat, walked out of the courtroom, and went to the bathroom. Upon my return, Hunker was still talking. "Did I miss anything?" I scribbled on a note to Hardesty. Ed shook his head.

"There was no warning sign," Hunker bellowed. "Nowhere did it say, 'Wet Paint.' And then, when I complained to the defendant—in polite fashion, of course—he became violent. He pushed me back against the wall and threatened to splatter the entire bucket of yellow paint over my head—on my face, in my eyes. I leave it to you, the members of this jury, to determine what type of serious injury an act like that could have caused. I might have been blinded for life." Hunker paused for effect, then went on. "I don't know what type of image this defendant will project when he takes the witness stand. But I can tell you how he appeared to me. Anthony Pisano is a thug. He's a reckless, no-good thug who lives off the people of this city, taking your tax dollars and mine, and then threatens to assault the very citizens who pay his salary."

"Very effective," the Judge mused when Hunker was done. "An opening statement, testimony, and summation all rolled into one. Mr. Pisano, would you care to cross-examine the witness?"

"No, Judge. I just want to tell what happened."

"Very well, then. Mr. Hunker, you may take a seat at the counsel table. Mr. Pisano, please take the witness stand."

As Pisano stood up to testify, Hunker rolled into the chair beside me. "Where the hell did you disappear to?" he whispered.

"To the bathroom."

"Did you have to go during the middle of my testimony?"

Fulcher rapped his gavel twice.

"Do you promise to tell the truth, the whole truth, and nothing but the truth so help you God?" the court clerk intoned.

"I do," Pisano answered.

"Please state your name and address for the record."

"Anthony Pisano; 12-65 Grand Avenue, Brooklyn."

"Mr. Pisano," the Judge instructed. "Will you tell the jurors in your own words your version of what happened?"

Nervously, the little man looked around. "I don't speak English so good," he began. "I never been to court before. Mr. Hunker, he's the big shot, and me, I'm the little shot. But I'm gonna tell you what happened. I'm gonna tell you because this is America. It's my home and, when I pass the test to become a citizen, they tell me how anyone can come to court and talk to the jury and the judge. So now it's me, Tony Pisano, talking to the jury and the judge."

I tried to catch a glimpse of Hardesty, but Hunker was sitting between us, blocking my view.

"Seventeen years, I been working for the city," Pisano said. "Seventeen years, and this is my only trouble. What I do the day I see Mr. Hunker, it's the same I do every day. I put a rope around the stairs, I hang a sign that says 'Wet Paint,' and I work. Maybe Mr. Hunker, he's in a hurry so he comes under the rope instead of going to the other stairs. Lots of other big shots ride the same subway, but they all use the other stairs on account of the rope and the sign. Then Mr. Hunker, he come where I'm painting. He go *boomf* and knocka into the rail. Then he yell at me. That's all what happened. If the law says I gotta pay, then it's-a wrong."

That was it—short and sweet, and I could see that Hunker was a little nervous. Pisano had been pretty effective and, unless old fatso did something fast, the jury just might find for the defendant.

"Your Honor," Hunker announced, "if I may, I'd like to cross-examine the witness."

"Go ahead."

Slowly, Hunker rose to his feet and approached his prey. "Mr. Pisano, you claim to have a fairly thorough recollection of our little incident, do you not?"

"Yes sir."

"And you wouldn't lie to this court on cross-examination, would you?"

"I wouldn't lie never."

"Just answer my question, please. If I ask an honest question, will you give me an honest answer?"

"Yes."

"Very well, then. Isn't it a fact that, after I complained to you about getting yellow paint on my suit, you threatened to dump the entire bucket of paint on my head?"

Obviously wrestling with his conscience, Pisano glanced around. "It's-a true," he said at last, staring directly at the jurors. "When I say it, I know I never do it. But when Mr. Hunker yell things at me, he make-a me mad."

"Thank you," Hunker smirked. "I have no further questions."

"It's twelve-thirty," Fulcher said, looking at his watch. "We'll break for lunch and finish up at two. In the interim, I'd like to caution the members of the jury not to discuss this case among themselves or with anyone else. Court is adjourned."

"Come on," one of the reporters said to Tony. "I'll buy you a pizza for lunch."

Juries are extremely unpredictable. Thousands of attempts have been made to analyze their behavior, but in the end each case must be separately resolved. After lunch, Judge Fulcher read a brief statement to the jurors explaining the law of negligence and assault: "If you find that the defendant Pisano failed to exercise reasonable care in cordoning off the work area and that this failure was the proximate cause of damage to plaintiff's suit, then you must find for Mr. Hunker on the issue of negligence. If you determine that the defendant Pisano unjustly placed the plaintiff in fear of imminent bodily harm, then you must find for Mr. Hunker on the issue of assault. If you decide that the defendant Pisano's conduct was so outrageous as to warrant special punishment, then you may award the plaintiff punitive damages. Mr. Hunker is seeking a total of twenty thousand dollars. You may award him anything up to that amount or you may award him nothing. The choice is yours."

Forty minutes later, the jurors were ushered back into court. Hunker, Hardesty, and I sat together at one table. Anthony Pisano sat alone.

"Mr. Foreman," intoned the court clerk, addressing the lead juror. "Have you reached a verdict?"

"We have."

"And what is that verdict?"

On all counts, we find for the defendant Anthony Pisano."

Hardesty and I stared straight ahead. Three or four spectators applauded.

"Shit," Hunker muttered. "Let's get out of here."

On our way to the door, I cast a glance back toward Pisano. There were tears on his cheeks. "America," he said to no one in particular. "It's-a the best."

That night, Hardesty and I got very drunk. "Here's to lawyers," Ed boomed, hoisting a glass on high. "They're all schmucks."

The piano player next to the bar was playing "I'm Gonna Sit Right Down and Write Myself a Letter." I couldn't quite remember the last time I'd heard it.

"Let me tell you about lawyers," Ed slobbered. "The constitutional law professor I had at Harvard was so bad he made civil rights cases boring for black students. My fellow associates at Ashworth & Palmer—and some of them are sweet guys—don't know the difference between illusion and reality. As for Lonnie Hunker, all I can say is that he had a very expensive Brooks Brothers suit. Two hundred hours we spent on his case. Two hundred hours at seventy dollars an hour is fourteen thousand dollars. Fourteen thousand dollars plus the time of one judge, one court clerk, one court stenographer, one court security guard, and six jurors—all at the taxpayer's expense. And you know something? It was worth it. It was worth it because we proved something. *Pisano won. The system works.*"

"The system works." Long after I staggered home that night, the thought echoed in my mind. Too much was weighing down on me . . . Hunker . . . Beth . . . Moffitt . . . Jordan. . . . Beneath the covers in bed, I knew it would be a long night. I lay on one side, then the other, then switched back to the first side again. Despite being drunk (or maybe because of it), I couldn't sleep. It was too hot with the blanket pulled over me and too cold without it.

I had to talk with someone. Beth was the only one. I'd been too long at Ashworth & Palmer. I had started to look at people like pieces of office machinery. I'd been told I was better than everyone else, and I'd fallen into the trap. I had believed them. It was the greatest mistake I'd ever made. Beth was as good as any of them, myself included. She had made me happy. She was the one. I had to see her, now. She'd talk to me. She had to. Three A.M. I couldn't wait any longer.

Desperately I dialed Beth's number . . . five rings.

Without speaking, I hung up the receiver. A man had answered.

XX

Katherine Whittle switched off the intercom and looked up from her desk. "Mr. Moffitt will see you now."

"Thanks," I told her. "I know he's busy. I won't take much of his time."

Inside, Moffitt sat surrounded by glass and chrome. "Have a seat," he offered, gesturing toward a chair directly opposite his own.

It had been a long, mostly sleepless weekend, and I didn't look so hot.

"What can I do for you?"

"I've decided to leave Ashworth & Palmer."

If my message struck an emotional chord, it didn't register on Moffitt's face. Instead, he leaned back in his chair as if measuring an adversary, taking longer than necessary to respond. The pause, it seemed, was calculated to intimidate, and I realized that this was a man I had been afraid of for two years.

"Why are you leaving?" he said at last.

"Because I don't want to spend the rest of my life at Ashworth & Palmer. I've seen what it's like, and the time has come for me to close this chapter of my life."

"What will you do?"

"I don't know. Right now, I'm not even sure I want to be a lawyer. But I do know it was wrong for me to come here, and I don't want to stay any longer."

"Is this at all connected to your relationship with Beth Anders?"

"She was the catalyst."

"I've heard you're no longer together. Is that right?"

"I'm not sure it's any of your business, but your information is correct."

"And now you're willing to throw away your entire career as some sort of penance?"

"If you're suggesting that leaving Ashworth & Palmer is the easiest way to put Beth Anders behind me, I suppose that's right."

"And you're telling me that the memory of a twenty-three-year-old secretary from Queens means more to you than your future at Ashworth & Palmer?"

"I guess so, only I found out a little too late. Also, if it makes you feel any better, with or without Beth Anders my decision would be the same. I've decided it's not always necessary to make it to the top, and I don't think I'd enjoy spending the rest of my life here."

"I'm not sure you're in a position to judge that," Moffitt answered. "You've had a bad experience with Lonnie Hunker. I wouldn't want you to repeat what I'm about to say, but Lonnie isn't one of our stronger partners. I wish you'd stay on for another two years to see what the good side of Ashworth & Palmer is like. I'm really counting on you for the National Industries case."

"Your interest is flattering, but my answer is no."

"If you leave now, you'll have wasted two years of your life."

"That's better than wasting the next forty."

"You look tired," Moffitt said, changing his tack. "You've been working awfully long hours. Maybe a week's vacation would brighten your outlook."

"I doubt it."

"American Steel has a subsidiary in the Virgin Islands. I could arrange for you to do some wrap-up work down there on the antitrust case we just settled. It would be an all-expenses-paid trip. You wouldn't have to work more than two or three hours a day."

"No thanks."

"Is there anything I can do to change your mind?"

"I'm afraid not."

"Well, at least you can stay through the first of the year. That way, you'll pick up some paid holidays."

"I'd like to be gone by November first."

Very briefly, Moffitt's face took on the look of an angry father whose child has rebelled. Then anger gave way to a fatherly visage. "Tom," he said, "I'd like to tell you a story.

"Back during the depression, a man was looking for work. Jobs were scarce, and some people even had trouble getting enough to eat. Well, this man came to a farmhouse, knocked on the door, and asked the farmer's wife if there were any odd jobs he could do in return for a square meal. It was nine in the morning. The woman looked at her watch and told him, 'All right. If you plow the north field, I'll give you lunch when you're through.' Now, ploughing the north field was a job that ordinarily took five or six hours but, forty minutes later, the man was done. 'My goodness,' the woman told him. 'I'm afraid lunch won't be ready for another two hours but, if you cut the logs piled out back and stack them by the barn, I'll give you an extra portion of potatoes with your meal.' There were enough logs to keep two men busy for a day, but half an hour later that task was completed too. 'You're the fastest worker I've ever seen,' the woman told him. 'But it's only ten-fifteen, and lunch still isn't ready. The only thing I can do is give you another chore. Next to the silo, you'll find a big pile of potatoes and two burlap sacks. Why don't you go out and separate the potatoes into two piles? Put the large potatoes in one sack and the small potatoes in the other so I can take them to market.' "

Looking straight at me to make certain I was following his tale, Moffitt went on. "As soon as the man got out to the silo, the woman began to cook lunch. After all, the latest task was one that could be performed in less than an hour. By eleven o'clock, the meal was ready, but there was no sign of the man, and the woman put lunch in the oven to keep it warm. At twelve o'clock, there was still no sign of him, and the woman decided to give him a little longer. When he hadn't appeared by one, she went out back and found him sitting by the silo. Both burlap sacks were empty. The pile of potatoes was still there. In his right hand, the man was holding one medium-sized potato, flipping it up and down. 'I don't understand,' the woman told him. 'You did two very difficult jobs so well. Why couldn't you do this one?' And the man answered, 'Lady, work is easy. Decisions are hard.' "

His story complete, Moffitt stared rather coldly at me. "Tom, no one can make your decisions for you. But if you leave Ashworth & Palmer, you'll be making the biggest mistake of your life."

Ten minutes later, I was in Hardesty's office. "You'll never guess what I just did," I said.

The next four weeks passed more quickly than I had thought they would. In anticipation of my transfer to the National Industries case, Ira Kamenstein had taken over my duties on the UCC litigation, so there wasn't much work for me to do. At one point, Hunker asked for some revisions on a memo I'd written six months earlier, but the job only took two days. More and more, I found myself leaving work in mid-afternoon, going home, and being bored when I got there. My head felt like a repository for stagnant water.

The biggest problem with my head was that I missed Beth. I can't convey the sense of loneliness and despair that surrounded me, and I won't try. I was unable to sleep more than four or five hours a night. Having a gift for the ironic, I began leaving my hair brush on the shelf bristles down (the way she liked it). Whoever had answered her telephone at three o'clock in the morning would doubtless make fewer mistakes than I had. Their life would be long and happy together.

My last day at Ashworth & Palmer was largely ceremonial. The books I had shipped from Nebraska two years earlier lay neatly packed in boxes on my office floor. Like the other belongings I'd accumulated over the preceding two years, they would be delivered by messenger to my apartment after a firm file clerk searched through them to make certain nothing improper was being removed. The office walls looked very bare.

Arlen Cohen, Ira Kamenstein, and Carole Shiner dropped by to say good-bye. They were followed by Jordan, who also bid me farewell. Ed took me out to lunch. As a sentimental gesture, we went to Lindemann's. "Who would have thought you'd leave Ashworth & Palmer before I did?" he mused.

"Maybe you'll stay and become a partner," I suggested.

"No way! I'll be gone by Christmas."

After lunch, we walked back to my desk. "I'll miss you," he said. "Your being here improved the quality of life at Ashworth & Palmer."

That afternoon, I made my final rounds. "You're the first person I met at Ashworth & Palmer," I told Katherine Whittle. "I just wanted to say good-bye."

"It's been a pleasure," she said. "I'm sure Mr. Moffitt would like to wish you well in person, but at the moment he's tied up in a meeting."

"That's all right. Just give him my best."

One by one, I paid my respects to people I'd worked with for two years. At four o'clock, I returned to my desk. "You can leave early," I told my secretary.

"I'll miss you," she said. "You've been a very nice boss."

"Why have I been a nice boss?"

"You're the only lawyer here with legible handwriting."

Hardesty wandered by to chat. "Have you said good-bye to Hunker?" he wanted to know.

"Not yet."

"Will you?"

"I haven't decided."

We reminisced for the better part of an hour—about the day we met, our trips to Unger, and the time Ed crammed a softball down Hunker's throat; everything but Beth.

"Will you have dinner with me?" I asked.

"I can't tonight. I have plans."

I nodded.

"I'll change them if you want."

"That's okay," I said. "We'll make it for sometime next week."

Ed left. The office seemed emptier than ever. In a matter of days, some bright-eyed first-year associate would be sitting at my desk. Suddenly, it was very important that he not find my nameplate the way I had found Peter Forrest's. Very carefully, I slid the narrow brass strip from its holder by the door and dropped it in the wastepaper basket. Only one act remained. I had to say good-bye to Lonnie Hunker.

Just after five o'clock, the telephone on my desk rang. "Mr. Hunker would like to see you," a secretary said.

His office looked the same as it had two years earlier.

There were a few more papers on his desk than when we first met and the number of Harvard Law Review volumes on the shelf had grown by two, but otherwise everything was unchanged. Hunker looked the same too—a shade heavier, perhaps a line or two more on his face, but that was all.

"Sit down," he said.

I did as instructed.

"I don't have much to say," he began. "Good-byes have always been difficult for me, and I usually avoid them. However, in your case there are a few things on my mind, and I want you to hear me out. I know you don't like me very much. That's been apparent from day one and, while I find it disappointing, there's nothing I can do or say in five minutes that will eradicate two years' resentment and hostility, so I won't even try. But you also seem to have developed a very negative attitude toward Ashworth & Palmer, and this firm is very important to me. In fact, it's the most important thing in my life and the lives of most of my partners, so I'd like to explain a few things to you.

"I came to Ashworth & Palmer twenty-three years ago, an unhappy, lonely kid who tested well and didn't have much else going for him. For almost a quarter of a century, this firm has been my home. It's provided me with the brotherhood of forty partners and hundreds of associates who have been my co-workers and friends. It's given me the opportunity to become part of the legal profession's grandest legend and to shape the way law is practiced in the United States. Not everything is perfect here. Sometimes we represent a client we think is wrong, but that's life. Occasionally, personal excesses, hardships, and even cruelties occur. But we try our best to perpetuate the traditions we've inherited, and we try our best to bring young lawyers like you along. At every juncture, we've been tolerant and given you the benefit of the doubt. We've done everything we possibly could to make you happy and keep you here, both for your benefit and our own. Obviously, we've failed. But I wish you well in whatever you do, and I hope that in time your resentment fades. That's all I have to say."

We shook hands, and for the first time it occurred to me that maybe Hunker wasn't so bad, after all. Very often, I'd seen a look on his face that I'd been unable to place. Now I recognized it for what it was. Lonnie Hunker was perpetually afraid that someone was going to punch him in the face and break his glasses.

Two years to the day after I arrived, I left Ashworth & Palmer.

* * *

That night, my apartment seemed particularly empty. The hotshot lawyer from Nebraska had failed. I'd never felt more alone in my life. I wanted to cry. I wasn't able to.

Slowly, I made the rounds of my domain—a tiny foyer, a walk-in kitchen, living room, the bedroom with its teak dresser and spruce green carpet. From the wall above the bed, my parents looked down at me. I looked back at their pictures, and then the tears came. I cried for them and everything that had happened the past two years; for what I had lost and the things I'd never gain. I cried until I ran out of tears, and then I cried some more. And when the telephone rang late that night, I picked up the receiver hoping to God it was Hardesty who had gotten home and would come over to talk with me.

"Congratulations! I hear you're a free man," Beth said.

AFTERWORD

Ten months have passed since I left Ashworth & Palmer and, like the sea, the firm rolls on. Jordan Caine became a partner in June. Shortly thereafter, Ed Hardesty left to take a job with the District Attorney's office in Boston. His departure went largely unnoticed, overshadowed as it was by the impending arrival of thirty new associates. Under James Moffitt's guidance, the National Industries case has become the biggest revenue producer in the office, with twenty associates spending most of their time sticking blue dots on documents. "The work will be more interesting when the document phase is complete," Moffitt told them recently. What he didn't mention was that the document phase is expected to last three to five years.

As for Lonnie Hunker, the fates have been less than kind. Moments before his partners assembled last June, he was approached by James Moffitt, who asked to see him in private. The two men retired to Moffitt's office, where

Hunker was told that the Ashworth & Palmer formula of equal pay for all partners was about to be amended. "Several of us have discussed the matter," Moffitt explained, "and we think it would be appropriate if you took a slightly smaller share of this year's profits. We've arranged for your drawing to be adjusted accordingly. Needless to say, you're free to raise the issue with the full partnership if you like. However, we've canvassed the group rather thoroughly, and sentiment for the adjustment appears overwhelming."

Hunker, of course, did not contest the issue. Two months later, he resigned from the firm to accept a federal judgeship. Jordan Caine is now in charge of the UCC litigation.

As for my own future, I do want to practice law again. Despite (or maybe because of) my experience at Ashworth & Palmer, I believe the system works. I don't know where or when I'll re-enter the profession, but I suspect the time is near. Much of what I do depends on Beth.

I've tried awfully hard these past ten months, and the gulf between us has narrowed. We still have separate apartments and a residue of anger remains, but in many ways we're closer now than ever. We see each other three or four times a week, which isn't as often as I'd like. But Beth is almost ready to trust me again, and I've come to accept her fully for what she is. For a while, I doubted we could make it, but not too long ago we had a conversation that gave me hope. "Maybe I'll go back to Nebraska to practice law," I told her. "With two years at Ashworth & Palmer under my belt, I could be a real hotshot at Hutchins, Culpepper & Woods. Would you come?"

"Maybe," she answered.

"I'm not particularly proud of the past few years. You know that, don't you?"

"Don't worry about it," she said, putting a hand on my shoulder. "When two people are right for each other, things have a way of working out."